Cronus Team

Ace Evans Book 3

by
TOBY NEIGHBORS

Cronus Team - Ace Evans book 3
© 2020, Toby Neighbors

ISBN:978-1-952260-11-7

Published by Mythic Adventure Publishing, LLC
Idaho, USA

Copy Editing by Julie Duke

Books By Toby Neighbors

Avondale
Draggah
Balestone
Arcanius
Avondale V
Wizard Rising
Magic Awakening
Hidden Fire
Fierce Loyalty
Crying Havoc
Evil Tide
Wizard Falling
Chaos Descending
Into Chaos
Chaos Reigning
Chaos Raging
Controlling Chaos
Killing Chaos
Elder Wizard
Lorik
Lorik the Defender
Lorik the Protector
Spartan Company
Spartan Valor
Spartan Guile
The Vault Of Mysteries
Lords Of Ascension
The Elusive Executioner
Regulators Revealed
We Are The Wolf
Welcome To The Wolfpack
Embracing Oblivion

Joined In Battle
The Abyss Of Savagery
Dragon Team Seven
Uncommon Loyalty
Total Allegiance
Kestrel Class
Jump Point
Gravity Flux
Modulus Echo
Zero Friction
Planet Fall
Charter
Jack & Roxie
Third Prince
Royal Destiny
The Other Side
The New World
Zompocalypse Omnibus
My Lady Sorceress
The Man With No Hands
ARC Angel
Battle ARC
Broken Crucible
Lost Kingdom
War INC
Carthage Prime

Toby Neighbors Online

www.TobyNeighbors.com

FACEBOOK

www.Facebook.com/TobyNeighborsAuthor

INSTAGRAM

Instagram @TobyTheWriter

Prologue

The drill bot chewed through the massive pillar of concrete with a steady grinding sound that echoed through the engineering space deep in the bowels of the Ahzco universal headquarters building. The man working the small, robotic tool looked around nervously. It was clear that he was up to no good, but he was one of the few people in the company who even knew where the engineering space was. All the executives and managers depended on him, even if they didn't know his name.

Hundreds of people worked in the Ahzco building. They were dependent on the massive machines that propelled fresh air up into the towering building. The transformers in the dark, narrow engineering space provided electricity to power their computers and devices. Water, sanitation, networking, heating and cooling—it was all run by massive machines under the building. The building itself relied on dozens of support pillars that created a steady foundation for a structure that was over a kilometer tall, and these were all located in a space slightly taller than two meters with bare concrete floors and poor ventilation.

The man looked around his domain and smiled. He had served Ahzco faithfully for years. His job was to keep the big machines under the building functioning. No one liked it down in the hot, crowded engineering space, but that was finally working in his favor. The odds of getting caught drilling into the support pillars was very low. A beep sounded once the drill bot had reached the desired depth inside the thick column. The man pressed a button, and the drill bot reversed, quickly propelling itself out of the hole it had made.

He took the small, robotic tool and returned it to the case it was kept in. From a separate bag, he took a long, cylindrical explosive device. He hadn't made it himself; the explosives had been delivered to him by someone outside the company. He slipped the explosive into the pillar. It had a small detonator with a wire receiver to pick up the signal that would arm and eventually set off the explosion. The man packed the hole with putty that perfectly matched the concrete. The only trace of what he had done to the pillar would be the short wire protruding from what appeared to be seamless concrete.

With his work done, the man began to gather his tools. No one knew what he was up to. He could have spent the entire day loitering in the engineering space without raising suspicion, but no one spent more time down in the engineering space than absolutely necessary. It was hot, humid, dark, and foul down in the bowels of the massive building. Yet his job required him to monitor and maintain the machines that kept the building functioning. Unfortunately, his compensation was not equal to the conditions he endured to ensure that those at the top of the company's workforce had the essential elements needed to do their job. It was the primary reason he had been approached with an offer that far exceeded his yearly wages. All he had to do was plant the devices, then take the small fortune he was being paid and leave the system. Others would do the truly dastardly work.

Chapter 1

"Where are we going?" Alex asked.

Executive Vice President of Security Loman Haley turned around and took a sip from the flask he kept inside his coat pocket before answering.

"To Arcadia," Loman said once his sip burned down his throat and began to spread heat through his body. He found that alcohol helped him to relax in stressful situations. While he didn't mind confrontation, his job required him at times to utilize his skills of manipulation. He found it a distasteful practice.

"Arcadia? I don't understand," Alex said.

"You're the hero of Carthage," Loman said, as if he were announcing Alex's new title to the world. "You saved the company, Alex. There needs to be recognition for that."

"You said we weren't supposed to talk about it," Alex said.

"And you aren't...not the details, anyway," Loman confirmed. "We'll come up with a suitable cover story. But the bottom line is that you and your team, in our state-of-the-art Titan battle suits, saved the day. That's what the people want to hear."

Loman looked at the small group he had summoned to the captain's study on the carrier ship *Republic*. Three operators and three controllers—the optics were perfect.

"So, we're in marketing now?" Ash asked.

She was the one he worried about. The fearless operator who had no filter might be a problem, but she also played the perfect counterpoint to Alex's "good boy" image.

"You are employees of a galactic corporation that has many, many needs," Loman said. "Your first priority is the security of the company's employees and assets. To that end, I need to put you together with some of our top security administrators. There has been a systematic attack against us, and if we don't find a way to fight back, we could all be out of work." It was a grandiose statement but true nonetheless.

"But while you're on the Ahzco homeworld," Loman continued, "we can let the company and shareholders know that they're in very capable hands. Think of it as a mini-vacation. Have any of you ever been to Arcadia?"

They shook their heads. Loman already knew the answer. Arcadia was an old world, one of the first colonized planets, and essentially one massive city. It wasn't just a level-one planet; it was *the* planet, home of the rich and famous. Every major corporation had their headquarters on Arcadia. Most holo-films were made there. It was a planet of dreams and opportunities. If you could make it on Arcadia, you could make it anywhere.

"It's a fabulous place, and you'll have plenty to time to explore," Loman said. "We'll give you all a bonus for your heroics on Carthage Prime. You'll have credits to spend, and everything you ever wanted or thought you might possibly want is available there. Trust me—you're going to love it."

"Sounds good to me," Sly said.

"That's the spirit," Loman said.

"We're appreciative—don't get me wrong," Alex said. "But I thought we had work to do. You tasked us with finding who was behind the false information about Carthage Prime."

"That's right," Loman said. "Which is why I'm setting up a meeting with you and my top investigator, Ciara Prince."

"Can't we do that from anywhere?" Nyx asked.

"You could," Loman agreed. "But we need to keep this quiet. Whoever is behind the attacks and false reports almost certainly has agents watching and listening. Even an encrypted holo-conference doesn't guarantee that someone isn't listening in. I want you in a room that we know is secure. And Alex, I want you to have access to our full suite of systems."

"And those of every other business on Arcadia," Ash said. "It's not a bad plan."

"Hacking is a major crime," Nyx pointed out. "And Arcadia's laws are incredibly strict."

Loman wanted to say he couldn't agree more. The flask in his inner pocket was a prime example of just how strict a planet's laws and restrictions could be.

"We aren't going to hack anyone," Loman said. "You cannot do anything other than meet with Security Admin Prince. Only time will tell. So, let's just try to enjoy ourselves, shall we?"

Alex nodded, along with the rest of the group. They had their meager belongings packed, and they followed Loman out of the captain's study as the *Republic* began docking procedures with the New Wales Transit Station. When Alex had come aboard the carrier ship, it had been in a shuttle that ferried five squads up from Helena Prime. This time, they would exit using the officers' exclusive airlock from the ship's command level.

Loman was joined by Colonel Chastain, who, with her new promotion, was his top military advisor. He had a lot to do and had been gone from his office for nearly three weeks. Loman trusted his VP assistants, but he didn't trust Zan Fordham, who had been elevated to equal rank with Loman himself. The greedy puppet had taken Loman's office and filled it with expensive furnishings and even elevated his desk on a platform. There was no doubt that the foolish Zan would run the entire security division into the ground if he was allowed to. Loman fully expected to have to clean up after Zan, whose position hadn't even been defined before Loman left Arcadia.

They passed through the airlock, out of the ship, and down the space station docking corridor. At the end was a woman in a dark suit with pale, white skin. She stepped up to Loman and spoke quietly.

"Mr. Haley, the transport is waiting on docking arm seventeen, slip J."

"Thank you," Loman replied.

The woman stepped aside, and Haley continued into the heart of the station. The *Republic* was docked on the big ship side of the station. Their transport would be on the opposite side, one of the docking arms reserved for smaller vessels.

"Wouldn't mind hanging out a while," Sly said from behind the executive VP. "There's plenty to do here if you need to take care of some work, sir."

"You really want to spend the day on a transit station?" Ash asked.

"I wouldn't mind getting something to eat," Sly replied.

"He's always hungry," his controller said.

"The food on board a spaceship isn't really up to my standards," Sly said. "I have a discerning palate."

"Nothing on this station will be any better," Loman said over his shoulder, "but I've chartered a first-class transport. The meals on board will be prepared by a private chef with fresh ingredients."

"Now we're talking," Sly said.

Chapter 2

Alex hurried to keep up with the VP's pace. His leg was healed, according to the medical staff on board the *Republic*, but Alex still felt pain. The medical scanner showed the bone to be fully restored, and the incisions had healed nicely, but Alex was convinced that something was still wrong with the leg. The medical staff suggested that perhaps his complaints stemmed from a psychological issue, which Alex brushed off. The pain wasn't just in his mind, no matter what the doctors said.

"You okay?" Nyx said, walking beside him.

They were behind the others, and she spoke quietly, which he appreciated. He was already getting more attention than he was comfortable with for their mission to save the VP's transport in the Carthage system. He understood that his newfound abilities had kept the ship from being captured by the Zen Tech forces and saved the passenger and crew as well, but he didn't like being singled out. The last thing Alex wanted was to create discord with his teammates. Even the sympathy from being wounded made it seem like he was getting undue attention.

"Fine," Alex lied. "Just trying to keep up."

"You aren't getting soft on me, are you?" Nyx teased.

"No," Alex said with a grin. "But I do miss my Titan suit."

"Some rest is good for you," she said, tapping the side of her head and raising her eyebrows.

"It's fine," he said. "Just background noise, as usual."

"Nothing strange or unusual?"

"No," he said.

She was referring to his ability to hear the EM waves produced by electrical devices. The truth was, Alex could hear everything. Not that he couldn't before; it was a function of the Implanted Neural Controller (INC) the medical staff on Helena Prime had surgically implanted into the back of his head, which was intended to give him greater control of the mechanized battle suits he wore in combat situations. The INC was designed to be incorporated by his brain, which translated data like a sixth sense. But Alex's mind was somehow doing more. He was not only able to sync the INC to his battle suit, but to other computerized devices, as well. In orbit above Carthage Prime, he had taken control of Zen Tech ships and even the private transport that VP Haley had entered the system in.

Fortunately, the EM waves weren't overwhelming him. They faded into the background like the sound of rain pelting a thin roof. He could focus on the sounds if he wanted to. He could even pick one sound out of the various waves that his brain "heard," for lack of a better word to describe his awareness of the waves. Yet they were more than just noise to him since his abilities had increased; now he could hear each wave like a musical instrument in an orchestra. The background noise in his head had transformed into a soft, melodic song that was always playing.

"I'm good, really," he insisted.

Nyx smiled at him, sending a tingling sensation through his body. They both felt the chemistry, but they were both hesitant to move forward or declare their feelings. Alex felt like there was plenty of time for them to be together. They had both been promoted to sergeant, and after their missions in the Carthage system, no one could say they were rookies anymore.

They followed the VP across a wide concourse. There were kiosks selling a wide variety of goods on the station. The team of Titan operators and controllers looked around but didn't stop. The salespeople sat on stools, looking bored, waiting for someone to show an interest in their wares before expending any energy in selling their goods.

There was also a food court. Alex knew the food was all processed, yet the smells were enticing. Sly wasn't the only member of the group who was hungry, but Loman didn't stop. They were soon moving down a long corridor with airlocks leading to docking slips. When they finally reached J—the fifth docking slip on the left side of the corridor—Alex was starting to sweat.

"Here we are," Loman Haley said, pressing a button to activate the intercom to the transport.

"Yeah?," a voice said.

"This is Loman Haley. I'm here with seven other passengers ready to board."

"All right," the voice replied.

Alex thought the person sounded strangely informal for a private transport, but the airlock swished open, and Loman didn't hesitate to step through. Nyx looked at Alex, who shrugged his shoulders as the rest of the group followed the VP into the docking slip.

The passageway between the airlock and the ship had no gravity. After a few steps, they were floating through a tunnel that seemed to be made of thick plastic. The only lights came from each end. Alex thought the process was a bit frightening. It was completely different from what he'd seen in holo-films, but it was his first experience with private transportation.

The airlock on the charter ship was small. The group had to go through two at a time. Alex and Nyx were the last to enter the ship, and for the first time Alex was pleasantly surprised.

"That's everyone?" asked a scruffy-looking man in an ill-fitting uniform. "Welcome to the *Starchaser*. We're glad to have you on board. Glenda is our chief stew. She'll give you a quick tour of the ship, and then we'll get started."

"Tour of the ship," Sly said, elbowing Alex in the ribs. "This is fancy."

They were in what the stewardess called the main salon. There were sofas, a large video display, and windows on either side. A man with a tray of bubbly drinks offered one to each of them as they passed by. There were several crew members, a chief, an engineer, and the scruffy-looking man, who was the ship's captain.

The crew stood in line while the introductions were made but then quickly dispersed. Alex took his glass of golden bubbly liquid and gave the drink a sip. It tasted like he imagined the nail polish remover his mother had sometimes used would taste.

"Oh, that's not good," he whispered.

"Kind of like cleaning fluid," Ash whispered back.

Glenda took them down a very narrow set of stairs that led to a series of cabins. The master cabin was large, with a huge bed and a massive bathroom. It was bigger than the squad restroom facilities on the *Republic*. VP Haley claimed the room, went immediately to the built-in desk next to a large window that showed a view of the space station they were docked with, and used his PIL to log into the *Starchaser*'s network access portal.

"No rest for the weary," Sly said.

"I guess not," Alex agreed.

"Stop talking and pay attention," Nyx scolded him.

"He started it," Alex said with a chuckle.

"Hey! What did I do?" Sly said.

"You see what I have to deal with on a daily basis?" Ash said to Nyx.

Glenda continued the tour. The other rooms were luxurious, with large beds and private bathrooms. After touring the cabins, they were led to a level called the Rec Deck. There were game stations, exercise equipment, and even a library of old-fashioned paper books neatly arranged on thick, wooden shelves. Every surface gleamed. The wood was coated with lacquer and polished so that it shined from the ship's lighting. The metal was all chrome with a mirror finish.

From the Rec Deck they went up to the dining room. There was a bar with stools, a mirror behind the rows of liquor bottles, and a large, round dining table with an elevated center that could turn. Snacks had already been set out on the center portion of the table.

"Now we're talking," Sly said enthusiastically.

There were crackers with cheese and prosciutto, shrimp cocktail, fresh fruit, glazed nuts, and bite-sized cinnamon rolls. Everyone got small plates from a stack on the tabletop and filled them with the small appetizers.

"We'll serve lunch in a couple of hours," Glenda said with a dazzling smile. "But first, allow me to show you the observation deck."

She led the way up another set of stairs to a wide deck on top of the ship. It was covered with a transparent bubble that made Alex feel like he was outside. They could see the space station and a variety of ships moving toward or away from them.

"This is incredible," Nyx said.

"I may never leave," Sly proclaimed.

There was another bar, a U-shaped sitting area with thickly cushioned sofas, and finally a large, round hot tub filled with steaming water.

"The spa uses a natural ozonation process to clean the water," Glenda explained. "Feel free to use any of the ship's facilities as you like. If you need anything at all, just ask one of my stews. We're here to make your trip as enjoyable as possible."

"I've died and gone to heaven," Sly said. "Is there more food?"

"Certainly," Glenda said.

Sly followed her back down to the dining area. Ash's controller went down to his cabin, and Sly's controller mumbled something about looking at the books on the Rec Deck.

The ship started to move. There was no sensation of movement, but from the observation deck they could see the docking tube break free and retract into the station. There were small bursts of compressed air that pushed the transport forward.

Alex moved to the sofa and set his mostly untouched glass of bubbling champagne on a side table. Nyx and Ash joined him, along with Colonel Chastain.

"This seems a little excessive," Alex said.

"It was the only transport available at the last minute," Colonel Chastain said as she leaned back and sipped from her glass. "The VP spent his own money to charter this luxury yacht. It's probably the only time in our entire lives that we'll have a chance like this."

"Might as well enjoy it then," Ash said.

"I don't mean to complain," Alex said. "It's just not what I was expecting."

"You've got Neunhappin Syndrome, Evans," the colonel said.

"He's got what?" Ash asked.

"Neunhappin Syndrome is when a person goes from living in harsh conditions with very little to being in a place where life flourishes and there are many opportunities," Nyx said.

"Your controller's smart, Ace," Ash said.

"I know," he said proudly.

"I've never been to NP8261," Colonel Chastain said, "but no world without a name is ever a good place to be."

"We called it the Rock," Alex said. "The atmo was thin and toxic. No natural ground soil. It was essentially a big rock."

"Sounds terrible," Ash said.

"And now here you are," the colonel continued, "on a luxury space yacht, rubbing elbows with the executive vice president of a big-five company."

"Not to mention a colonel," Nyx said with a grin.

Chastain nodded. "It's a big change. Otto Neunhappin was a psychologist who studied planetary environments and their effects on the human mind."

"Sounds like edge-of-your-seat kind of stuff," Ash teased.

"How do you know about it?" Alex asked Nyx.

"My parents were scientists. They were constantly giving me books to read in almost every scientific field," Nyx said. "Neunhappin's theories were in one of them."

"Basically, it means that you're uncomfortable, Evans," the colonel explained. "That's not unusual. We all are, to some extent. You need to learn to adapt."

"I don't think Sly is having any problems with this ship or with being pampered," Ash said.

"We all deal with change in our own ways," Chastain said before finishing off her champagne. "You'll be fine. By tomorrow afternoon when we reach Arcadia, you'll be wishing you didn't have to leave."

Alex hoped the colonel was right. He watched her stand up and move easily toward the stairs. She had a confidence he envied. Beyond her, the space station appeared to be shrinking. He felt like he was in a dome theater rather than on a space vessel.

"Alone at last," Nyx said.

"Are we ever truly alone?" Alex asked, turning toward Nyx.

"No, but it is nice to have some time together," she replied, "…unless you don't want it."

"I want that more than anything," Alex said. "I just feel uncomfortable here."

"Me too, in a way," Nyx said. "But you've earned a break. Try to think of this and the days ahead as some much-needed R&R."

"I can't imagine being able to rest or relax, but I'll try."

"That's the spirit."

The two of them stayed on the upper deck, watching the ship fly through space toward what looked like a black hole. Space tunnels connected the various star systems, cutting down the travel time between systems from years to just a few hours. There were dozens of tunnels in the space around the New Wales Transit Station. Ships were disappearing into them or appearing out of them all the time. It made Alex feel like Nyx was right: anything was possible. He didn't have to force it or figure it all out on his own. He was part of a team, and he knew they had his back. All he needed to do was relax and try to enjoy himself.

Chapter 3

Dinner was a full production. They began with a cold corn chowder that was both sweet and savory. Alex felt like he could have just eaten the soup and been happy, but he didn't get nearly enough. The bowls seemed large, but they only held a small amount of the soup in a small depression right in the very center. The second course was a salad with grilled peppers and onions, topped with tiny tendrils of fried squid.

"Have you ever had calamari?" Sly asked as Alex eyed the salad dubiously.

"No."

"It's delicious," Loman said.

All eight passengers had been summoned to dinner by Glenda, who was busy serving the dishes and carrying away the plates and bowls when they finished. She filled their goblets with different wines as the dinner progressed, but Alex stuck with water. He didn't really like the taste of alcohol, and while Sly and VP Haley talked about the wine as if it were exceptional, Alex was satisfied with just a few sips.

Alex tried the calamari. He wasn't sure if he was tasting the squid or just the well-seasoned breading, but he liked it. The small, artfully arranged salad course disappeared quickly. The third course was a small cube of grilled fish on top of a circle of rice and covered with a small bundle of crunchy green beans.

By the time Alex polished off the third course, his hunger was completely satisfied, but the food was so good that he wanted more. The fourth course was the meat course. The chef prepared slices of beef filet with a buttery turnip puree, garlic roasted asparagus, and baby carrots. Alex was beginning to realize just how sheltered his life had been. He had thought the food in the cafeteria on Helena Prime was amazing, and yet compared to the meal he was eating on the *Starchaser,* it was the most basic fare.

"The final course," Glenda said once the table had been cleared of their empty plates, "is a chocolate soufflé with a raspberry drizzle and crème fraiche."

"Oh, so good," Sly said.

"Our compliments to the chef," Loman Haley said.

"I don't know if I can go back to regular food," Sly said. "You've ruined me."

"There are many fine dining establishments on Arcadia," Loman said.

"Don't encourage him," Ash said. "He'll get so fat, he won't fit into a battle suit."

After dinner, they all moved into the salon. The furniture was comfortable, but Alex wondered how many people had sat on it before him. Loman had a brandy, while Colonel Chastain sipped coffee. Alex was too full to eat or drink anything more. Sly promptly fell asleep.

"Alex, would you mind joining me for a stroll around the upper deck?" Loman Haley asked.

"Not at all," Alex replied.

Nyx raised her eyebrows when he looked at her, but she didn't speak up. He followed the executive VP out of the salon and up to the observation deck. They were in the space tunnel, and there was no light outside of the luxury yacht.

"When we get to Arcadia, I need your support," Loman said.

"Me?" Alex asked.

"Yes," Loman said. "It's no secret I have enemies. The chairwoman of the Ahzco Board is anxious to gain full control of the company. She's elevated people with no real merit into positions of power. Their only qualification is total allegiance to her."

"That sounds bad," Alex said, not sure what else he could say.

"Yes, and while that's my problem to deal with, if we can't find out who is behind the attacks, she'll have all the leverage she needs to push me out of the company."

"Is she behind them?" Alex asked.

"No," Loman said as he leaned against the rail. "I've had her checked out. She's a powerful woman, but she hasn't done anything that would adversely affect the company's profits. Whoever is behind the attacks, on the other hand, has no qualms about costing us billions."

"I'll do what I can," Alex said.

"That's all I'm asking," Loman replied. "Lead your team. Put on a smile and give our people something else to focus on for a while. I'm going to put my new counterpart in charge of a small PR campaign. Your team will be at the center of that effort and should keep Zan Fordham busy while we work to discover who is behind the attacks."

"I don't understand," Alex said. "A PR campaign? I thought you wanted me to help find who was behind the attacks."

"I do," Loman said, taking another sip of the brandy, "but there are a lot of plans in motion here. I need your team to smile and nod when the holo-cameras are pointed your way. I need you to go out on the town and enjoy yourselves so that our employees and stockholders will believe everything is as it should be. I need you to distract the man whose sole job is to make me look foolish. And yes, I need you to meet with the investigators. There may even be reason for you to do what no one else can do, but we'll just have to wait and see."

"And if someone finds out what I can do?"

Loman's face twitched, and he frowned.

"Should I be concerned?" Alex asked.

"I won't lie to you, Alex. You've saved my life, and I'll do everything I can to protect you as long as I live, but if I lose my job, there won't be much I can do. If the wrong people find out what you're capable of, well...you won't be safe. Neither will your team or your loved ones. You have a gift that in our day and age is incalculable..."

Loman continued talking about Alex's abilities, but he stopped listening. They had just exited the space tunnel. Alex had no idea what system they were in, but he could see a star and several planets in the distance. Yet what had his full attention was the fact that the loudest hum on the ship had gone silent.

"...wouldn't hurt for you to have a contingency—" Loman stopped talking when Alex raised his hand.

"The engines just powered down," Alex whispered.

"You sure?" Loman asked.

Alex nodded. He began syncing the ship's master computer to his INC.

"This could be bad. Let's get back to the others," Loman said.

They hurried back down through the Rec Deck and dining room to the main salon. Sly was slumped over, snoring softly. Nyx was talking quietly with Ash. Colonel Chastain and the other two controllers were not in the room.

"Where are the others?" Loman asked.

"In their cabins," Nyx said.

"Why? What's wrong?" Ash asked.

"Wake him up," Loman said, pointing at Sly. He turned around and looked at Alex. "Well?"

"They shut them down," Alex said. "All systems are good. There's no reason to stop."

"Stop?" Nyx asked in a whisper. She had moved beside Alex and was facing VP Haley.

"They've shut down the engines," Loman answered Nyx's question before turning back to Alex. "Can you check the radar?"

"There's a ship moving this way," Alex said. "It's still a thousand kilometers out. It could be moving toward the space tunnel."

"Not likely," Loman said. "We don't even have weapons."

Ash and Sly joined them. "Weapons?" Ash asked.

"Looks like there's going to be an attack," Alex said. "The crew have shut down the engines, and there's a ship coming this way. Mr. Haley, I can run this yacht. Just give me the word."

Loman was trying to decide what to do. The look on his face was one of bewilderment, fear, and just a little excitement.

"Wait a second," Nyx said. "Alex can only take control if the ship is functional. Once the crew realize what we can do, they might sabotage the ship."

"We have to get them all up here and under our control," Ash said. "Otherwise we're vulnerable."

"Go get Colonel Chastain," Loman said. "We have to do this quickly and quietly. Let's find something we can use as weapons just in case they try to fight us."

At that moment, the chief stewardess, Glenda, came into the salon. She gave the group a dazzling smile and offered to help them.

"I did have a question, up on the observation deck," Loman said.

"Certainly. How can I help?" Glenda asked.

"Could you show me how to use the spa controls?" he replied. Alex was impressed by the VP's calmness and quick thinking in the moment. "I'm ready to take a dip before I turn in for the night."

"Of course," Glenda said. "I'd be glad to."

"Alex, can you bring up the layout of the yacht?" Nyx asked. "Maybe send it to our flex PILs?"

"Yeah, I can do that," he said. It was a relatively simple matter. His INC was in control of the ship's computer system. He moved through the safety programs until he found the diagram and then sent it to his PIL. It only took a few seconds to send it on to Nyx, Sly, and Ash since they were already on his contacts list.

"Man," Sly said shaking his head. "I shouldn't have drunk all that wine."

Nyx stepped over to him and slapped him hard across the face. He stumbled back a few steps.

"Hey, what are you doing?" Sly said.

Nyx popped him again, then shook her hand.

"Stop!" Sly cried out.

"Pull it together," Nyx said.

"What's happening?" Colonel Chastain said as she entered the room with Ash.

It was a shock to see her out of uniform. She had on fuzzy pajama pants and a baggy tee-shirt that hung down past her waist.

"She hit me," Sly declared. "Twice."

"You probably deserved it," Ash said.

"The ship's engines are off," Alex said, "and there's a ship moving toward our position."

"Range?" Colonel Chastain demanded.

"Eight hundred kilometers and closing," Alex said.

"Where's the VP?"

"He just took the chief stew up to the observation deck," Nyx said.

"That would be the best place to move the crew," Chastain said. "I'm assuming you're synced with their systems?"

Alex nodded, but somewhere on the ship someone was typing a message using the ship's computer. He held up a hand as the words flashed somewhat slowly into his mind...whoever was sending the message wasn't accustomed to typing on the computer system.

Standing by for docking. Passengers are unaware. Should be a simple matter to transfer the primary to your ship.

"They're coming for the VP," Alex said. "The ship that's approaching is planning to dock."

"We need to get the crew all together," Nyx said. "Alex can fly us out of here, but only if they don't sabotage the ship's computer system."

"So we need to move them up here," Chastain said.

She walked across the room and hit a button on the wall. A moment later, the second stew appeared.

"How can I help you?"

"Sergeant West, escort her up to the observation deck," Colonel Chastain said.

The stewardess looked alarmed. "What?"

"There's a problem with the yacht," Nyx said. "We need to move everyone up to the observation deck as quickly as possible."

The stewardess nodded and hurried up the stairs, not waiting for Nyx.

"Evans, can you set off the fire alarm in this salon?" Chastain asked.

"Yes," Alex said.

"Do it," Chastain said. "That should get everyone moving. Corporal, you stay right by his side. If we lose him, we lose control of this ship, and we can't afford to let that happen."

"Yes, Colonel," Sly said.

His face was red on both cheeks, but his eyes looked clearer. Alex backed against the wall between a row of windows and the stairs leading up to the dining room. Setting off the fire alarm was simple; as soon as the thought crossed his mind, a blaring electronic wail rang out almost instantly.

"Is it possible to have a hangover this soon?" Sly said, cringing at the sound.

From the crew area below, the third stew, the bosun, and two deckhands appeared. They looked bewildered as they searched for the reason for the alarm to go off.

"I'm not seeing anything, Captain," the bosun said into a com-link.

"Tell him there's an electrical fire," Colonel Chastain said as she pulled a small blaster from the waistband of her pajamas.

The bosun looked at her, his eyes flashing down to the gun in her hand. It was clear he wasn't happy. For a moment it seemed like he was weighing the possibility of challenging the colonel, but instead he nodded and tapped his com-link.

"Looks like an electrical fire," the bosun said. "We need all hands in the main salon."

"Take your people up to the observation deck, and no one needs to get hurt," Chastain said calmly as Nyx returned.

"Okay, just take it easy," the bosun said.

"Corporal Timmons," the colonel ordered. "Join VP Haley upstairs and help keep the crew on the observation deck."

Ash stepped forward as the third stew followed the bosun and two deckhands up the stairs. "Yes, Colonel," Ash said, hurrying after the crew. Her controller followed along.

"Sergeant West," the colonel continued giving orders. "Move to the other side of the hatch. Use that lamp as a weapon if you have to."

Nyx ripped the shade off a table lamp and lifted it up. Alex could see that it was heavy. Nyx held the lamp upside down, the thick base of which was like a club.

They heard the rest of the crew before they saw them; footsteps pounded on the stairs, and heavy, wheezing breaths belted out curses. The captain of the yacht charged into the room past Colonel Chastain and Nyx. His eyes were wide, and he was looking around for danger—only to realize too late that it was the passengers, not a fire, that were the real threat.

"What the—"

"Shut up!" Chastain said in a commanding voice.

The chef and engineer were the final two crew members to come rushing into the salon. They both held fire extinguishers.

"Drop those," the colonel ordered. "We're all going up to the observation deck."

"What's this all about?" asked the gruff captain.

"It's about you stopping the ship," Chastain replied.

"We're making repairs," the engineer piped up.

Chastain chuckled. "It's good to know you've got your story straight," she said. "You'll be answering for your crimes here."

"The only crime I can see is a mutiny by the passengers," the captain replied. "You have the gun, not us."

"Why don't you tell me about the ship that's approaching?" Chastain asked.

"We're near the space tunnel. It could be anyone."

"Good, then they won't mind if we keep moving. Now get upstairs."

She waved toward the stairs with the blaster. The captain's eyes narrowed, but he started for the stairs.

Alex, through his link with the ship's systems, knew that everything was online and ready to go. He brought the engines up and started the vessel moving. The navigation system showed exactly where they needed to go, and while the yacht seemed bulky and sluggish, flying it was not difficult.

"You're making a mistake," the captain of the yacht said as he started up the stairs.

"Only if you mean that we shouldn't protect ourselves," Chastain said. "We know you planned to turn over Vice President Haley to whoever is on that approaching ship."

Nxy took hold of Alex's arm. "Can you walk and fly at the same time?" she whispered.

"Sure," Alex said.

Dividing his attention wasn't easy at first, but the yacht took no actual skill to fly. It was a fully automated vessel, and the course was already set. Once Alex got the ship moving again, it took very little of his attention.

They followed the colonel up the stairs, with Sly and his controller bringing up the rear. No one did anything foolish, and soon they were all on the observation deck. The crew were lined up on the U-shaped modular sofa. Most looked frightened, and Alex guessed that they had no idea what was going on. The captain and the engineer, on the other hand, were glancing out to starboard.

"We're all here," Colonel Chastain said.

Alex and Nyx sat on the edge of the spa. Lights inside made the water look green and inviting. He could feel the heat rising up his back.

"How close is that other ship?" Haley asked.

"Four hundred kilometers," Alex said. "They're sending messages."

"Don't respond," Chastain ordered.

"Have they changed course?" Haley asked.

"Yes," Alex said. "They're following."

"Can we outrun them?" Nyx asked.

"We'll be at optimal speed soon," Alex said. "Unless they fire on us, we should be fine."

"Now that's a cheery thought," Sly said.

"I wish I had my Titan," Ash said.

"They won't fire," Haley said. "It's too dangerous. This type of ship wouldn't survive, and we're in a populated system. What's our ETA on Arcadia?"

"Sixteen hours," Alex said.

"Good, we have plenty of time to find out what they know," Haley said. "Let's start with the captain."

Chapter 4

"Tell me what you know," VP Haley said in a calm voice.

"I don't know anything," the captain of the *Starchaser* said angrily. "I have a job to do, and you are risking all our lives with this ridiculous display."

"Don't lie to me," Haley said. "You sent a message to that ship."

They were on the Rec Deck now, just one level below everyone else, yet the room was quiet. Loman sat in a chair facing the captain with nothing between them. Loman wasn't an interrogator, but he was a good negotiator, and he didn't think there was a lot of difference between the two skills. He sat up straight, his eyes watching the captain's every move. The yacht captain was looking nervously around the room, avoiding Loman's steady gaze.

"That is a lie."

"You told them it would be a simple matter to transfer me onto their ship," Loman pressed. "Who are they?"

"I don't know who you're ta—"

Loman smashed his fist into the armrest of his chair. "Stop lying to me," he snapped. "Trust me when I tell you that Colonel Chastain will have a very different method of extracting information from you. A very painful method."

The captain was starting to breathe hard. He looked scared.

"No one is coming to the rescue," Loman insisted. "You've made your bed, and now you'll have to lie in it. So tell me what you know, or..."

He let the captain's imagination run away with the idea of what might happen. The truth was, Colonel Chastain was not as scary as Loman was making her out to be. It was a bluff, but an effective one. Ursula Chastain was what Loman considered to be a serious person with a laser focus. It made her a good officer, and yet at times she was considered overbearing and unnerving. He had no qualms about using her idiosyncrasies to his advantage when it suited the situation.

"I don't know who they are," the captain finally snapped. The words tumbled out of him as if holding them back had taken all his strength and he was verbally collapsing under the strain. "We were paid twice our normal rate to take you on at short notice. It was a simple credit transfer with instructions via personal messaging. The other party listed themselves merely as 'client' and said we would be met here. We were to pretend that we had engine trouble, and if any questions were asked, we should tell you that the approaching ship was coming to help with repairs."

It was a plausible story, but one with no real answers. Loman thought about it for a moment before asking his next question. "And what were you supposed to tell the authorities?"

"Authorities? I don't know. I hadn't thought that far in advance."

"A charter ship like this could lose its license over an incident like you're describing," Loman said. "Leaving the rest of the passengers behind would be too many witnesses. You couldn't have possibly hoped that my people wouldn't file a complaint."

"I didn't know there would be more passengers," the captain snapped. "Not until you actually booked passage. By then I had already taken the money."

"What were your plans for the rest of us?" Loman asked.

"Nothing yet," he said, his head drooping. "But I was considering leaving them at a port or station where they couldn't make trouble."

"You were going to kill them," Loman said with a chuckle. "Fortunately for you, we caught on to your betrayal."

The captain looked up in surprise. "Fortunately?"

"Yes," Loman said. "Because whoever was trying to get me off this ship wouldn't have let any of you survive. They would have destroyed this vessel and killed everyone on board."

"No, that was not the plan."

"It's the only thing that makes sense," Loman said. "Once they had me, you would all be a loose end that could neatly be dealt with—an accident in space that kills everyone on board, and there are no more witnesses to the truth."

"But they paid us," the captain snapped.

"Because they needed your cooperation," Loman replied. "And odds are good that they won't just let us go, either."

"What do you mean?"

"I mean they're still out there, following us. And they won't let you go. Not now that you're a link back to whoever sent them in the first place."

"I don't know what you're talking about," the captain wailed.

"That much is obvious," Loman said. "I hope it was worth it."

He stood up, grabbed the captain by the collar of his white officer's shirt, and tugged him up out of the chair. The man was shaking all over, clearly terrified. His gruff demeanor was a sham to conceal the coward inside. Loman shoved him toward the stairs.

"Let's go."

They climbed back up to the observation deck. Loman looked out across the darkness of space, trying to see the ship pursuing them, but it was either too far away or running dark so as not to draw attention. They were in the Humphries system, which was part of the Free Trade Association's open route of space tunnels but otherwise unremarkable. There wasn't a habitable planet in the system, but there were several gas-mining space stations. The star was a white dwarf and didn't cast much light. Other stars filled space in every direction, but there was no sign of the ship pursuing them.

"Update?" Loman asked Colonel Chastain.

"We're almost up to speed," she replied. "The yacht isn't very fast."

"She's a luxury ship," the engineer spoke up. "Speed isn't a high priority on a mega-yacht."

"What about the pursuer?" Loman asked.

"They're following," Alex replied. "Still over three hundred klicks out, but closing in. Once we reach top speed, they'll catch us in just under ten hours."

"By then we'll be through the next space tunnel and in the Greco System," Chastain said. "They won't dare attack us in a highly populated part of space."

"Unless they feel like it's better to take us out than let us go," Loman said. "In that case, they could fire on us long before we reach the space tunnel."

His words hung over the passengers and crew like a dark cloud. Loman could see the anger and frustration on the faces of his operators and controllers. They didn't like being stuck on a luxury yacht that had absolutely no defenses. A single laser blast could compromise the yacht's bubble hull and kill every person on board. The looks on the faces of the crew were even worse; they were clearly terrified. Several were casting hate-filled looks at the captain, who had clearly gotten them into a fix they were beginning to fear they might never escape from.

"Sir," Alex said. "I think I might have a solution."

"Let's talk about it downstairs," Loman said. "Colonel Chastain, give Corporal Timmons your blaster. I don't think the crew is going to be much trouble. I want you and Sergeant West to join us downstairs."

"Yes, Mr. Haley," Chastain said, handing Ash her pistol.

Loman waved the others down the stairs. "Let's go find a way out of this mess."

Chapter 5

The small group gathered together on the Rec Deck as far from the stairs as possible. Alex didn't think the crew would betray them or even had the means now that they were separated from the control center of the yacht, but it was possible—and he didn't want to take any chances.

"You have a plan?" Loman asked him.

Alex looked at Nyx, who gave him an encouraging nod. "I think we should let the ship catch up," Alex said.

"If they board us, at least we have a fighting chance," Chastain said.

"Better than getting blown to oblivion, I suppose," Loman said. "I don't even think they have adequate emergency gear on this vessel."

"No," Alex said. "I don't think we should let them board. We just need to let them get close."

"And then what?" Loman asked.

"Then he can sync with their ship," Nyx said.

Loman looked at Colonel Chastain. There were clearly some doubts in his mind.

"Do you have a read on that ship?" Chastain asked.

"Not yet," Alex said. "It's too far out to be more than a faint hum, but I know I can do it."

Colonel Chastain shrugged her shoulders. "It's impossible to know for certain what he can or can't do. But they have to know we're on to them. The only chance we have is to let them think they can get on board. If they can't do that, it's likely they'll destroy the yacht."

"So let's get the crew on our side," Loman said. "We'll do an inventory of their safety equipment and find out if they have any kind of weapons. Maybe whoever is on that ship won't expect us to fight back."

"You don't want me to sync to their ship?" Alex asked, more than a little bothered that they were dismissing his plan so easily.

"No, you're plan A," Loman said. "But we can't help you, so we might as well focus on plan B just in case you aren't able to sync to their ship. Alex, if you do get access, we need to know as much as possible. Who are they? Who are they working for? That sort of thing."

"I can't read minds," Alex said. "But I'll look at their communications log. Maybe we can get some information from that."

"How much time do we have?" Colonel Chastain asked.

"I'll slow us down," Alex said. "They'll be close enough for me to sync in just under two hours."

"We should have the captain write them back," Nyx said. "Make an excuse for moving the yacht. Tell them that we're going to stop again."

"Good, we'll let you handle that," Loman said. "Ursula and I will take the engineer and chief stew down to look for emergency gear and weapons. Everyone else stays on the observation deck until Alex gives the word to move them out of sight."

They all nodded. It was a good plan—as long as the approaching ship didn't fire on them as soon as they were within range. Alex needed the ship close if he was going to sync with it. Until then, they were completely vulnerable.

The captain led the way down into the crew quarters of the ship. Unlike everything else on the mega-yacht, the crew quarters were small, cramped, and constructed of the cheapest materials. They passed the small cabins where the crew slept. They were tiny rooms with multiple bunks built into the sloping bulkheads. In stark contrast with the rest of the ship, the cabins were messy and unkempt, with clothes and personal items littered on the beds and hanging from makeshift racks. The galley was small but pristine. A small common room was barely large enough for the table that took up most of the space. Alex was reminded of the housing on NP8261 where he had grown up, but he'd never seen his family home in such disarray.

The captain was the only member of the crew who didn't share his quarters with another person. He had a tiny room just off the bridge, which was deep in the bowels of the ship. The vessel's engines and life support systems took up the bulk of the area on the lower decks. The bridge was well put-together, with video feeds from the ship's exterior and radar that showed everything around the ships for hundreds of kilometers. The ship had a simple drive system. Other than docking, the navigation system did most of the heavy lifting. All the captain had to do was input a destination, and the nav system would take it them there.

Alex had already slowed the ship, using the thrusters to counter the speed built up by the ship's main engines. He had been forced to bypass the ship's autopilot and shut off the nav system's warning alarms. He had to admit that watching the captain as he checked the various systems on the bridge of his mega-yacht was satisfying; the man had no idea how they were controlling his vessel.

"You aren't here to fly us," Nyx warned him. "Check the messages."

There were only three, each sent by tight-beam, ship-to-ship transmission. All three were from the ship following them.

Why are you leaving the designated area? The first message was simple enough. The second repeated it and requested even more information.

Why are you leaving the designated area? Does the target know we're coming?

Alex wanted to write back that the target did in fact know —that they would soon be under his control and that he would have all their secrets. But that wasn't smart; the last thing he wanted was to tip his hand and reveal that the small group of fighters from Ahzco's CDF were in control of the ship and expecting them.

The third message was more direct: *Respond,* Starchaser, *or we will fire on your vessel.*

"They aren't very conversational," Alex said. "I could have replied already."

"They might know if you did it," Nyx said. "They've been talking with the captain."

She put a hand on the captain's shoulder and leaned close. "Keep in mind," she said, "that they're willing to fire on us if they think something's wrong."

"Yeah," he said in a tremulous voice. "I see that."

"Tell them you had an issue with the autopilot," Nyx said, "and don't do anything stupid. You'll just get us all killed."

The captain nodded. He punched in a quick message.

We're having problems with the autopilot. It's offline now. We're slowing down. Proceed as planned.

"So there was a plan," Alex said.

"Only for the primary," the captain said. "I had no idea the rest of you would be in danger. I thought it was just a kidnap for ransom."

"And you were okay with that?" Nyx said as they waited for a reply.

"We needed the money," he said in a voice laced with shame.

The computer beeped with a new message: *You're in range now. Try anything, and we'll fire on your ship. Deliver the target, and you're free to do whatever you want with the rest.*

Alex tapped into the navigation computer. It already had a course set for the Greco system. He wanted the mega-yacht ready to move as soon as he disabled the approaching ship. The systems on the luxury vessel were simple to use, and he didn't think it would take too much effort to control both ships, but he didn't want to take any chances.

"Can you stay here with him?" Alex said. "Just in case I need you to get us moving again?"

Nyx nodded. "I could pilot a ship like this in my sleep."

"It's not as easy as it looks," the captain said, but it was just a lame attempt to justify his career.

"The entire ship is automated," Alex said. "All she has to do is push a button."

"Well, yeah, on a cruise like this," he answered with a little more conviction. "But most of the time we're chartered for vacation spots. You get close to a nebula, and the gravity fluctuations render all the automated systems useless. That's when you need an experienced captain at the helm."

"I guess it's too bad that honesty isn't a requirement for making rank," Nyx said. "Aren't you charged with the safety of your passengers?"

The captain's shoulders slumped. "Nobody's perfect," he grumbled.

"Don't worry, I've got this," Nyx said to Alex.

The look in her eyes was total confidence. A shock raced through his body. The way that she looked at him made him feel weightless, and he couldn't help but smile.

"I never had a doubt," he said.

She smiled, and he realized that all he really wanted in life was to see that smile every single day.

Chapter 6

"How much time do we have?"

The executive vice president of security was clearly nervous. Alex was beginning to think he was a control freak. Of course, the fact that they hadn't found any weapons beyond kitchen knives didn't put the older man's mind at ease, but Alex had complete confidence in his abilities. The approaching ship was only fifty kilometers away and slowing down. It would only be a few more minutes until he could take control of her.

"I'll be able to sync with them soon," Alex said.

"And if you can't?" Loman asked.

"I can," Alex said.

"It's always smart to have contingency plans," Colonel Chastain said. "How long until they can board us?"

"Twenty minutes," Alex said. "Maybe twenty-five."

"We just have one blaster, two fire-suppressant canisters, and some knives," Loman said. "If this goes south, we're in trouble."

Alex would have argued that he could handle the approaching ship, but the EM waves coming from the approaching vessel were getting louder by the moment. He had no problem hearing them, but they weren't like other ships. There was no harmony to the sounds. It was more like a small group of instrumentalists all playing different sounds.

"What's wrong, Evans?" Colonel Chastain asked.

"I'm not sure," he said.

"Damn, I hate waiting," Loman grumbled. "It's the worst."

Alex turned all his attention to the approaching ship. It was only forty kilometers away, but it was unlike anything he'd experienced before. The EM waves picked up by his INC were clashing. It was almost painful, and it reminded Alex of when he'd first come out of the medical center after having his INC procedure. There had been a lot of different sounds then, too— different frequencies, speeds, and pitches. But the sounds from the approaching ship were worse; they were much louder and almost grating, as if someone were rubbing sandpaper across the surface of his brain.

He bent over, covering his ears, but it didn't help. The cacophony wasn't really a sound at all. There was no way to stop it.

"Is he okay?" Loman asked.

"I don't know," Colonel Chastain said.

They were on the Rec Deck stairs. The VP wanted to see the ship approaching. Colonel Chastain was right beside Alex and took hold of his arm.

"What's wrong, Sergeant?"

"I don't know," Alex said. "The waves are so loud."

"They're running unshielded," Loman said. "It's an outlaw ship. They're probably transmitting a dozen different transponder codes. It's an old trick to keep from being properly identified."

"Can you sync with them?" Colonel Chastain asked.

"Trying," Alex replied through clenched teeth.

"Most of those types of ships are cobbled together," Loman went on. "The systems probably aren't integrated. They'll be pieced together and overpowered. I never met a hacker who didn't overbuild their computers."

Alex synced with one system. It was the ship's life support. He powered it down with a thought. The other systems were a jumble of constantly moving frequencies. It felt like he was trying to pluck a single hair from a person's head in zero gravity. The systems seemed to move around him, eluding his efforts. The next system he found was merely an overpowered identification broadcast. He shut it down, and the noise in his head subsided a fraction. The ship was transmitting dozens of ID codes and playing a variety of pre-recorded messages. It was like being in a dark room with a hundred different people shouting at him all at once.

"They're still coming," Loman pointed out.

"Go tell Nyx to get us moving," Alex said, "before they collide with us."

"Is that a possibility?" Loman asked, but Colonel Chastain was already moving. She rushed past Alex and down the stairs.

He continued syncing with the various systems and shutting them down, but there were so many. When he finally found the weapons system on the ship, he flinched. They had no gravity or even light to see by, but the crew were preparing to fire on the yacht. He shut down their weapons systems. An instant later, their life support flickered on like an old lightbulb.

"They're fighting back," Alex said.

"Don't give up, kid," Loman said. "You can do this."

Alex thought the VP's change of heart was refreshing, but perhaps a little too late. Alex had to fight his way through the noise to find what he was really looking for. The ship's power system was massive. Syncing to it felt like he was putting his head inside a giant speaker. But once he was in, shutting down the ship's power silenced everything else. He breathed a sigh of relief.

"I shut them down," he said.

"Good work," Loman replied.

But Alex knew he wasn't done. He had cut the power, but the ship used a chambered fusion core reactor to produce the electricity that powered the vessel's systems. He had turned it off, but it could easily be turned on again. If Alex couldn't disable it, the approaching ship could quickly regain power and fire their weapons. He pushed his way deeper into the system. There were safety systems in place to keep the reactor from overloading and destroying the ship. Alex bypassed the safety features one by one. When he finally had them all down, he withdrew.

"That's it," Alex said.

"You shut them down?" Loman asked.

"For the moment," Alex said.

"We need more than a moment, Sergeant," Loman argued. "If they regain control, they could fire on us."

"I know," Alex said. "I'm counting on it."

The truth was, whoever was aboard the approaching ship couldn't be stopped—not by Alex using the power of his INC to take control. He needed to be close to control the vessel, and yet being close negated their ability to escape. Worse still, whoever was on the ship clearly had experience with their systems. Most ships were controlled by a master computer that synchronized the various shipboard systems and acted as a gateway to each individual module, but the approaching ship had no central control system; all the computers were separate and run by technicians who knew them well. To Alex, it was like trying to fight six different people with six different weapons, all at the same time. As soon as he shut one down, someone on the approaching ship went immediately to work bringing the system back online.

"You're what?" Loman said.

"I just hope we're far enough away," Alex said.

He synced with the *Starchaser*'s system again. He was beginning to feel tired. A pain had blossomed behind his eyes that felt like a red-hot coal had been stuck in his brain. He couldn't remember how long it had been since he had slept, but he suddenly felt incredibly tired. Perhaps it was just the stress of the attack, but he felt weak.

"Far enough away for what?" Loman demanded. "What did you do?"

Alex checked the yacht's radar. They were moving away from the approaching ship, but it was still moving in their direction. The *Starchaser* was a slow vessel, and it wasn't gaining the distance Alex hoped for. They were still only twenty-five kilometers from the ship.

"I bypassed the safety systems on their fusion reactor," Alex said. "If they power up their lasers, it will destroy their ship."

"And if they fire missiles?"

Alex hadn't thought of missiles. They were preparing their lasers when he had been connected to them. The noise from the other ship was still loud and grating on his mind. The thought of syncing with them again was loathsome, yet what choice did he really have? He reached out with his mind, enduring the cacophony of noisy EM waves radiating from the ship. It felt like he was removing his clothing and stepping out into a hailstorm. The burning sensation behind his eyes intensified.

Then—before he could sync with the ship—it exploded without warning. Light flared in the darkness behind the yacht, and Alex was hit with a powerful EM wave that felt like a physical blow. He collapsed. The last thought that went through his mind was the realization that he was falling down the stairs.

Chapter 7

Loman had seen a lot of things in his lifetime. Spaceships didn't explode often, but when they did, it was spectacular. The explosion of the ship that had been pursuing the *Starchaser* was unforgettable. With nothing between them but empty space, Loman had an unobstructed view, and yet he turned away from the brilliant flash as Alex tumbled down the steps.

There was no way for Loman to catch the young operator. He was already below him, only halfway up the narrow stairs that were edged in polished chrome. There was a single handrail, but Alex didn't even try to grasp it. Loman saw his eyes roll back in his head as he flopped backwards. He hit the stairs hard enough to flip his legs over his head and came crashing to a halt at the bottom.

"Alex!" Loman shouted as he hurried down the steps.

Something had happened. It made the VP nervous just thinking about it. What if Alex was dead? The boy was his best hope of finding out who was behind the attacks on Ahzco, and he couldn't deny his hope that Alex's new abilities could be replicated. It was too much power for anyone to have, and yet an army of operators capable of taking control of rival ships would make Ahzco the most powerful organization in the galaxy. Loman had always been ambitious, but the thought of total control—the likes of which no one had ever imagined—being at his fingertips was heady indeed. The very thought of it made him giddy.

A shutter vibrated through the ship: the shockwave from the explosion. The lights flickered, then went off. He halted on the stairs, holding onto the handrail just in case some piece of the exploded ship impacted the mega-yacht. If it did, chances were high that it would compromise the ship's hull. They could all die if luck wasn't on their side. He held his breath, waiting for disaster, but nothing happened. The lights came back on, and there was no crash. Loman decided to continue down the stairs.

He reached Alex but didn't move him. The young man was lying crumpled on his side, but nothing looked broken. Loman reached out a hand and felt for breath. A slight puff was detectable. Loman breathed a sigh of relief. Whatever was ailing Alex, he wasn't dead. Perhaps he had just over-exerted himself. Once upon a time, Loman had been an operator himself. It seemed like a different lifetime, but he still had an INC chip in the back of his head. With his INC, Loman could still sync to his work computer, a powerful AI that helped him keep tabs on the company's vast resources. Yet Loman had to be in the same room with the device. He couldn't imagine what it would be like to sync with something thirty kilometers away.

"Alex, can you hear me?" Loman gave Alex's arm a gentle shake. There was no response. The fall down the stairs wasn't terribly far, but falling wrong could still cause major damage. Loman worried his young star could have broken his neck. Moving him could be dangerous, so instead he called for help. "We need help down here!" Loman bellowed.

Ash and Sly came running. They slowed as they descended the stairs from the observation deck.

"What happened?" Ash asked.

"He collapsed," Loman said, "just when the other ship exploded."

They continued down and stepped over Alex's prone body.

"It could have been the EMP," Sly said. "Was he synced to that other ship when she blew?"

"I'm not sure," Loman said. "Maybe."

"We need to move him," Ash said. "They probably have a portable scanner on this ship."

Sly bounded back up the stairs and called for Glenda. The chief stew hurried down the steps.

"It he okay?" Glenda asked.

"That's what we need the scanner for," Ash said.

"Oh, right," the stewardess said. "I'll get it."

She hurried away, and Loman looked at Ashton Timmons. "Not the brightest bulb, is she?"

"I think they hire based on looks, not IQ," Ash said. "At least she's not belligerent."

Loman had to agree. Most of the crew seemed to know nothing about the deal to hand him over to the pirates following them. They were shocked and scared, but not duplicitous. It was, he realized, a lucky break.

"She's coming back," Sly said.

Glenda appeared with a medical scanner. She turned it on and held it over Alex's crumpled body, while Loman and Ash moved away.

"No broken bones," Glenda said. "I'll need more time for a thorough scan."

"That's good enough," Loman said. "Get him something to drink. Something with a little kick."

He gently tugged Alex's shoulder while the young operator's teammates straightened his legs out. Alex groaned. Loman could see his eyes moving through his eyelids, but they didn't open.

"Should we move him?" Sly asked.

"Yeah," Loman agreed. "We can put him on that sofa. The rest of the crew has to go back to work."

Sly picked up Alex's legs, and Loman held his arms. Ash supported his head, and they set him gently on the sofa.

"If it was the EM pulse that knocked him out," Ash said, "is it possible it scrambled things in his head?"

"Or disabled his INC," Sly suggested.

Loman felt a cold knot of fear in his stomach. The thought of losing Alex before they even had a chance to find out what his new abilities could do was terribly frightening. Guilt over his concern for Alex's ability was even worse. Loman didn't think of himself as a greedy person, but if he cared more about what Alex could do than for the person he was, what did that say about him?

"What else can we do?" Glenda asked.

"Nothing," Loman said, taking the medical scanner from her. "Your people can go back to work."

"We're not in danger?" the stewardess asked.

"No," Loman said. "Not from us."

"And not from the ship that was coming to take us away," Ash said.

"All right," Glenda said. "I'm sorry about that."

She moved quickly back up the stairs to the observation deck where the rest of the crew waited with Ash's and Sly's controllers.

"Should we try to wake him up?" Sly said.

"I think rest is the best thing for him right now," Loman said. "We all need some rest, but we'll need to do it in shifts. I'll stay with Alex for now. Sergeant West and Colonel Chastain will make sure the ship stays on course. We'll wake you in a few hours."

"Roger that," Ash said.

The crew came down from the observation deck along with the controllers who had been watching them. They all looked relieved, and he didn't blame them. It was a relief to have escaped whatever trap was set for him, but his worry for Alex tempered that relief. If saving him had cost Alex his new abilities, Loman wasn't entirely sure it was worth it.

Soon everyone was below. Most of the passengers and crew had returned to their cabins. The third stew had prepared some coffee for Loman. He sat in a chair near the sofa where Alex was sleeping, sipping his hot, caffeinated beverage and hoping for a miracle, when the young operator finally woke up.

"What happened?" Alex asked.

"You passed out," Loman told him, leaning toward Alex, "and fell down the stairs."

"I believe you," Alex said. "Everything hurts."

"We ran a medical scan. No broken bones."

"What happened to the other ship?"

"She blew, just like you predicted," Loman said. "It happened right when you lost consciousness."

He helped Alex sit up. The younger man began rotating his joints, checking to make sure everything was still working. He winced a little as he rolled his head around, stretching the muscles in his neck.

"You're bound to be pretty sore," Loman said. "The stairs are steep on this ship."

"At least we're not in danger, right?" Alex asked.

"That's right," Loman said. "I don't suppose you had a chance to find out who they were or why they were after us?"

"No," Alex said. "All the systems were isolated, and there was so much noise."

"More than the Zen Tech vessels in the Carthage System?"

"Much more," Alex said. "It was like a hundred different systems all projecting at once. It didn't make sense. There was no central control."

"Outlaw ships don't have any continuity," Loman said. "Some ships are just a jumble of cobbled-together computer systems. Most are built by the crew members who use them, and few can even sync together. The fact that you could is astounding."

"It wasn't a pleasant experience," Alex said.

"Well the good news is, you're alive. I hate to ask it of you, but do you think you might just test out your INC? We need to know if anything got scrambled by the electromagnetic pulse that was generated when the ship exploded."

"An EMP," Alex said, considering the idea. "I guess that might affect me if I was synced to the system."

"It's just a theory," Loman said. "Can you sync to the *Starchaser*'s systems?"

Alex closed his eyes and sat very still for a moment. Loman's fears were surging, but after a pause, Alex nodded.

"Yeah, I'm synced," he said. "I've got a read on all her systems."

He grinned, and Loman felt a surge of relief. "We're on course?"

"Yes, sir," Alex said. "Still gathering speed, but we're headed for the space tunnel to the Greco system."

"Excellent. I'm going to bed. I've had enough excitement for a month," Loman said. "I suggest you do the same."

"Yeah," Alex said. "I'll do that."

Loman stood and began a slow shuffle toward the stairwell that would take him down to this cabin. Even though the *Starchaser* was a luxurious mega-yacht, he couldn't wait to get off.

Chapter 8

Alex was ready to go to sleep. Sly was already snoring softly on the twin bed in their shared cabin. He sat on the soft bed and bent over to unlace his boots. Pain suddenly slashed through his head—an agonizing, piercing agony, as if someone had jammed a knife straight through his brain.

He groaned as he slowly raised back up. His teeth were clenched tight, and his hands were gripping the bed sheets into tight wads on either side of him. The pain he'd had in his leg and now his whole body after falling down the stairs was nothing compared to this new pain in his head. As he moved back up into an upright position, the pain eased slightly. He sat like a statue, barely daring to breathe as the pain slowly receded.

Something was wrong; that much was obvious. Fear was poking around trying to find a way into his mental calm. He thought about what he knew for sure. It was easy to link his new abilities to the sudden issues he was struggling with, but he didn't know for certain that one had anything to do with the other. Perhaps the EMP had damaged something, but Alex didn't think so. There had been pain behind his eyes before he had synced with the outlaw ship. He could still remember the burning feeling, and he knew he'd take that deep, aching burn over the sharp stab he'd just endured any day.

After a minute had passed, the pain dissolved completely. He still didn't move. Fear was threatening to bring back the pain if he moved. It was absurd, he knew, but he couldn't deny the fact the he was loath to repeat what had happened when he'd bent over to untie his boots.

I'm alive, he told himself. *Everything's okay.*

He wasn't sure if he really was okay, but he knew that his thoughts had power. He focused on being okay and lifted his right foot up. It felt like he was breaking an unwritten rule to put his boot on the soft sheets of the bed, but he wasn't going to bend over again, and he didn't want to sleep in his boots. His fingers untied and loosened the laces. After repeating the process on his left boot, he used the toe of one to push off the other. With his boots off, he slid back on the bed.

Fear told him the pain would return if he lay down, but he pushed the thought away. There was no truth in the thought that lying down would hurt him. His mental training came back to him. He had to focus on what was true: he was alive, and the pain in his head was most likely just a result of stress and overwork.

Lying down brought no new pain. It actually felt good to relax. He closed his eyes and let the tension melt away. Sleep came quickly, and Alex didn't resist it. The sweet release of sleep swept him away from the threat of pain and his concern for the safety of the people he cared about—worries that seemed to be hanging over him like a dark cloud. If there was a storm coming, he would weather it. Until then, he could sleep. And he did.

Six hours of sleep doesn't sound like much until you've gone without any for days. When Alex woke up six hours later, he felt better—and hungry. Sly was sitting up on the other bed, pulling his socks up.

"The shower on this ship is like a dream," Sly said.

"Hot water?"

"Loads of it," Sly said. "And from what I hear, the chef is up and taking orders for breakfast."

That got Alex moving. After a hot shower, he shaved, dressed quickly, and made his way up to the dining room. The second stew was busy seeing to everyone. Loman Haley and Colonel Chastain were already eating. Alex asked for orange juice and eggs.

Nyx wasn't there, and after eating his breakfast, he set out to find her. She was still asleep in her cabin that she shared with Ash. Once he was certain she was all right, he went down to the crew quarters and stepped into the bridge. The gruff captain was there with Ash's controller, who had Colonel Chastain's blaster.

"You here to relieve me?"

"Sure," Alex said.

The controller stood up, handed Alex the pistol, and started to leave. "Are they still serving breakfast?"

"Whatever you want," Alex said. "Made fresh to order."

The controller grinned and left the bridge. The captain never looked away from the instruments. Alex knew he could sync to the ship's systems and know everything there was to know about the ship, but he preferred not to. He was feeling good, and while there was no hard evidence to suggest that using his INC was the cause of his headaches, he didn't feel like taking the chance.

"How's it going?" Alex said.

"We're on schedule," the captain said in his gruff voice.

"We're in the Greco system?"

"That's right. Just a few hours and we'll reach Arcadia's spaceport."

"What happens to you then?" Alex asked.

"I suppose I'll be taken into custody and have my captain's license revoked. I'll be lucky to get a job swabbing the deck on a backwater space station."

"At least you'll be alive," Alex said.

The captain grunted, clearly not in agreement with Alex's assessment. It didn't seem likely that the gruff, older man had ever been in real danger. Alex could still see Newt's body, the way it had looked after being shot down in his Titan battle suit on Carthage. The memory haunted him. There was no doubt in Alex's mind that his friend would rather be swabbing a deck somewhere than dead in the cold ground on Carthage Prime.

The bridge was little more than a computer station. There were large display screens above the work surface, where a variety of controls were available. The captain sat in a large chair directly in front of the workspace, but there was a bench seat and table behind him on the port side of the bridge. Alex sat on the thickly padded seat, the blaster and his PIL on the table in front of him. The four hours passed quickly, especially after Nyx turned up a couple hours before they were scheduled to reach the station. They spent the remaining time talking quietly. The captain was no real threat at that point. He merely kept the ship on course and followed the directions of the flight controllers in the Arcadia port.

When Loman Haley poked his head into the bridge, they were less than fifteen minutes from reaching their destination.

"You said you'd never been to Arcadia before, right?" Loman asked. They both nodded. "Well, you should head up to the observation deck then. You don't want to miss it. I'll keep an eye on things down here."

Alex and Nyx didn't hesitate. Alex handed the executive vice president the blaster and hurried out. It was his first trip to a level-one planet, and there was no denying his excitement. When they reached the observation deck, what Alex saw was like nothing he'd ever even imagined.

Chapter 9

The Greco system was incredible. Alex had seen it in holo-films and documentaries, but they did not compare to the real thing. There were huge solar sails glowing with golden light. Ships of every make and model were in the system, from luxurious personal spacecraft to massive freighters. The Arcadia spaceport was more than just a transport hub; it was a huge city with hundreds of docking ports for ships coming into the system. It looked to Alex like a gigantic, manmade snowflake. It was geometrical in design, with spokes standing out in all directions.

As impressive as the station was, it didn't hold a candle to the planet itself. Arcadia was one giant city. From orbit, the blue seas contrasted with the glimmer of sunlight from ten thousand skyscrapers made of metal and glass. The world looked as if it were made of polished chrome, and there were so many orbital satellites that they formed a ring around the planet.

"It's amazing," Nyx said.

"I've never seen anything like it," Alex said.

Arcadia had three moons, and two were visible from their perspective: Apollo and Artemus. Apollo was used as a shipyard. The gravity of Apollo was so low that most spacecraft could land and take off from the moon, even if they couldn't from any other celestial body. Some of the finest and most expensive ships in the galaxy were built there. Artemus was a wildlife sanctuary. After being terraformed, the moon was a miniature twin of Arcadia. As the massive cities on the planet expanded, the wildlife and native flora were transplanted to Artemus, where they could live without the threat of mankind destroying their habitats. It was an emerald gem hovering above the sparkling silver planet.

Ash and Sly were already on the observation deck. The four of them stood by the spa and took in the sights of the level-one planet. There were other space stations, too, all on Arcadia's orbital plane. Those within sight were spectacular feats of architectural design.

"What are the space stations for?" Sly asked.

"Upscale resorts," Ash said.

"Really?" Alex replied. "They're just for tourists?"

"Arcadia is all business," Ash replied. "There's plenty to do down there, but business interests have purchased all the properties. Tourists usually stay off-world and just take day trips down to different parts of the city."

"The world that never sleeps," Sly said. "I can see why."

Alex could too. The incredible number of people on Arcadia and in the Greco system made him feel small and insignificant. He could hear the EM waves from a hundred different ships, and the roar from the spaceport alone was stupendous. He had to tamp the noise down and push it to the back of his mind for fear of being overwhelmed by it. He flinched when Nyx touched his arm.

"You okay, Alex?" she asked.

"Sure," he said, although in truth he was completely overwhelmed.

"Ya know, I could get used to this," Sly said.

"It's the most expensive planet in the galaxy," Ash said. "You wouldn't last a day without us."

"So we stick together," Sly said. "I think we can make it work."

Alex wasn't so sure, but he couldn't deny he was anxious to see what Arcadia was really like. They all returned to their cabins and gathered their personal belongings. They didn't have much, and it wasn't long until they were gathered in the main salon. The entire crew minus the captain were there too, lined up to say goodbye to their guests. Alex could feel the tension, and he didn't blame them. The passengers had taken control of the ship, and the crew probably felt as if their futures were in jeopardy.

They shook hands with the crew members, and then Loman Haley, executive VP of Ahzco security, led them off the ship. The only person who stayed behind was Colonel Chastain. She was seeing to it that the captain was held accountable for his crimes and probably interrogated to see if he knew anything more about the attempt on VP Haley's life.

The Arcadia spaceport was immaculate. There were people everywhere hurrying to and from the various storefronts and docking arms. Loman didn't waste any time locating a shuttle that would take them down to the surface. Alex knew he could have spent a month exploring the spaceport. It was bigger than any city he'd ever been in before, but they spent less than ten minutes on the space station. The shuttle departed as soon as they were on board and strapped in.

The shuttle had rows of captain's chairs in plush leather. Once they left the spaceport, they were in zero-gravity for almost ten minutes. There were no windows on the ship, but there were video displays on the back of every seat. Advertisements played on the screens, and with only a tap, a person could learn more about whatever was being advertised. Alex focused instead on his Flex PIL. He brought up a map of Arcadia and zoomed down to the massive Ahzco building. In total, Ahzco owned eighteen blocks in the massive city. Sixteen were located around their HQ building, but two were on the coast. There was only one building with temporary housing. Executive suites for visiting business professionals or talented management-level personnel being recruited by the company overlooked the bay where cargo ships had once carried goods from around the globe. Alex wanted to know exactly where he was going and how to get from the Ahzco building to their quarters overlooking the bay.

It was early morning in the central district, which was the part of Arcadia's massive metropolis they would be in. The shuttle came down on a private landing pad on a short but broad structure near the Ahzco building. Loman stood up and went immediately to the exit. Alex and the others scrambled to keep up.

"Just leave your bags here," Loman said. "Our people will move them to your quarters."

Alex made sure he had his Flex PIL snapped onto his forearm and his company ID on a lanyard around his neck. Everything else he owned was in the thick rucksack with his name stenciled on the side.

"Welcome to Ahzco universal headquarters," Loman said as they walked down the ramp onto the roof of the wide building. "This is the heart of the galactic corporation we are tasked with protecting. You're standing on the Product Display Building. Everything we produce is represented in the eight stories below us here. I'm sure you'll have time to tour the entire campus, but for now, let's get you to the HQ building. There are people there I want you to meet."

It was warm, and the air was rich with oxygen. Alex could smell the briny scent of the ocean not far away. Despite the multitude of people living in Arcadia's global city, there was no stench of machinery, exhaust, or garbage. An open-air hovercraft rose up beside the Product Display Building. Loman led the group over and got them all on board the transport, which then descended between the towering buildings and wound its way to the tallest structure for miles around.

The Ahzco universal headquarters building was a dazzling mega-skyscraper with over two hundred stories. The group of operators and controllers, recently given the name Cronus Team, followed the VP of security off the transport and across the perfectly manicured courtyard that fronted the massive building. They went through a large revolving door into the lobby of the building. Alex looked up at the ceiling that was thirty meters above their heads.

"We'll need to get your IDs logged in as visitors," Loman said. "Then we'll go up and meet CEO Ian Gentry."

"We're going to meet the CEO?" Nyx asked in surprise.

"Oh yes, he'll want to meet the team that saved our investment in the Carthage system," Loman said. "Just relax, he's harmless. Once you've met the CEO, I'll introduce you to Zan Fordham. You're going to have an amazing day."

Chapter 10

At the same moment that Alex and his Titan team were riding up the executive elevators of the Ahzco universal headquarters building, down in the engineering space a different sort of work was being conducted. The final explosive charge was being laid inside the support pillar of the massive building's foundation. In the gloom, the man who had labored long to complete his assignment was giddy despite the heat and humidity in the narrow workspace. He was dreaming of a new life far away. Once he reported his success to the agent who was already waiting for him nearby, he would receive more credits than he could earn working for Ahzco in ten lifetimes.

He filled the last hole—which had been drilled by the small robotic tool into the stalwart, concrete pillar—with putty, making sure the wire receiver was more than ten centimeters long. When he finished, he wiped his dirty hands on an old rag and put everything into his small, portable toolbox. There was something so gratifying about completing a job—not that he could take any real joy in preparing the Ahzco building for what could only be a terrible act of terrorism. Still, he felt good about his life. If people died, it wouldn't be from him pulling the trigger. He had been paid to prepare the charges, nothing more. And if Ahzco security ever paid him more than the faintest passing recognition, he wouldn't have been able to do that much. He was invisible. There were hundreds of people working in the building above his head, each one of them dependent on the work he did, yet he made a fraction of their wages. No one outside his department even knew his name. In his mind, whatever they got was no less than they deserved.

After leaving the dank engineering space, he climbed the stairs to the communication terminal and put a sign on the cage that showed it under repairs. He set his tools down beside it. If the building was destroyed, whoever dug through the rubble would find his belongings and assume he was dead too—if his tools could even survive the blast. After leaving his things behind, he slipped out a maintenance door on the ground level. It wasn't like the opulent lobby with polished floors and glass walls; he was forced to use the rear maintenance door which was dull, gray steel, the walls and floor bare concrete. When the heavy door closed with a *thunk!*, he actually felt a sense of relief. It was the last time he would ever sweat through his clothing in the stuffy engineering space or climb stairs until his legs burned just to plug in someone's holo-projector because they were too dense to realize it wouldn't power on without being connected to the electrical grid. His work was done, and he was looking forward to his retirement.

He walked briskly between the buildings, following the route he took every morning and evening, until he came to the public transportation hub. Working on Arcadia was an achievement for most people, but it only made the laborer's life harder. He couldn't afford a personal transport, and he was forced to live in a squalid, sub-basement apartment. The cost of living on Arcadia was ridiculous, but what choice did he have? He was a tiny cog deep inside the unseen depths of the galaxy's glitziest planet.

Another man waited on a bench just inside the public transportation hub. He looked like every other business professional. There were millions of them in the central district alone. Sitting on the bench just inside the station, studying his PIL, he was completely forgettable. The maintenance worker joined him.

"Is it complete?" the businessman asked quietly.

"Yes sir, every pillar is set," the worker replied.

"And no one knows?"

"Not a soul, just as we discussed."

"Very good. I have your compensation."

The worker pulled his own PIL from the inner pocket of his coveralls. It was old and outdated, but still serviceable. He already had his banking info pulled up. His Personal Information Link didn't have the proximity transfer capability that the newer models had, but all the businessman needed was the banking info. The worker's hands shook a little as he imagined all the credits that were about to be transferred into his account. He would be rich and never have to work another day in his life. He could leave Arcadia and spend his life on a resort planet being pampered by beautiful women. In that moment, he felt like a child on Christmas morning.

But the businessman didn't take his PIL or make a financial transfer. Instead, he casually reached over and injected a fast-acting neurotoxin into the worker's thigh. It was over in less than a second. The sting of the injection made the worker jump. He dropped his PIL and grabbed his thigh.

"What was that?" the worker demanded.

"Payment in full," the businessman said, without any emotion in his voice.

"You were supposed to..."

The worker had suddenly lost his train of thought. He was angry, but he couldn't remember why. The businessman stood up and walked away without another word. The worker watched him go. He thought briefly that he should follow for some reason, but couldn't think of why, and he was tired. His arms and legs felt heavy. Thinking was hard, and his eyelids were drooping. All he wanted in that moment was to sleep, and he couldn't think of any reason not to.

The worker slumped over on the bench, took one last shallow breath, and died. People passed by without a second glance. In the dirty coveralls, he looked like a homeless person who had passed out from alcohol or drugs. The busy executives assumed a security officer would roust him out of the public transportation hub soon enough. The man was, in many of their minds, just another example of why the vice laws on Arcadia weren't stringent enough.

Chapter 11

The lift opened into a large waiting room. It was completely unlike anything Alex had ever seen before. Large, leafy green plants were growing near a soothing waterfall that flowed from the tall ceiling down over large chunks of polished stone. The sitting area was made up of tufted leather chairs with thick armrests. A polished reception desk gleamed in the soft light, and behind it sat the most perfect-looking woman Alex had ever seen.

"Oh man," Sly whispered.

"She's cosmetically enhanced, you dolt," Ash whispered back.

"Who cares?" he replied.

Loman walked straight to the receptionist and told her that the heroes from Carthage Prime were there to see Ian Gentry. The rest of the group stayed close to the lift, almost as if they were afraid of getting into trouble.

Alex remembered the waiting area in the security hangar on NP8261. It had seemed to him then like the most lavish accommodations in the galaxy, but compared to the CEO's waiting area, it was more like an old, smelly barn.

"Have a seat," Loman said, turning back to the group from the reception desk. "We'll be called in when the CEO has a free moment."

Alex and Nyx settled into two of the chairs. The leather creaked beneath them yet felt almost slick to the touch. Alex couldn't believe how comfortable the chairs were.

"This place is amazing," Nyx said.

"You can say that again," Alex said. "Can you believe that waterfall?"

A large video wall rotated through advertisements for various Ahzco products. Everyone spoke in hushed tones like they were afraid of being overheard. Alex felt so out of place that he assumed at any minute he was going to be found out and sent packing.

"Can I offer you refreshments?" the receptionist said as she came out from behind her desk.

She was tall, with a figure that looked almost cartoonish. Her waist was narrow, her legs long and thin, yet her backside and chest were large. Her eyes were larger than any eyes Alex had ever seen. Her cheekbones protruded from her angular face in a way that he could only describe as severe. She seemed sculpted, with certain features overemphasized. Her hair was blond and gleamed in the light. She wore it pulled into a tight ponytail, and not a single strand was out of place. Despite the fact that she had been altered in the extreme with high-end cosmetic surgeries, Alex still found her astonishing to look at. It was almost impossible for him to look away.

"How about mineral waters?" Loman answered for the group. "With a twist of lime."

"It would be my pleasure," the receptionist said.

As she walked away, Loman leaned toward the Titan team. "Gentry keeps her to unsettle his visitors. Don't let her get in your head."

It was too late for Alex. He couldn't get the strange-looking woman out of his mind. There was something oddly appealing about her—something almost intoxicating.

"Are you okay?" Nyx whispered to him.

"Yeah," he lied. "Sure. Never better."

He knew he wasn't believable, but he didn't want Nyx to think he was attracted to someone else. Wrenching his mind away from the receptionist was difficult, but he managed it by focusing on the EM waves picked up his INC. The city was filled with electrical devices. It was almost like he was drowning in the myriad sounds all around him, even though the waiting room was actually very quiet. Alex focused on the harmonizing tones of Ahzco's electric devices. They merged together like the various instruments of a massive orchestra.

The receptionist returned with waters. Alex only looked up to take his drink and then immediately turned his attention back to the tones created in his mind by the EM waves. It was tempting to look up and stare at the cosmetically enhanced woman. She reminded Alex of holo-films about androids created to be perfect human companions. Those movies almost always ended with the android malfunctioning and killing the people around them. He wondered if that thought had somehow manifested itself in his mind when he suddenly heard a dissonance in the harmony of the EM waves. It was faint at first and far away, like a single instrument playing out of tune among a host of other perfectly tuned instruments. Yet the more he focused on it, the louder and more dissonant it became. The sound wasn't merely out of tune; it was low and pulsing with menace. The other waves were higher-pitched and seemed productive.

"Can you hear that?" Alex leaned toward Ash and Sly, who were sitting opposite from him.

"Hear what?" Ash asked.

"That throbbing tone," Alex said. "It's strange."

"Man, there's so much noise here I have to push it all back," Sly said. "It's just a jumble of noise to me."

"I don't think I could pick out one sound from another," Ash said, wrinkling her face in concentration. "It gets too loud."

Nyx put her hand on his arm. He turned and looked at her.

"Are you okay? You're shaking."

"I'm all right," Alex said. But the strange dissonance persisted, even when the large wooden doors opened and a tall, dark-haired man appeared. Loman stood up, smoothing his clothes.

"Mr. Gentry," Loman said. "Thank you for meeting with us."

Alex and the rest of the Titan team stood up.

"It's a pleasure to meet your team of Titan operators and controllers," the CEO said. He had a deep, rich voice. "Why don't you bring them into my office, Loman? We'll get some pictures together."

They shuffled into the office, which was twice the size of the waiting room. The furnishings were few and very minimalistic. The walls were made of transparent material. The views of the surrounding city out toward the bay were incredible.

"I'm sure Loman has told you that I'm the CEO of Ahzco," Ian Gentry said. "In fact, I'm a direct descendant of the Baum family who founded Ahzco nearly three centuries ago."

There was more talk. Loman and Gentry went back and forth, but Alex could barely hear them. The strange noise from far below was consuming his attention. The next thing he knew, Alex was lined up between Nyx and Ash as Loman introduced each one of them to Ian Gentry.

"And this is Sergeant Alex Chester Evans," Loman said. He was giving Alex a strange look as Alex snapped out of the fugue he was in. "Callsign Ace. He's the leader of the Titan operators."

"It's a pleasure to meet you, young man," Ian said, extending his arm to shake Alex's hand.

Alex looked directly into Ian Gentry's eyes and said, "You have to get out of this building. It's going to explode."

Chapter 12

"What?" Ian Gentry said.

"The building," Alex said. "I think it's going to blow up."

"Is he insane, Loman?" the CEO barked angrily.

"What is it?" Loman Haley asked as he took hold of Alex's shoulders.

"I've got something down low, underground maybe," Alex said. "It's not Ahzco tech. It's something else. Something sinister."

"Someone better tell me what's going on," Ian Gentry said angrily.

"Sir, get out of the building," Loman said. "You've got a transport on the roof, don't you?"

"Yes," Gentry said. His deep, confident voice started to sound shaky.

"Then move, quickly. Take the controllers with you."

"Look, Loman, if this is some kind of trick—"

"No sir," Loman snapped. "Just do it. Get in the air and stay clear of the building."

"I picked it up when we were waiting," Alex said. "It may have just come online."

"What?" Loman asked. "What are you reading?"

"Multiple units," Alex said. "They're all on the same wavelength, but it's completely different from everything else in this area. And it's deep underground."

"How the hell does he know that, Loman?" Gentry demanded.

"Sir, we have to do what he says," Nyx said. "You're in danger."

"Should we give the order to evacuate the building?" Ash asked.

"No!" Alex said. "I can't be sure, but I think the explosives are remote-detonated. If they see people leaving the building, they'll blow it."

"Can you pick up any more details?" Loman said.

"They're small electronic devices," Alex said. "A lot of them. They just activated a few minutes ago. They have a power cell with a single function. I can't tell exactly, but I think they're detonators."

"If he's right, a lot of people are going to die," Ash said.

"We have to help," Sly said.

Loman felt his insides turn to water. An attack on a rival corporation's interests off-world—especially on those outside the FTA—were expected. But an attack on Arcadia was unheard of. Whoever was behind it wanted more than increased market share. Somehow, Ahzco had become the target of financial terrorists. If the HQ building fell, the entire company would be devastated, perhaps even forced into bankruptcy. Their competitors could pick them apart piece by piece. But even more frightening was the thought of how many innocent lives would be lost; besides the executives and staff in the HQ building, the damage from a mega-skyscraper falling would affect the central district for blocks and blocks. It would be catastrophic for anyone within five kilometers of the building.

"All right—Ash, Sly, you get communications going," Loman said. "I want contact with your controllers in the CEO's transport. Gentry, if you don't get moving, I'll order the controllers to leave without you."

"Okay, yeah," the CEO said, his calm demeanor shattered.

"I need to go down," Alex said. "I think I can block the signal, but I've got to get closer. There are a lot of them."

"Ash, you stay with the receptionist," Loman said as he swiped the side of his PIL to activate it. "She has total communication control of the building. If we have to evacuate, you can order it from there. Sly, you're with us. I'm mobilizing a security team now. If Alex can locate the source of the signal, we can catch whoever's doing this."

Loman took hold of Alex's arm. Every instinct was telling him to run, to flee the danger, but he knew he couldn't. If the building went down, his career was over. As executive VP of security, he would personally be named in every lawsuit brought against Ahzco. His fortune would be seized, and he would be a pariah. Better to die trying to stop the destruction than to survive only to be flayed alive by the media.

He hit the button for the lift, which opened immediately. Loman pulled Alex inside. Sly stayed with them. Using his PIL as a com-link would work for a while, as long as they didn't get separated or have too much interference between them. Loman sent a message for Raz Goreman to get a full spectrum communicator and meet him in the basement.

"Okay, we're going down," Loman said. He could feel pressure around his chest, as if someone had wrapped cargo straps around him and was pulling them tighter the lower they descended. "Any changes?"

"None so far," Alex said. "I've got forty-two devices."

"How is that possible?" Loman said, his mind spinning at the very thought of forty-two explosive devices being smuggled into the Ahzco HQ building right under their noses. "Are you sure of that number?"

"No," Alex said. "There could be more."

"Sir, the controllers are in the air," Sly said.

"Good, at least Gentry is clear," Loman said. "So much for keeping your abilities under wraps, Evans."

"Sorry, sir," Alex said.

"Don't sweat it. Save the building, and you can write your ticket," Loman said.

He had two security teams in the building. They were both using MP Patroller battle suits, which were essentially battle armor with surveillance tech. They were tied into a control center on the one hundred and fiftieth floor. They had access to the sensor suite built into the building, including radar. They also had all the company employee records for the entire campus.

"Sly, stay with Alex. No one but me gets near him," Loman ordered.

"Roger that, sir," Sly replied.

Loman hit a button on his PIL and spoke quietly into the device. "This is a red alert. I repeat: a red alert. Loman Haley, ID number 4862971, password scotch and soda."

A tiny voice replied from his PIL. "We read you, Mr. Haley. Red alert authorized. Alpha and Bravo team are standing by."

"Good," Loman said. "Get them on ground transports immediately. One on the west side of the HQ building. One on the east side. Stand by for further orders."

"Copy, mobilizing security teams Alpha and Bravo."

The lift was fast, but it still had eighty floors to go just to reach ground level. Loman pulled up the building's schematic on his PIL. There were two maintenance floors below the secret executive meeting lounge. Loman knew that there would be so much concrete between them and the control center—not to mention the executive lounge's anti-spying construction—that it would be almost impossible to stay in contact with his security operators if the explosives were down that deep.

The future was balanced on a knife's edge, with just one man capable of saving thousands of innocent lives and trillions of credits in property damage. Yet all that paled in comparison to losing Alex himself. The boy was the future—not just of the company, but of the entire human race.

Chapter 13

Alex felt sick. The lift was descending fast, but that wasn't what bothered him. It was fear. He had identified forty-two devices and synced with them. If a signal came in, he could block it—as long as he didn't lose his concentration. But what if he had missed one? What if there were forty-three explosive devices? If just one went off, it would probably trigger the others.

The elevator finally slowed down and came to a stop. They were on the ground floor, but the EM waves were rising up from beneath them. Alex was amazed that he could hear them at all. When he opened himself up to the devices, the cacophony of noise from hundreds of thousands of electronic devices bombarded him. It was like trying to hear a person five rows over in the middle of a rock concert. He had to focus all his attention on the signals and continually sift through the massive wall of sound for anything that might be trying to signal them.

"You okay, man?" Sly said. "You're looking shaky."

"Yeah," Alex said, talking much louder than he needed to. The blast of sound in his mind was overwhelming his other senses.

The truth was, the burning sensation behind his eyes was back. Sweat was springing up on his forehead and down his back. Part of him wanted to shut down. His physical body seemed to be taking second place to the input overload in his mind. He felt like he might vomit.

Just as the doors opened, Loman's com-link buzzed. Alex and Sly stepped out into the hallway that led from the lobby to the executive elevator. Sly led his friend to a padded bench and sat him down. Alex wasn't trying to eavesdrop on the VP, but it was impossible not to hear him.

"What?" Loman barked. His PIL was acting like an intercom, and Alex could hear the person calling.

"Loman Haley, listen very carefully. There's a bomb in the Ahzco universal headquarters building."

The caller paused to let his message sink in. A man with bulging muscles was approaching. Sly stepped in front of Alex protectively.

"What do you want?" Loman said, sounding as if he didn't believe a word he was hearing.

"To ruin you."

"Many have tried," Loman said. "All have failed. Do you know how many phony calls like this we get every week?"

As the big man approached, Loman pointed at Sly. The man had a communication unit hanging from a strap over his shoulder. He handed the unit to Sly, who took it and immediately slipped the earpiece into his ear. As he turned around, Alex saw a look of relief on his friend's face. Sly obviously hadn't relished the idea of defending Alex from the big man. He was grateful the man turned out to be friendly.

"This isn't a prank. I suggest you take this seriously. I'm on your personal com-link, Mr. Vice President of Security. You know what I'm capable of."

"Yeah, hold on," Loman said, sounding busy and slightly disinterested.

He hit the mute button on his PIL and pointed at the big man.

"Alex, this is Raz Goreman. We go way back," Loman said quickly. "Raz, you take these two operators wherever they need to go. I'll keep this nut talking, Alex, but you've got to find a way to disarm those explosives."

The big man looked surprised at the word explosives, but to his credit he reached out a beefy hand, which Alex took, and pulled him to his feet.

"Tell me what you want," Loman said, speaking into the PIL again. "I don't have all day here."

"I don't want anything other than to watch your life and the Ahzco empire go up in smoke."

"You and a billion other people, pal. What makes you so special?"

Alex didn't stick around to hear the rest of the conversation. "I need to get to the engineering sub-basement," Alex told Raz.

"Follow me," Raz said in a deep voice.

Alex and Sly followed the big man back to the lobby. Despite everything going on, Alex couldn't help but be dazzled by the building's glitzy lobby. Raz led them to a side door. It blended into the wall so well that a person couldn't see it unless they were really looking for it. Raz flung the door open, and Alex saw that it led to the maintenance sections. The floor went from polished marble to bare concrete. Gone were the wide-open spaces, the wall decorations, and the leafy, green plants in ornate pots. The maintenance section consisted of a bleak hallway that was narrow and confining. Pipes and conduits ran along the ceiling. It reminded Alex of the crew quarters on the *Republic*. There was such a stark contrast between the public spaces of the company and the actual working conditions.

Alex had no illusions about Ahzco or any of the mega-corporations. They were big businesses with millions of employees, yet despite their massive profits, most company employees barely made a living wage. Those living on company planets like NP8261, where Alex grew up, made even less. Yet it was still surprising to see the harsh reality that the maintenance staff endured on a regular basis.

As if to confirm his suspicions, a short man in dirty coveralls with hair sticking out from his head as if he hadn't washed or combed it in weeks came out of a doorway. He had the look Alex had seen many times on the miners who worked with his father; they were trapped in a job which they couldn't afford to lose yet which didn't offer them enough money to improve their lot in life, either. He stared at the strange trio and stood aside.

"Where are the stairs down to the engineering basement?" Raz asked the man.

"Over there, it's marked," the man replied. "Don't know why anyone would want to go down there, though."

Raz hurried past the man, and Alex followed. They opened a door with a diagram of a stairwell on it. The smell of stale air and metal was strong in the confined space. Their feet echoed on the metal steps and off the concrete walls.

"This is ominous," Sly said as the light flickered.

Alex didn't disagree, but the deeper they went, the less noise from above pounded his brain. He knew they were going underground and that the earth and thick concrete walls of the building were absorbing the EM waves. He could still hear them, but they receded like the buzz of a nearby insect. It was shocking that he had picked up the EM waves from the explosive devices at all. If not for their dissonant tones clashing with the harmony of the Ahzco-generated electronics, he never would have. Or perhaps it was the fact that there were forty-two devices—enough to break through the wall of sound even though Alex had been over a kilometer above them.

They came to a landing with double metal doors. A sign warned that only authorized maintenance personnel were allowed beyond that point. Raz yanked the door open, and they went through the portal into a room with large, humming machinery.

Alex couldn't hear the EM waves being generated, but he felt them. It was like walking through something that scrambled every atom in his body. The corridor was well-lit. Most of the machines were inside cages and marked with large signs warning of electrical shock. They passed one such cage with a metal toolbox near the door and a temporary sign that listed the unit as under repair.

"I've got almost no signal down here," Sly said. "There must be a ton of interference. Any chance the explosives are on timers?"

Alex didn't sense any timers. He could sense that the explosive devices were simple: just a power cell leading to a detonator. If not for the potency of the batteries, he wouldn't have noticed them at all. The electronics were essentially just a digital circuit switch that, once activated via a remote control, would allow the power from the batteries to flow into the detonation rods, which would then ignite the explosives.

"No," Alex said. "No timers."

Raz opened the door at the end of the corridor. Another set of stairs led down even further. The final stairwell was lit only with a single, dim bulb. They hurried down and found themselves in the maintenance space. Alex had to stoop a little to keep from banging his head on the pipes that crisscrossed the low ceiling. He felt the oppressive heat and humidity immediately. Alex was already sweating; he could feel the moisture being sucked from his body and saturating his compression fatigues.

"Holy crap," Sly said. "This place is a dungeon."

There wasn't much light in the narrow space. The few dim lightbulbs were overwhelmed by the shadows from the huge machines and barely cast any illumination. But Alex could see a few thick, concrete pillars and knew immediately that the explosive devices where planted deep inside them.

"The explosives are in the support pillars," Alex said.

"How can you tell?" Raz asked.

"I'm synced to them," Alex said.

"That's impossible," the big man argued. "I was an operator for over twenty years. You can't sync to regular tech."

"He can," Sly said in a teasing voice. "He's special."

"Trust me," Alex said as he hurried forward. He circled around the nearest pillar and found what he was looking for: a tiny wire protruding from the concrete. "This is it."

"What is it?" Sly asked.

"An antenna," Alex said.

Sly looked at the communication unit hanging from his shoulder. "No way, man, there's no signal down here. I don't think anything could get through the concrete or past the electrical interference."

"Why plant bombs," Raz said, pressing his finger into the putty that surrounded the wire, "if you can't set them off?"

"Well, I picked up the EM waves coming from the explosives," Alex said. "Even from the top floor."

"Yeah, but you're not normal," Sly said. "Everyone knows that."

"They're using a frequency that can get past the interference and reach down this deep," Alex insisted.

"They're not close, either," Raz said. "Not unless they plan to die carrying out their plan."

"It's possible," Sly said. "For all we know, they could be in the building."

"What happens if you pull out the antenna?" Raz asked. "Will they blow?"

"Yeah," Alex said. "They've got a failsafe. We need to pull the whole thing out and remove the power cell."

"We'd need a drill or something," Sly complained.

"No," Raz said. "Look at this."

He was pulling out the putty covering the hole in the pillar when the door opened behind them. The trio moved around the pillar and saw a man in a business suit. He looked like every other executive working in the massive building, but Alex saw the device in his hand. He reached out with his mind just as the man pushed the trigger to detonate the explosives.

Chapter 14

Alex felt the signal reach out to all forty-two explosive devices at once. It took all his mental strength to prevent the circuits from connecting. It felt like he had just managed to slip his hand between the closing doors of an elevator. They didn't crush him, but they continued trying to close. He dropped to his knees, straining to keep the bombs from going off and killing everyone in the building above him.

Raz charged forward with the bellow of a raging bull. Sly grabbed Alex's arm for support. The man at the doorway pulled out a nasty-looking, curved, ceramic blade. As Raz closed on him, the man slashed the blade toward his face. For a big man, Raz was fast and agile. He swayed back out of reach, then twisted his hips as he lashed out with a well-aimed kick. His foot smashed into the side of the stranger's knee. The man with the detonator crumpled to the floor and broke the extremely hard but brittle ceramic knife blade in the process. Raz could have ended the fight safely, but instead he spun around behind the stranger and wrapped his thick arm around the man's neck. Alex saw the stranger's eyes bulge. He hacked back at Raz's wide, muscular body with the broken knife blade. Blood dripped from the broken handle that still had several centimeters of sharp blade above the guard. Raz grunted with the impacts, and the stranger soon lost all his strength. The knife and remote detonator fell to the floor as the man passed out from Raz's chokehold.

"Get the detonator," Alex said through clenched teeth.

He felt as if he were trying to hold back a flood of water with just his hands. The signal was relentless; keeping forty-two devices in his mind at once taxed him more than he thought possible. The burning sensation behind his eyes was growing hotter. It felt like part of his brain was melting.

Sly dashed toward Raz and the stranger. He scooped up the detonator and looked at it.

"It's got a combination," Sly said. "I can't stop it."

"Give it!" Raz shouted.

He took the device from Sly and turned it over. With one quick motion he removed the back panel that covered the detonator's battery. It was a good idea, but the stranger had planned for just such an act. A boom sounded. It was so loud in the concrete-lined basement that Alex thought his ear drums had surely burst. He dropped to the ground and rolled over, still keeping his mind on the explosives. It was like he was juggling a ball as he fell, and it took all his mental capacity to keep the bombs from going off.

From what seemed like far away, a horrible, blood-curdling scream echoed through the basement. Alex struggled to his hands and knees, looking toward his friend. Sly was slumped against the wall, unconscious. The stranger lay not far away, still incapacitated by Raz's choke. The big man was still standing, but both of his arms were gone from the elbow down. Blood poured from the stumps, and smoke rose in an acrid cloud in front of him. Alex wasn't sure if it was pain or despair that caused the man's screams, but he wailed. As Alex watched, he dropped to his knees, holding his ruined arms out in front of him.

There was no doubt that Raz needed help, but Alex couldn't help him. He had to stop the explosives from going off, and while the detonator had been destroyed in the explosion, the signal had triggered the devices. If Alex relaxed—even a tiny bit—the circuits in the explosives could close, sending power to the detonation rods and destroying the mega-skyscraper that was over their heads.

Alex staggered to his feet and wiped the grit from the explosion from his eyes. The hole on the pillar was still exposed. Alex leaned against the concrete support and slowly pulled the device from the hole. He had to be careful not to pull the antenna out of the device, which would trigger the failsafe and cause it to explode. He removed the half-meter-long tube. It was mostly explosive, but there was a round power cell at the end. Alex looked at the device carefully, searching for any sign of a trap. He didn't want to make the same mistake Raz had, and yet he knew he couldn't just wait for help. Holding the forty-two devices in check felt as if it were ripping his mind to ribbons. The fiery pain behind his eyes was spreading; it felt like someone had poured molten metal into his head.

With a shuttering breath, he pulled the battery free of the explosive device. It immediately shut off. Alex felt the connection in his mind end as if someone had flipped a light switch and cut the power. There were still forty-one active devices, but the one in his hands was disarmed. He set both the explosive and the battery on the ground gently, but far away from each other, then staggered to the next pillar.

Raz's screams had turned into rasping wheezes. They sounded far away, which Alex guessed was due to the damage his eardrums had suffered when the detonator exploded. He hoped the stranger had been killed, but he doubted he was so lucky. Raz was dying, and Sly might be dead too—Alex couldn't be sure. There was no time to help them and no time to secure the man who had tried to destroy the building. He had to get to the other devices.

The basement was dark, but that didn't stop Alex. He wasn't really using his eyes to find the next pillar. His link with the devices guided him, and his eyes were only used to keep him from running into something along the way. It was so hot that he felt faint. Sweat was running down his face, stinging his eyes and dripping from his nose and chin. He reached the next pillar, found the wire antenna, and began poking his fingers into the putty. It was soft in the hot, humid sub-basement. He guessed that if conditions were different the putty might have hardened, making his job much more difficult. It felt like he was pulling old chewing gum from where some mischievous student had wadded it. The putty came free, and he gently pulled the second explosive out of the pillar. Just like the first, he examined it and found no trap to the battery. It popped out with a simple tug, and Alex once again felt the device go silent in his head.

He soon lost track of time. Raz's wails dwindled, then stopped. The only other sounds were the hum of the machinery and the undulating of the explosive devices' EM waves. Alex followed them, one by one. He was thankful that the space was gloomy. There was very little to distract him. At one point, a rat raced through the darkness and over his foot. He jumped and nearly lost control, with well over twenty explosive devices still under his control. Fortunately, with each one he disarmed the task became a little easier, and despite his fright from the rat, he didn't lose control.

By the time he was down to the final few explosive devices, he became aware of other people in the sub-basement. He could hear their murmurs and the EM waves from their battle suits. It was tempting to connect to them, just to see who they were and what types of suits they were in. Yet he couldn't risk losing his connection with the last few explosives. He was fairly certain that if the devices went off at this point, the building wouldn't fall. But he was also sure that if they did, he would be killed, so he kept going.

The pain in his head had eased slightly with each device he decommissioned, but the hot lump behind his eyes was still burning. He was certain now that it had something to do with using his new ability. It scared him to think that he might be causing himself permanent brain damage, but what else could he do? If he hadn't used his new INC ability, thousands would have been killed.

When he pulled the last explosive device free and disarmed it, he felt his body sway. There was nothing else in his head but his own thoughts. He was free, untethered, and he slumped to the ground, his back against the pillar. Thirst was all he could think about. His tongue felt thick in his mouth, and he had no strength left. After a few moments, a figure emerged from the shadows. It was a woman in an MP Patroller battle suit. Alex could see the segments of armor that covered her body. There was a stun baton hanging from her belt on one hip and a blaster on the other. She had a heavy, reinforced case. She set it on the floor near Alex.

"Hi there," she said, her voice projecting from her helmet's small speakers. "Are you okay?"

"Water," Alex croaked.

"We'll get you some soon," she said encouragingly. "Are there any more explosives?"

Alex shook his head. She picked up a disarmed explosive and set it gently in the case, then sealed it up.

"I'll be back," she told him.

He watched her go. She moved slowly, holding the case out away from her body as she went, as if she feared it might explode at any second. Alex turned over onto his knees and used the concrete pillar to pull himself up. Someone had taken their time drilling holes into the pillars and setting the explosives. Just getting them into the building must have been a chore. Alex was glad the threat was over. He needed help, hydration, sleep, and time to clear his mind. He longed for a space free of EM waves, someplace he could quiet the throbbing hum in his mind. But Arcadia was not that place.

He staggered back through the dark engineering basement, following the sounds of voices until he could see the exit. Sly was gone, and so were Raz and the stranger. Alex stumbled and was caught by a man in a Patroller MBS.

"Easy there," the man said. "I got you."

"I want...out," Alex said in a raspy voice.

"No problem, Sergeant. We'll make that happen," the operator said.

Alex saw the name on his chest read "Kipper." He leaned into the man as the group of patrollers parted to let them through. The light from the corridor beyond was blinding, and the climb up the stairs was exhausting. When they reached the power facility, Alex couldn't walk. Another operator, the woman from before, joined them, and they basically carried Alex out.

He never would have made it up the stairs on his own in his condition. When they reached the ground floor, Alex was taken into a prep room. He could see lockers and old, cheap tables where employees undoubtedly ate lunches and had breaks. Sly was sitting up, being scanned by someone with a medical device. Raz lay on another table. The stumps of his arms were sealed in bags, but the big man had bled to death before help arrived. He looked pale, his face waxy—the same way Newt's face had looked when Alex found him on Carthage Prime.

Alex felt his eyes stinging, but he was too dehydrated to cry. The patrollers sat him down on a bench across the table from Sly, who didn't look at Alex. There were burn marks on his face, and Sly looked shaken up.

"Here, drink this," a woman in a lab coat said. "I'm Dr. Patrice Tarken. Do I have your permission to examine you, Sergeant?"

"Yes," Alex croaked.

She put a bottle of vitamin water into his hands, and he drank it eagerly while she began to scan his body for signs of trauma.

"Looks like you're just dehydrated," she said.

Her voice seemed to come from far away.

"I'm having trouble hearing," he said, his voice still raspy after sucking down half the bottle of water.

"It's just trauma, but no damage," Dr. Tarken said. "Your eardrums are intact."

Alex leaned across the table. "Sly?" he said.

His friend didn't respond. Alex grabbed Sly's shoulder and shouted. "Sly!"

"He can't hear you," the doctor said.

"Ace?" Sly said.

"Are you okay, man?" Alex asked.

"Ace? I can't see," Sly said in a tremulous voice. "I can't see."

Chapter 15

"The threat is neutralized," Ash's voice sounded far away over the transport's communication headsets.

"Any casualties?" Nyx asked.

"I don't have a reliable answer to that yet," Ash said. "I should have gone with them."

"What have you heard?" Nyx asked.

"Someone died," Ash said. "But it's just a rumor. I don't even know who they're saying got hurt."

Nyx felt her blood run cold. It was frustrating to be cut off from Alex. She much preferred to be at her controller console when he was in action, where she felt connected to him and she knew she could help. What if Alex was dead? What would she do? The thought made her feel sick, and the transport suddenly swooping down didn't help.

"It's okay to go back, right?" Ian Gentry said.

He was sitting beside her in the plush passenger cabin of the luxury transport. He was handsome in the custom suit he wore, and he even smelled nice. His cologne was both sweet and masculine at the same time. His every word sounded confident and self-assured, but the words themselves revealed that he was actually quite frightened by the situation. Nyx didn't know if he was scared of being hurt himself or that so many people could be killed by the bombs that had been planted in the building.

"Yes," Nyx said. "They have the threat contained. There's no more danger."

The CEO visibly relaxed. He gave a quick order to the pilot, but Nyx could tell from the movement of the transport that they were already descending toward the rooftop for a landing.

The other two controllers looked even more disconcerted than Nyx felt. They didn't have access to the communication from Ash. Only Nyx, the transport pilot, and Ahzco CEO Ian Gentry had headsets. The luxury vehicle wasn't designed for combat situations. Communications were limited, and while the transport had full flight capabilities, it was a short-range vehicle. The interior was plush and included a bar as well as full access to Arcadia's news networks. Yet for all that it offered, Nyx felt blind and helpless. They were still above the city. She could look out the windows and see the buildings below them, but she had no idea what her operator was doing down in the bowels of the Ahzco universal HQ tower.

"We're descending," the pilot said. "ETA sixty seconds, Mr. Gentry."

"Thank you, Ron," Ian Gentry replied.

"Ash," Nyx said using the transport's communication system, "we're headed your way."

"Good, I want to go down and see what's happening."

"I'll go with you," Nyx said.

The transport spiraled down and landed without incident. Nyx couldn't get back into the building quickly enough. She hurried through the CEO's private rooftop entrance, down a flight of marble-tiled stairs, and through the hallway lined with ancient paintings that she guessed were worth billions.

When she finally made it to the CEO's waiting area, Ash was standing by the elevator. The digital display showed the lift to be rising up to them.

"Took you long enough," Ash said.

Nyx knew Ash's impatience wasn't really with her. She was anxious to get down to where her companions were, and the elevator was taking longer than she liked.

"Any news?" Nyx asked.

"No," Ash said sourly. "Where are the others?"

"They aren't going down," Nyx said. "Gentry offered to have them escorted to a waiting area before being shuttled over to the building we're staying in."

"I'm not surprised," Ash said. "My controller is a real buzzkill. She thinks I'm too reckless."

"Everyone thinks that," Nyx said, just as the elevator doors opened.

They got on the lift and hit the button for the ground floor. They descended in silence, the tension building with every passing moment. Nyx watched the floor display counting down. It was maddening to have to wait so long to get answers. She was used to having an entire ship's worth of scanning and communication at her fingertips, and being cut off from Alex made her feel as if a huge part of her were missing.

"I guess we could have stayed with Gentry," Nyx said. "He's the CEO. He'll probably find out what's going on before we will."

"I don't like waiting on the sidelines," Ash said, "especially when it's my team on the field. We already lost Newt."

The statement hung in the air between them. The lift suddenly seemed tiny and stifling. Nyx felt like her heart was going to beat its way out of her chest if she didn't find out soon whether Alex was okay.

The door opened with a pleasant chime, and the two young women rushed out. They turned down the hallway toward the lobby, searching desperately for any sign of their friends, and almost bowled straight into executive VP Haley. He looked grim.

"Is Alex okay?" Nyx blurted.

"He wasn't injured in the blast," Haley said.

"The explosives detonated?" Ash asked. "Is Sly okay?"

"Knoxx," Haley called out. A grim-faced man in a security uniform came hurrying toward them. "Take these two over to the staging area. They have full access."

"Yes sir, Mr. Haley," the man named Knoxx said.

Loman Haley wasn't alone. He was followed by a striking woman with dark skin and hair. She didn't speak, but Nyx felt the woman studying everything about her. It was as if nothing missed her intense gaze. The VP moved on down the hall toward the executive elevator, and Knoxx led Nyx and Ash across the lobby toward the hidden maintenance door. They passed through the opulent area for guests to the stark hallway used by the building maintenance crews. They were taken to a set of double doors that were propped open, leading to the employee locker room. It took dozens of people to ensure the building was clean and running at peak performance. There were tables where the maintenance personnel could take their breaks and eat their lunches. Benches lined the locker areas, and vending machines filled the space between the men's and women's bathrooms.

Nyx saw Alex and Sly sitting at one of the tables. A group of medical professionals were clustered around Sly. Operators in Patroller battle suits were moving in and out of the big room. One stopped the two women as they started in.

"Can I help you?" the operator asked.

"They've been cleared by VP Haley," Knoxx said.

"I'm Sergeant West," Nyx said, pulling out her CDF identification. "This is Corporal Timmons. We're with them," she said, pointing at Alex and Sly.

"Very well, Sergeant," the operator in the Patroller battle suit said.

Nyx thought she heard a note of jealousy in the operator's voice. She noticed the double stripes on the MBS denoting that the operator was a corporal, even though he sounded older. But there was no time to worry about whether her field promotion in the Carthage system had been premature. She had been in the field, which was more than ninety percent of controllers could say. She didn't relish being in danger, but she felt she'd earned her promotion.

"Alex," she said, as she and Ash hurried up to the table where he sat slumped over, resting his arms on the tabletop.

He looked up, a weary expression on his face. "Hey," he said.

She recognized his tone—it was complete exhaustion and pain. Something was wrong with him, but he wasn't admitting it.

"What happened?" Ash asked. "You were supposed to stay in contact."

"There was too much interference," Alex said.

"So how did the explosives get armed?" Ash shot back, as if she didn't believe him.

"The perpetrator was in the building," Alex said. "In the sub-basement."

"A suicide bomber?" Nyx said.

Alex nodded. "Raz took him out."

"Who's Raz?" Ash asked.

"A former operator," Alex explained. "Mr. Haley sent him with us. The bomber tried to detonate the explosives. Raz took him out, and Sly was trying to stop the detonation."

"You couldn't?" Nyx asked.

"I was blocking the signal with my INC," Alex went on. "But it was straining me to the limit. We thought if we could stop the signal, it might disarm the explosives. But when Raz went to take the battery out, it exploded."

"Oh no," Nyx said.

"He lost both arms and bled out before help could arrive," Alex said. "Sly was hurt."

They all looked across the table. Dr. Tarken was wrapping bandages around Sly's head, covering the burns on his cheeks and eyes.

"Is he..." Ash started but couldn't finish.

"I don't know," Alex said. "They were still running scans when I got here."

"You disarmed the explosives?" Nyx asked.

"Yeah, all forty-two of them. And the security team has the bomber in custody."

"He wasn't hurt by the explosion?" Ash asked, a serious edge to her tone.

"No," Alex replied. "It knocked him against a wall and unconscious when it went off. He's got a few scrapes and bruises, but he got off easy."

"He won't get through the interrogation so easily," Nyx said, glad that she wasn't the one being held in custody by a very hostile security force.

Chapter 16

Loman watched the bomber, who sat alone in an interrogation room deep beneath the CDF security hangar. There were two squads of operators stationed on the Ahzco campus. They patrolled the sixteen blocks in the middle of the Arcadia Central District, but they were also prepared to switch over to heavier MBS's should the need arise. There was also a holding cell and interrogation room underneath the hangar.

The bomber's name was Riley Roark, according to his DNA file, but Loman was sure it wasn't his real name. Whoever was behind the attack had deep pockets and serious resources. They had sent in a man willing to die to bring down the iconic Ahzco universal HQ building. There was little doubt that they would hide their tracks.

Loman watched the man on a holo-projector inside his tiny office. He was furious about the death of Raz Goreman. The man had been a loyal employee for decades and the perfect face of the security executives on the hundred and ninety-sixth floor. He could intimidate almost anyone—not just with his imposing size but also with the look in his battle-tested eyes. The man had killed, that was obvious, and everyone who met him knew he wasn't someone to trifle with.

The only upside to losing Raz was the fact that he hadn't lost Alex. The young operator was irreplaceable, and while the loss of Raz was painful, the man had done his job. He had subdued the bomber and saved Alex's life. In that regard, his actions had been successful.

The door to the interrogation room opened, and Ciara Prince went inside. The interrogation room was stark white, designed to make the occupant feel as if nothing could stay hidden. With her dark hair, dark skin, and dark clothing, Ciara Prince was the opposite: a shadow, a minion of Death to whom nothing was denied. She stood near the door, watching the bomber. There were no questions and no accusations. Loman didn't need a confession; the bomber had been caught red-handed. What they needed was the link back to Riley Roark's handlers—the people who had sent him on his mission. Pain might not motivate a man who was prepared to die, but fear was always effective. Ciara Prince, standing silently by the door and watching him with her intense gaze, would spark whatever fears the man had.

Loman wished he could be in the room with them, but that wasn't a good idea. He would lose his temper. He didn't have the patience for interrogation. It wouldn't take long until he was screaming at the subject, making vile threats that would never be carried out and thus ruining the credibility of the interrogators. He sat in his chair, wishing he had a drink, and feeling a nagging, inescapable grief that he couldn't deny.

"Go ahead," Riley Roark blurted. "Do your worst. I don't care. You don't scare me."

Loman couldn't help but smile. The man was already starting to crumble. He was afraid, but not of torture. It was something else. Ciara Prince stood as silent as a statue, just staring at him. Riley looked away, but he couldn't keep his gaze from the shadow by the door for long.

"I don't care what you do to me," he said, a note of desperation clear in his shaky voice. "I won't talk. You might as well kill me now."

Loman tapped a button on his PIL and activated the com-link that Ciara Prince had hidden deep in her ear canal.

"Tell him about the chair," Loman said.

Down in the interrogation room, Ciara Prince finally moved. The bomber flinched as she quickly approached the small table. He was sitting on a metal chair that was designed to be uncomfortable. His legs were shackled to the legs of the chair. A strap wrapped around the back of the chair and across the bomber's stomach. His arms were on the metal tabletop, held together by a set of plastic security straps.

"The chair you're sitting on," Ciara Prince said in a cold tone, "is made of copper. Do you know why?"

"Copper?" the bomber asked. "No, why?"

"Copper is an excellent conductor of electricity," Ciara Prince said. "We don't kill people here, Mr. Roark. Dying is easy. Living is hard—especially with, say, a hundred volts racing through your body."

The man began to shake. Loman could see the sweat running down his face. His lips were trembling. Yet despite his obvious fear, he refused to make things easy for them.

"I won't talk," he said, his voice barely a whisper.

"Everyone talks," Ciara Prince said. "You're talking now. Tell us what we want to know, and you'll be treated humanely. The authorities have found the maintenance man you bribed to plant the explosives. You'll be turned over to them once we're though with you—in what condition is completely up to you."

"I want a lawyer," the man said. "You can't keep me here. You have no authority."

Ciara Prince pulled out a device from her pocket. It was small with a dial built into the side and a small, digital screen on the front. She adjusted the dial, then set the device on the table in front of the man. Loman could just make out the numbers: *100v*. A green button on the front activated the device.

"I don't bluff, Mr. Roark. And repeating myself only makes me irritated. Tell me who you are working for or you will feel what a hundred volts feels like."

The bomber set his face, the muscles and tendons in his neck standing out. Ciara Prince didn't wait. She picked up the device and pressed the button.

Riley Roark grunted with pain as every muscle in his body spasmed. His eyes bulged with pain, and his jaw clenched. Ciara Prince released the button, and Roark slumped forward, breathing hard.

"One hundred volts for one second," Ciara Prince said. "Every time you refuse to answer or lie to me, I will increase the voltage and the duration." She made a show of dialing up the voltage. "We're at one hundred fifty volts, Mr. Roark. Who are you working for?"

He looked up, fear and anger in his eyes. Loman knew what was coming next. Denial was the first step in breaking a person under enhanced interrogation.

"I don't know what you're talking about," he said.

"You decided to blow up our building all by yourself," Ciara Prince said. "You obtained illegal explosives and enough credits to bribe one of our maintenance staff. You planned the destruction of a mega-skyscraper all on your own. That's what you're telling me?"

He shook his head. Ciara didn't hesitate. She pressed the button and sent the voltage racing through his body for three seconds. His face turned red, and when she released the current, he slumped to the table, panting.

"Once again: refuse to answer or lie to me, and I will shock you," she said. "Tell me the truth and this can all be over. It's your choice, Mr. Roark. I know you weren't working alone. Who were you working for?"

"I don't know," he said with a note of desperation in his voice. "I don't know. I never met them."

Ciara Prince was a professional. She knew the second phase of enhanced interrogation was to lie. She lifted the device. The man shook his head, but she wasn't there to show him mercy.

"No, no, plea—"

She pressed the button again. The man stiffened, a gurgling sound emitting from his tight throat, his eyes watering. She held the button down for four seconds. When she stopped the electrical shock, the bomber began to weep.

"We're going to find out who you really are," Ciara Prince said. "It's obvious that you were desperate to help someone you care about. You were willing to die to carry out this plan. We'll find them and find out why you accepted the task of blowing up our building. And we'll intervene, Mr. Roark. We'll stop the surgery, call the sudden windfall of credits into question with the authorities, bring the people you care about into a room just like this and—"

"No!" he shouted. "You can't. You can't do that."

"We can," Ciara Prince said.

Loman knew she was lying, but the bomber didn't. The CDF had a lot of power, but they couldn't swoop in and kidnap innocent people. Even if they could, he wouldn't approve it. The bomber had been willing to kill thousands of people. He had cast aside his rights as soon as he involved himself in a heinous attack on the innocent employees of the Ahzco Corporation. Loman had no qualms about questioning the man. He was lucky his plan had been thwarted and that only his accomplice and Raz Goreman had been killed. Otherwise, Loman might have seen fit to make the bomber's death as slow and painful as possible.

"No," Roark said. "Please. I'll do whatever you want."

"I thought you might see it that way," Ciara Prince said.

Chapter 17

The commotion in the maintenance locker room ended quickly. Alex was cleared to leave but waited with Nyx and Ash to find out about Sly, who was eventually taken to a nearby hospital for treatment. Alex felt as though he had run nonstop for hours and been awake for days. When he got up from the table, he was shaky.

"Just lean on me," Nyx said.

"This isn't right," Ash said. "Has it crossed your mind that what you're doing isn't good for you?"

"I didn't think you were the cautious type," Alex said.

"Yeah, me neither," Ash said. "But first Newt, now Sly...he'd be dead if he had opened the battery compartment on that detonator instead of Raz."

Alex didn't like to think about how close their friend had come to be being killed. He was trying to shake the frightening image of Sly with his arms blown off from his mind. Imagining it was all too easy, since he'd seen Raz Goreman die in exactly that manner. Then a master sergeant with the patroller squad came into the room with his helmet off, looking chagrined.

"Looks like this party's over," he announced. "The explosives were fakes."

"What?" Alex said, even though the master sergeant couldn't hear him.

"They were only blasting rods in modeling clay, not explosive material," the master sergeant went on.

"Why would anyone plant fake bombs?" one of the patrol operators asked.

"Probably trying to extort money from the company," the master sergeant said. "Call in a bomb threat, make it look real so the company pays up. Anyway, there's no more threat here. We're calling it a day." The patrol squad left the room quickly, leaving Alex with Nyx and Ash.

"That doesn't make sense," Alex said.

"Maybe," Ash said, "if the bomber knew there was security on site, they might want to make it seem like they had the capacity to carry out their threats."

"No, I get that," Alex said. "What I mean is that the explosives were hidden. They were drilled into the foundation pillars, and then the holes were covered with putty."

"So?" Nyx asked.

"So we never would have found them if I hadn't been able to sync to them with my INC," Alex said. "Why do that? Why plant fake explosives?"

"Maybe it was just to scare us," Ash said.

Alex walked toward the double doors, trying to understand. Nothing made sense to him, and the pain in his head was still there. It had diminished over time, but he could still feel it lurking behind his eyes. The doctors had done a full scan on him. The portable med scanners weren't as powerful as the larger ones in medical centers, but if there was a problem with his brain, they should have found it. Still, the idea that the explosives were fake made no sense to him.

"Maybe the person planting the bombs thought it was real," Nyx said. "Most criminals are well below average intelligence."

"You think he thought he bought explosives and it was just modeling clay?" Ash said. "People died over nothing?"

"Not nothing," Alex said. "And the explosive in the detonator was real. I don't think it was an accident. There has to be a reason—we're just not seeing it yet."

"Where should we go?" Nyx asked. They were moving slowly down the hallway toward the building's opulent lobby.

"Once we get Ace settled, I'm heading to the hospital to stay with Sly," Ash said. "He'd do the same for me."

"We should all go," Alex said.

"No," Ash replied. "You need rest. And Nyx can keep an eye on you."

"Of course," Nyx said.

"Then we'll come as soon as I get some rest," Alex insisted.

They were met at the lobby doors by the same security guard that had led them to the maintenance locker room. Alex saw the name Knoxx embroidered on a patch that was sewn to his shirt.

"Mr. Haley wants the three of you upstairs," Knoxx said. "Come with me and I'll get you on the executive lift."

They followed without argument. Alex was ready to crash. He felt so tired that he could have lain down on the marble floor. He could imagine the cool stone against his hot and dirty skin. But when the executive VP of security sent a request, it wasn't really a request but an order. Perhaps, Alex thought, Mr. Haley had a comfortable sofa that he could stretch out on.

The lift took a while to reach them. It had to descend almost two hundred stories. When the doors opened, Alex and his friends stepped inside.

"Floor 196," Knoxx said. "Someone up there will show you to the VP's office."

"Thank you," Nyx said as the doors closed.

Alex sagged against the wall. Using his INC outside of his Titan MBS seemed to take a greater toll on him, or perhaps it was the fact that he'd been forced to divide his mind between forty-two separate explosive devices for so long. Whatever the case, his head throbbed with pain, and his body felt shaky. In the end, it was all for nothing. He had pushed himself to the breaking point over a hoax.

"This place is massive," Ash said.

"And it's just one building in the complex," Nyx said. "Hard to imagine anything keeping so many people busy."

When they finally reached the one hundred and ninety-sixth floor, the lift door slid open to reveal an empty reception area. They walked forward toward the receptionist's desk, and Alex saw a name plate that read "Raz Goreman." He felt a lump of grief rise up in his throat. He hadn't known Raz, but he still felt responsible for the man's death. Why hadn't he recognized the threat in the detonator? If he could sense the devices in the fake explosives, why hadn't he noticed the real device inside the detonator?

His focus was elsewhere, of course. His mind had been so consumed with keeping the explosives from going off that he hadn't even tried to sync with the detonator.

"Who are you?" said a short man in a ridiculous-looking outfit, who came trundling into the waiting area.

"Sergeant West," Nyx said. "This is Sergeant Evans and Corporal Timmons. VP Haley sent for us."

"You're the operators that were involved in the fighting on Carthage Prime?"

"That's right," Nyx said, "but I'm a controller."

"It's all the same to me," the man said. "Just have a seat. I don't know what has happened to Raz Goreman. He's not at his desk. Some days it's as if this place is falling apart."

He left the reception area. Alex couldn't tell if he was waddling or trying to strut, but he moved like a chicken whose legs were too long.

"Who was that?" Ash asked.

"Beats me," Nyx said.

There were several comfortable chairs in the corner of the reception area, near a large window. Alex sat down. He could see a tiny thread of water in the distance between the towering buildings. Nyx and Ash sat on either side of him. It didn't take long for Loman Haley to appear.

"I suppose you've heard," he said as he sat down in the otherwise empty waiting area across from Alex.

"About the explosives?" Alex replied.

Loman Haley nodded.

"Why would the bomber use fake explosives?" Ash said.

"He didn't think they were fake," Loman said. "We've been questioning him. He expected the building to come down."

"And the bomb in the detonator?" Nyx asked.

"I believe it was intended to kill him," the VP said. "Once he tried to set off the explosives, he would probably check the detonator to see what went wrong and..."

"And no loose ends," Ash said.

"Exactly," Loman said. "Only whoever is behind the attack didn't count on Alex being able to find the explosives, or Raz being able to subdue their perpetrator, may he rest in peace."

"So, what do we do now?" Nyx asked.

"Now we put on a show for the public and for the company. All is well that ends well, or so they say," Loman explained. "I know you're tired. After you meet Zan Fordham, I'll have you transported to your quarters to get cleaned up for a night on the town. It's a cruel and unusual punishment, but at least the food will be good."

"I want to go see Sly," Ash said.

"And Alex needs to rest," Nyx said.

"We all have our duties to perform," the VP said. "I know it's been a taxing day for all of you. But Corporal Lasiter is in one of the best medical facilities in the galaxy. I've already got someone there giving me regular updates. I'll contact you as soon as we get more information on him. In the meantime, have an energy drink and put on a smile. The PR folks will have spread the word that the CDF heroes are being wined and dined. Expect some attention. All you have to do is smile and be polite."

Alex didn't feel like smiling. His head throbbed, his eyelids felt heavy, and he was desperate for sleep. He felt like he'd been awake for three days straight. It seemed that using his new abilities taxed his body at a rate he had never experienced before. Still, he wouldn't disobey an order, and orders didn't get any more official than from the mouth of the executive vice president of security.

"We'll make it work," Alex said.

Chapter 18

Nyx stood at the window of the room she was sharing with Ash and her controller. The entire wall was transparent, and far below, the dark blue of Arcadia's ocean surged against the massive stone walls that lined the shore. She wore the dress uniform that had been delivered to the suite of rooms before she had even arrived. It was form-fitting, which was a change from the baggy controller fatigues she normally wore. The silky fabric was black with gold piping that was a little flashier than she was comfortable with, but the sergeant stripes were welcome.

The sun had gone down, but light from the city illuminated everything—even the wide expanse of the harbor below. Nyx could see buildings across the water: tall structures filled with light that were built right up to the water's edge. Arcadia was an architectural marvel, yet the massive global city made Nyx feel small and insignificant.

"You ready?" Ash said, coming up behind Nyx. "Ace should be here soon."

He was coming from across the hallway, where the boys had their own suite of rooms. Nyx couldn't help but think about how far she had come. Her family was thousands of light years away on a tiny scientific space station studying astronomical phenomena. Her parents were happy with their lives, but Nyx couldn't help but feel sorry for them. They were missing so much. A life could be spent studying the galaxy's marvels, or simply exploring a single world like Arcadia.

"Yes," Nyx said. "I'm as ready as I'll ever be."

"Maybe Zan won't be so bad out of the office," Ash said. "Sly is going to be angry that he missed dinner."

"I hope it's worth being angry about," Nyx said.

"VP Haley promised the food would be good," Ash said.

"It's the company that I'm concerned about," Nyx said.

"So he's a little strange. Tell me you didn't ever hang out with a dork in high school."

"I didn't go to school," Nyx said. "I grew up on a scientific space station and learned from computer courses."

"Okay, well, trust me," Ash said. "We'll have Zan Fordham eating out of the palm of your hand before the night's over."

"Yeah, that's what I'm afraid of," Nyx said with a grin.

They both laughed, just as the door chime went off. Ash hit a button on the wall that opened the sliding door. Alex stood at attention just outside. Sly's controller was behind him, but Nyx only had eyes for Alex. She felt awkward in her dress uniform, but Alex's uniform looked custom-made for him. His shoulders were broad, his waist narrow, and the fabric clung to the bulge of muscle at his biceps and across his chest.

"Someone cleans up good," Ash said.

Alex looked down at his uniform a little self-consciously and tugged at the hem of the dress shirt to smooth a wrinkle. "It's a little tight," he said.

"I think it's supposed to be," Nyx said.

"You both look great," Alex said. "Are you ready?"

"Just as soon as my controller gets finished with her hair!" Ash said in a loud voice.

"I'm coming," a voice said from the bathroom.

Once everyone was ready, they rode the lift up to where a company transport was waiting on the VIP landing pad. Most people in the city used the public transit system, but the wealthy had their own multimillion-credit transports. Zan Fordham was waiting in the Ahzco luxury vessel that looked as if it were made entirely of dark-tinted glass. Nyx followed Ash inside and sat on a short-backed, plush, leather seat as far away from the executive as she could.

Zan was an odd man. VP Haley had explained that he'd been brought in from a management position and given equal status with the executive vice president but that he didn't have an actual title yet. Zan wore a glistening overcoat that reached his ankles. It was open at the top, revealing a silky, red shirt beneath, which only made the skin of his face look splotchy. Nyx wasn't sure if he was blushing, nervous about something, or if he just looked that way all the time.

"I hope you're hungry," Zan said. "We have a reservation for a seven-course tasting menu at Zatoria's Food Designs in the historic Bleaker building."

"Sounds good," Alex said.

Zan ignored Alex and stared at Nyx. He had the look of a hungry jackal who had just spotted his next meal. Nyx couldn't tell if Zan considered himself to be a ladies' man or if he thought she was low-hanging fruit, but she didn't want any part of the smarmy executive.

"Any word from Sly?" Ash asked.

"Who?" Zan asked.

"Corporal Lasiter," Alex said. "We've been waiting on news from the hospital."

"Oh, yes, your...companion. I've been told to have the driver take you to the med center as soon as we finish our meal."

"Do we really need to have a fancy dinner?" Ash asked. "I don't know about everyone else, but I'd really rather just get to where Sly's at."

"Of course we're having dinner," Zan said. His voice was loud and clipped, almost like a bark. "We have reservations."

"I think we all appreciate that," Alex said, "but we're worried about our friend."

"He's in the med center," Zan snapped. "It's the safest place on the planet. I think he'll be fine. Besides, the meal is prepaid and cost over a thousand credits per person. I've got half a mind to charge Corporal Lasiter for his share. The chef won't be happy when we show up a person short. The menu is designed for a party of seven."

"He was injured in the line of duty!" Ash said, her voice rising. "You aren't going to charge him anything."

"Injured? On Arcadia?" Zan chuckled as if Ash were exaggerating. "Corporal, perhaps you're out of your depth on a level-one planet."

"What did you hear happened to him?" Alex asked.

"Oh, I heard about some type of training exercise, but to be honest I have more important duties than keeping up with visitors. This dinner is a PR stunt that my colleague put together. The press wants to see more executives with the everyday man...and woman," Zan said, giving Nyx a clumsy wink. "So be prepared for pictures, but let's not talk. If there are questions, I'll answer them."

"You don't want us to talk at dinner?" Nyx said. She knew what the executive meant, but she couldn't help but tease him a little. Zan needed to be knocked down a few pegs, in her opinion. And if he was going to make it easy for them to humiliate him, she was game.

"Of course you can talk at dinner," Zan said, flashing her a smile with artificially whitened teeth. "I was referring to the reporters who will meet us outside the Bleaker building."

The Bleaker building was part of the historic district, a wide swath of old-style, forty- and fifty-story buildings that were part of the original colony settlement on Arcadia. On most planets, colonies turn into city centers over time, but Arcadia had grown continuously until the entire planet was one large city. What set the historic district apart was primarily the space between the structures. Wide city streets flanked the old buildings—a necessity back when most of the populace had traveled by ground transports. There were large spotlights shining up into the sky and crowds of people. The entire city block seemed to be caught up in a celebration.

Zan tried to act disinterested, as if it was all a bore to him, but Nyx caught him looking down almost as much as the Titan team members.

"Lot of people down there," Alex said as the transport descended toward a roped-off area for private vehicles to land.

"Is it some kind of celebration?" Ash asked.

"Every night is a celebration in the historic district," Zan said. "Holo-film premiers, celebrity author events, concerts, even old-fashioned stage plays all take place in the old buildings. Most nights it's a who's who of the rich and famous."

"Strange place for a military public relations event," Nyx said.

"Oh, no, my dear," Zan corrected her. "They're not here because of your accomplishments in battle. They're here because you represent Ahzco. And everyone loves a winner."

Nyx looked at Alex, who shrugged his shoulders. She supposed that it was true. Ahzco was more than just a company making gadgets. They created devices that shaped culture, spanned star systems, and influenced the course of human history. The Flex PIL she had snapped on her forearm was proof of that. It was a communication device, an entertainment platform, her banking and personal identification bona fides, a ticket for transportation, and access to the various information networks no matter where she was in the galaxy. She didn't feel like a representation of all that Ahzco created, but if it was her duty to be the face of the company for just one night, she would do what she could.

The transport settled, and a man in a lavish outfit hurried forward and opened the door. Zan was the first person out. He turned toward a crowd of reporters who were waiting nearby and held up his hands.

"Ladies and gentlemen," he said, trying to sound important but producing only a squeaky whine. "Let me be the first to introduce you to the CDF Titan team who saved the Tunis colony on Carthage Prime."

Nyx followed Alex and Ash out of the transport. The other controllers were behind her. The reporters surged forward. Large lighting units were already set up and bathed the area in shining brilliance. Nyx could hear the artificial shutters snapping away as pictures were taken. And then the questions began.

"Can you confirm reports of multiple civilian casualties on Carthage Prime?"

"How many lives were lost in the war for profits, Sergeant?"

"Do you think wasting billions of credits in unregulated corporate violence is inhumane?"

"One at a time, one at a time," Zan bellowed over the crowd of anxious reporters.

He seemed completely unfazed by the questions, but Nyx could tell that something was wrong. She had long been a follower of galactic news, and rarely were the corporate militaries treated as anything less than heroes.

"You first," Zan declared, pointing to a woman with gold hair.

"Sergeant West," the woman called out. "What is your response to the claims that multi-global corporations are out of control? Is it time for centralized government oversight and regulations to rein in corporate military forces?"

Nyx stood transfixed for a second. She certainly wasn't prepared for the question, and she didn't feel like she was qualified to speak for the entire company. Yet when she glanced at Zan, he stood smiling, as if the ambush were his idea.

"I know we have extensive training," Nyx said. "The CDF takes its job very seriously."

The golden-haired reporter seemed completely unsatisfied with that answer. "But people died on Carthage Prime—some were civilians," the reporter snapped. "What gives you the right to kill the innocent?"

"We weren't there to kill anyone," Alex said in a firm voice as he stepped closer to Nyx. "We were there to protect Ahzco employees."

Ash stepped up on Nyx's other side and put a hand on her back. "It was Zen Tech that sent explosive kamikaze drones toward Tunis and later tried to take control of the colony. If anyone is to blame, it's them."

"And yet," the golden-haired reporter continued, "it's Ahzco forces that have seized the colony of Tunis, trampled the rights of the citizens there, destroyed their property, and left dozens dead or injured by the mechanized war machines that Ahzco is so proudly displaying."

The reporter pointed. Nyx turned, along with the rest of the team, and saw three Titan MBS's lined up under a bank of lights. She saw at a glance that Alex, Ash, and Sly's names were printed on the gleaming, armored chest plates.

"Isn't it true," barked out a male reporter with tattoos rising out of the collar of his shirt to cover his neck and parts of his face, "that you turned the FTA colony into a battleground?"

"We didn't start the fighting," Alex said. "Zen Tech did that. Just think of what might have happened if we weren't there."

"But that's exactly my point," the tattooed man said. "If you hadn't been there, Zen Tech wouldn't have sent war machines to the new planet, and the citizens of Tunis would still be alive."

"I believe we had a contract that gave us the right to be on Carthage Prime," Nyx said. "We went through the proper channels and were only there to mine for minerals."

"Isn't stripping a planet of its natural resources a crime against humanity?" shouted an older man.

"What do you say," another reporter shouted before they could answer the last question, "to the people who believe it's time for a centralized government to rein in multi-global corporations and their military forces?"

"Aren't people like you oppressing entire worlds?" the golden-haired reporter jumped into the fray again. "You claim that you keep the Ahzco employees safe, but who is keeping us safe from you?"

Nyx felt her mouth go instantly dry. She had never been the target of such seething hatred.

"You aren't the solution," someone shouted. "You're the problem."

"We did our duty," Alex said bravely.

Alex didn't seem cowed by the anger and unpredictability of the crowd, which was growing. There were more than just reporters, and Nyx knew that the velvet ropes that separated the mob from her friends wouldn't hold them back if things got out of hand. She instinctively took hold of his arm as the crowd began to bellow and scream.

"All you did was murder the innocent!"

"Down with corporate greed!"

"You owe the people for the destruction you've caused!"

"Let's get out of here," Ash said.

Nyx turned, but the transport was gone. It had flown away, and she hadn't even noticed. Alex took the lead and pointed to a building constructed of thick, brown masonry stones. Above the wide, glass doors the word "BLEAKER" was carved into the stone.

"That way," he said.

The crowd was pressing in against the ropes. Many were shaking their fists and shouting. The group of CDF personnel, five in total, hurried toward the old building. Nyx couldn't help but wonder what was going on and when her world had been flipped upside-down.

Chapter 19

The interior of the building was dimly lit with warm yellow light along the walls. The floor was polished stone, and the walls were covered in thin slabs of granite. A large sign on the wall listed the dozens of businesses who called the Bleaker building home. On either side of the sign were two lifts, their metal doors shining gold. All the fixtures in the grand lobby were accented with polished gold, although Alex doubted that it was real. Any number of less expensive metals could be colored and polished to look like gold.

They all breathed a little easier as the noise and chaos outside the building faded. After a moment, the questions began.

"What was that?" Ash asked.

"I don't think it's what the VP was expecting," Alex said. "Also, what happened to Zan doing all the talking?"

"It's like he wanted us to be caught off guard," Ash said.

"Were there civilians killed in the fighting at Tunis?" Nyx asked.

"Not that I know of," Alex said.

"Of course not," Ash demanded. "It's all BS—just some hippy, anti-military crap conjured up to make us look bad."

"But why?" Nyx asked.

Before anyone could answer, Zan Fordham burst through the doors. He was red-faced, panting, and clearly angry.

"What was that?" he said. "How dare you simply leave in the middle of a press conference!"

"That wasn't a press conference," Alex replied. "It was an ambush."

"We invited those reporters," Zan said, throwing his hands up in the air. "This is what I get for trusting Loman. He said you were ready for this."

"Ready for questions about killing innocent civilians?" Ash said. "We didn't do that. We saved that colony from being destroyed by Zen Tech thugs."

"She's right," Nyx said. "I don't think the VP knew the questions—"

Zan interrupted before Nyx could finish speaking. "No, no, no, that's not right at all. I've read the reports. Your actions nearly destroyed the colony."

"Hey, whose side are you on here?" Ash said.

"There are sides," Zan said. "You are subordinates, and I expect you to act like it."

"What did you want us to say?" Alex asked. "We didn't kill civilians on Carthage Prime. We don't know anything about government oversight, but it doesn't sound like something the company would want."

"You don't get it," Zan muttered. "That's the problem. You think you're all above the law."

"Sir," Nyx replied, "we aren't trying to be disrespectful, but what those reporters were implying about the action in the Carthage system isn't true."

"We had the permits to be there," Ash said, "and we fought to protect the colonists. Our friend died in that battle. Don't you dare stand there in that ridiculous outfit and say we don't understand. If you haven't picked up a weapon and stepped onto the front lines, I suggest you keep your fat mouth shut."

"Ash!" Alex said.

Zan's face was so red, it looked like his head might burst. There was a malicious look in his eye, and his mouth curled into a sneer.

"You are the embodiment of everything that's wrong with the CDF," Zan said. "Your arrogance is deplorable. You think because you have an INC chip in your brain that you're somehow better than me? Or better than the rest of society? What do you think, that we should all just bow and scrape because you were chosen to be operators? Well, let me tell you something. I'm in charge now, and none of you have a future in the CDF. Those reporters are right about you, and I'm going to make sure they know it."

He stormed from the lobby back outside.

"I don't think this is what the VP had in mind when he sent us out with that slug," Nyx said.

"I can't believe he's an executive in the company," Ash replied. "He clearly hates us."

"But why?" Alex said. "What is going on?"

He pulled out his PIL, which was stuffed into the back pocket of his dress uniform, and swiped the sensor to activate it. The others did the same. Alex brought up the news feed on Arcadia's planetary network. The headlines made things a little clearer.

MORE CARNAGE FROM PRIVATE MILITARY FORCES — *The truth from Carthage Prime comes to light.*

CORPORATE MILITARY RUN AMUCK — Why we need oversight of all military and law enforcement.

TIME FOR CHANGE — Private corporations have too much power.

The list of news articles and videos went on and on. The news networks were in an uproar on Arcadia, and there were reports from other worlds, as well. Someone was fanning the flames of discontent, and corporate defense forces were at the heart of the outrage.

"Is this for real?" Ash said.

"Looks real," Nyx said. "It's all over the network."

"There have always been naysayers and people complaining about private military forces," Alex said, "but I've never seen anything like this."

"My gosh, the vitriol on social media is deplorable," Nyx said.

"So everyone hates us," Ash said.

"They don't just hate us," Nyx said. "Look at this post..."

She held out her PIL for the others to see. Alex, Ash, and the other two controllers leaned in.

If you aren't speaking out against private military, you are part of the problem. The Arcadia Actors Guild supports central government oversight of all private military. Mega-corporations have too much power and hoard too many resources. It's time for a change.

The picture beside the post was of a famous actor named Allany Frost. His trademark smile, for which he was known on dozens of worlds, had been replaced with a stern look of disapproval.

"I don't know which is worse," Ash said. "What that airhead is saying, or the fact that Nyx follows Allany Frost to begin with."

"I don't follow him," Nyx said, although Alex thought she said it a bit too fast. "It was shared by someone else."

"The point is," Alex interrupted the teasing. "We aren't going to be welcome if people know who we are."

"The dress uniforms were the perfect fashion choice for this evening," one of the controllers said.

"Yeah, there's no hiding what we do for a living while we're wearing these monkey suits," Ash said. "So what do we do?"

"I, for one, don't have much of an appetite anymore," Alex said.

"Yeah, me neither," Nyx agreed.

"You don't want to stay around for the tasting menu?" Ash said. "Sly would be so disappointed."

"Speaking of Sly, I say we get out of these uniforms and go check on him," Alex said.

"How do we get back to our quarters?" Nyx asked. "The transport is gone, and I don't want to go back out there."

"There's got to be another way out of this building," Alex said. "There's no need to go back to the rooms we're staying in. We can buy new clothes."

He walked over to the sign between the elevators. It didn't take long to find a department store in the posh building.

"It's probably expensive, but we can get new outfits," Alex said pointing to the store.

"If we're in civilian clothes," Ash said, "we can take public transit to the med center."

"Good idea," Nyx said.

"I could shop," Ash's controller said.

Alex pressed a button to call for the elevator. He felt a slight sense of relief about having a plan of action, but in the back of his mind he knew he needed to contact VP Haley and inform him about what was happening in the historic district and on the networks. It was not a conversation he was looking forward to.

Chapter 20

Loman was in shock. For the last hour, he had watched the news and social media blow up with outrageous stories about private military forces across the galaxy. Ahzco was just one of hundreds of large corporations who employed military defense forces to protect their employees, assets, and intellectual property. The attacks weren't aimed solely at Ahzco, but Ahzco bore the brunt of the scathing condemnation, most of which appeared to be coming from people with absolutely no experience or expertise on the subject.

Even more frightening was the way in which the public was joining the outrage over perceived atrocities carried out by CDF forces. Loman knew many of the stories to be erroneous or even outright fabrications, but the public was in an uproar. The solution being presented was a call for a central governing body to preside over all known worlds. When Loman's phone buzzed in his tiny office, there was no doubt who was calling.

"Are you seeing this?" CEO Ian Gentry cried as soon as the call connected and his face appeared on the small display screen of Loman's desk phone.

"Yes, sir," Loman said.

"Centralized government oversight? Since when has more government ever been a good thing?" the CEO ranted. "I'm hearing rumors of monopoly busters and revocations of private space tunnels. People are calling for open accounting of all known worlds, Loman. This is unprecedented."

"I know," Loman said quietly.

His mind was consumed with the question of who was behind it all. It certainly wasn't the media or some grassroots non-profit organization; it was too big and happening too fast. The tide of public opinion had been turned, and there was no going back.

"How did this happen?" Gentry demanded.

"I can't say," Loman admitted. "But it's big. This isn't like anything we've ever experienced."

"We'll be ruined," Gentry said. "Ahzco has too much invested in celestial property. If they revoke our rights to own the worlds we discover, we're doomed."

Loman considered the idea of giving away the locations of their space tunnels. Ahzco had an extensive network of system-to-system passageways, some leading to level-two planets that could easily be colonized. Besides the security fears of having their systems easily accessible, if the company planets were populated, the residents would have inherent rights that might interfere with Ahzco's plans.

"We have to get the PR department working around the clock," Loman said, even though he knew on an instinctive level that it was already too late.

The die was cast, and truth had already been disregarded in favor of public opinion. Unfortunately, the ire of the civilized worlds was suddenly focused on mega-corps just like Ahzco.

"I've already sent the memo," Gentry said. "It feels too little, too late."

"There's nothing more we can do," Loman said. "Maybe the idealists will spend decades fighting over what type of government to create. And even when they establish something, each world will have to decide if they want to join or not. We have time."

"Yes," the CEO said, sitting back in his chair. "I want a full plan on what to do in the days ahead to protect our assets."

"I'm already working on it," Loman said.

"Very good, very good," Gentry said. "I'm glad I can count on you, Loman. We're in this together."

"That's right, sir."

The CEO reached forward and ended the call. Loman watched the screen go dark. It didn't occur to him until a few minutes later that he had sent Alex and the rest of his team on a PR dinner with Zan Fordham.

He snatched up his PIL and sent a quick message to the Titan group leader.

Alex, I had no idea the firestorm I was sending you into. Tell me where you are. I'll send someone for you. I need to know everything you said to the reporters.

All he could do was wait and watch what unfolded. In the meantime, he still had a mega-company to keep safe, and as of late he wasn't doing a very good job. He dictated a quick memo to all CDF commanders to double their security and consider every company asset a target. Then he busied himself looking for the best place to send the Titan team. Leaving them unsupervised on Arcadia was no longer a good idea.

His PIL beeped to alert him of an incoming message. He looked at the screen and saw a reply from Alex.

On public transit, heading to the hospital to check on Sly.

Loman had expected more information, but the reply was terse. There was no information regarding the interviews that had been arranged in the historic district. Loman had no doubt that whatever the team said was being twisted and taken out of context by reporters and news agencies to fit their agenda. At least he knew where to find the group. The hospital would be a safe place away from the media storm. He pressed a button to alert his transport that he was ready to leave, then left his tiny office and hurried to the lift.

The ride down the nearly two hundred stories seemed excruciatingly slow. When the lift reached the lobby, Loman hurried out through the grand lobby and found a small transport waiting for him. It was nothing like the luxury transport Zan had picked up the Titan team in. There was only a single row of seats covered in thin plastic, and there were no doors or windows. The top of the flying craft was some type of stretchy material pulled tight over the transport's open frame.

Most upper-level executives preferred the expensive, fully enclosed, luxury transports, but Loman was not the type of man to flaunt his wealth. All he really cared about was getting from point A to point B, and the economy transport did the job just as well as the luxury carrier.

They rose straight up and made the journey from the Ahzco campus to the medical center in just under five minutes. Loman paid the rate with his PIL, including a generous tip for the driver, and got out. He went into the massive hospital and found Alex sitting with Ash and the three controllers in a waiting room on a recovery floor. He felt a stab of guilt over not keeping tabs on Corporal Lasiter's condition.

"How is he?" Loman asked, taking a seat in the empty chair beside Alex.

"Burns on his face are being treated," Alex replied, "but only time will tell if his eyes will recover. They've been treated and covered. They gave him enough painkillers to keep him asleep while they work on the burns."

"What a disaster," Loman said. "I'm sorry I haven't kept up with his treatment like I promised."

"It's been a crazy day," Nyx said. "I suppose you heard about the reporters?"

"I've been on the net all evening," Loman explained. "Gentry's near panic. I expect an emergency board meeting to be called any moment now—which is why I came to speak with you in person. What did you tell the reporters?"

"Not a lot," Alex admitted. "They were hostile."

"They blamed us for things on Carthage Prime that we knew nothing about," Ash added. "Were civilians killed in the fighting?"

"No," Loman said. "There was only some property damage, but that's not what the news agencies are reporting. We'll repair the damage to the colony, of course, but the damage to us is done. And they aren't just coming after us. All the mega-corps are being painted as corrupt, greedy, blood-thirsty companies that only care about profits."

"People have said that all my life," Nyx admitted. "There are always stories about it floating around the global networks."

"But this time it's become major news—a social movement maybe," Loman explained. "There have been protests on all the level-one planets. In fact, I think it would be best if your team went to the Skandia system in the morning. The *Currency* is in orbit. It's a smaller ship, with just two squads of MBS's. There's room for your team, and hopefully Corporal Lasiter will be able to join you."

"I wouldn't want to leave him behind," Ash said.

"None of us would," Alex added.

"If he can't travel right away, I can have him join you later. There are always passenger vessels traveling between the highly populated planets," Loman said. "Of course, if he can't see, he can't pilot an MBS."

"But even if he can't see," Alex pointed out, "in the Titan his INC would translate the data straight to his brain as if he could see. Right?"

Nyx nodded, but Loman shook his head. "You're right, of course, but company policy forbids anyone with permanent injury from operating battle suits. I can't make an exception, not even for him. Besides, the ships aren't set up for people with disabilities. He wouldn't cope well and would be at risk of further injury."

The look on Ash's face was unbridled fury, but she held herself in check. "That's not fair," she said, her voice trembling.

"I know, I'm sorry," Loman said. "But it's a good policy, based on hard data from many years. He wouldn't be dismissed from the CDF. We'll always take care of the people who have sacrificed for us."

"So we're leaving in the morning?" Alex asked. "Can we stay here tonight?"

"Yes," Loman said. "Don't talk to any more reporters if they track you down. But you shouldn't be bothered here. I'll confirm your location once the shuttle is ready and provide a transport to get you to the launch pad."

"I'm sorry we can't stay and help more," Alex said.

"You're doing your jobs," Loman said. "That's all anyone can ask for. And you've already done so much. Today could have been a disaster if not for—"

He was interrupted by a doctor who stepped into the waiting room. He looked tired. There was sweat on his chest and under his arms, making his thin surgical outfit cling to his skin.

"You're here for Sylvester Lasiter?" the doctor asked.

"Yes!" Ash said, bounding to her feet with more energy than Loman felt like he could muster even if someone were chasing him.

"There's good news," the doctor said. "Preliminary tests show no permanent damage to his eyes."

"That's such a relief," Ash said.

"He'll still need to keep them covered for a few days and then wear dark shades for a week, but he should regain full sight," the doctor explained. "He'll need to rest as much as possible, and if he has problems with his sight after a week, he'll need to see a specialist. It's always possible that something might not show up in our testing, but the scans were all positive."

"That's great news," Alex said. "We're shipping out in the morning. Is there any chance he can go with us?"

"As long as there are no complications in the night," the doctor said. "I'll be back to check on him in the morning. I can't promise anything until then."

"Thank you," Ash said. "Can we see him?"

"He's resting, so perhaps just one of you," the doctor said.

Ash followed him without even checking with the others. Loman was beginning to think there was more than just friendship between the two of them, but that was the least of his worries.

"Alex, can I get a word with you and Ms. West alone?" Loman said.

"Sure," Alex replied. He and Nyx followed the VP to the corner, where he spoke to them in quiet tones.

"I don't want anyone to know what you can do," he said. "The CEO knows, but no one else. I can keep Gentry in line. He's probably already forgotten about it with this new crisis to deal with. I'm hoping you won't be deployed in the Skandia system, but we've got several factories building Titan MBS's there. If the riots get out of hand, we'll need to protect them, but I don't want you using your new trick. If word were to get out to the news media about what you could do, it would cause panic and make this entire media storm worse. The last thing we need is for people to think we can control them or hack into their computing systems at will."

"That makes sense," Nyx said.

"Good," Loman continued. "Hopefully things will calm down soon and we can move you on to more important assignments. I'm sorry things didn't work out here on Arcadia."

"I think we're all ready to leave," Alex said.

"I know it hasn't been the relaxing break we expected," Loman admitted. "If things calm down, there could be a chance for leave on Skandia Seven."

"I could see my parents?" Alex asked.

"Most likely, but I can't promise anything. We're still in unchartered waters here."

"Roger that," Nyx said.

"Yeah, whatever is best for the CDF, sir," Alex added.

"I appreciate your cooperation. I'll be in touch," Loman said.

He left the waiting room with a glimmer of hope. At least he hadn't lost another operator. The trio could stay intact. The last thing Loman needed was to have to bring in new Titan operators that might not see Alex's abilities as a gift. All Loman had left to do was to find a way to use Alex to get them out of the mess the company was mired in. If he could do that, he might just salvage everything. That tiny spark of hope kept him going, even though he was beyond tired. There would be no rest for him or any of the other executives, who were already being called back to the Ahzco universal HQ building.

Loman felt his PIL vibrate and pulled it from his pocket. What he read almost extinguished the tiny bit of hope he had left. Chairwoman Lynn Faulk had called an emergency board meeting. Just when he thought things couldn't get any worse, they did.

Chapter 21

Alex felt gross. He still hadn't slept, despite feeling exhausted. The entire team had spent the night in the hospital, trying to rest in the uncomfortable, plastic chairs in the waiting room. He was in new clothes that had wrinkled overnight. When his PIL showed the local time as 0630, he decided to start moving.

"You going somewhere?" Nyx asked.

"I'm going to find something to eat," he said, his voice croaking.

"Okay, sure," Nyx said as she closed her eyes again and leaned her head against the wall. He couldn't blame her for getting as much sleep as she could. Between the discomfort of the waiting room and the pain throbbing behind his eyes, sleep was simply out of reach for him. The pain in his head no longer felt like a red-hot coal, but rather a deep strain, as if he'd stretched his mind too far and it couldn't bounce back into shape.

He walked down the sterile corridor, resenting the bright white, artificial light that made him squint. His mouth felt gluey, and there was a film on his teeth. Eating would help, but what he really needed was a hot shower, a toothbrush, and a warm bed. Instead, he was forced to settle for food from a dispensary. The large unit was built into the wall and had a few options for every time of day. Alex selected a breakfast burrito and a bottle of orange juice. He paid for his food the same way he'd purchased his new, overpriced clothes. He held his Ahzco ID up to the payment reader and had the funds withdrawn from his account. Everything on

Arcadia seemed much too expensive. The money he'd spent on a pair of pants and T-shirt from the clothing store in the Bleaker building would have fed his family for a month growing up. But he didn't have many expenses, and once he was back on a CDF ship, he could store the civilian attire for use somewhere. He wouldn't always be on duty, and the new clothes were much nicer than anything he had owned growing up on NP8261.

The thought of free time made him wonder if he would really get the chance to see his family again on Skandia Seven. Being on his own and doing something he enjoyed was empowering, but he still missed his parents and baby sister. Seeing them and letting them see how well he was doing in the CDF would be welcome.

He pulled the wrapper off the hot burrito and sniffed it. The food seemed real. Eggs, peppers, cheese, and some type of sausage made from actual meat. It was better quality than ship food. He took a bite and let the thick tortilla clear the gunk from his mouth, then took a long swig of the orange juice. It had the unpleasant tang of preservation chemicals, but otherwise it was all right. He felt a little better with some hot food in his stomach.

Ash appeared in the corridor before he finished his breakfast. She looked tired, her eyes puffy and red.

"Everything okay?" Alex asked.

"Sly's fine. Sleeping like a baby, in fact. He never even knew I was there all night," Ash said. "I stayed awake—not that a person without drugs can sleep in the chairs here. It's like they were designed for aggressive interrogation or something."

"Tell me about it," Alex said.

"Not to mention the beeping machines and nurses coming in at all hours," Ash went on. "I don't like hospitals."

"Hopefully we'll be gone soon," Alex said.

"How's breakfast?"

"Better than ship food."

"That's not saying much," she said with a sigh. "Any word from our fearless leader?"

"You mean VP Haley?" Alex asked. "No. Not yet. What about the doctor?"

"Haven't seen him either," Ash replied. "The nurses say he'll be here in an hour or so, but there's no guarantee what time he'll make his rounds. If he has an emergency, it could be hours."

"I hate waiting on other people," Alex said.

"Me too," Ash said, as she purchased her own burrito and joined him against the wall.

They leaned beside a window, looking out over the city as the sun slowly filled the sky with pink light that reflected off wispy clouds high above.

It wasn't long before Nyx joined them. She rolled her head on her shoulders, trying to work out a kink. "I need to find a bathroom," she said.

"I'll join you," Ash said. She had already devoured the burrito. "Alex, if you see the doctor, I want to know everything."

"Sure," Alex said. He was starting to feel the effects of a full bladder himself, but he would wait until they returned. Several minutes passed—enough time for him to finish his breakfast—when his PIL buzzed on his forearm. He held it up and looked at the message.

Shuttle leaves at 0920. Will have you a transport at the hospital at 0900. - L. Haley

The PIL showed that they had just a little over two hours before they would need to leave. All Alex could do was hope that Sly would be discharged and could leave with them. When Ash and Nyx returned, he gave them the news. Ash bought another burrito and headed back to Sly's room. Nyx and Alex woke the other two controllers, then went for a stroll. They passed patient rooms, nursing stations, medical bots, and admin offices before discovering a balcony. They went outside and felt the cool morning air. Inside the hospital it was quiet, but outside, the sounds of the city were coming to life. Transports buzzed overhead. There were people walking in the streets below the balcony. Nyx sipped coffee from a disposable cup, and they both leaned against the railing, looking down at the people passing by.

"Can you imagine living here?" Nyx asked.

"Some people might say it's exciting," he said doubtfully.

"But not you?"

"Compared to flying a Titan? No way," he said. "I mean, you do what you have to. If I couldn't be an operator, I would find some type of work, but living in a place like this, working in a huge building surrounded by even bigger buildings…it would feel claustrophobic."

"What about Carthage Prime?" she queried.

"You mean live there?" Alex asked. "That would be better, I think. I mean, I know it's a way out from the level-one planets, but still, a person would have room to grow and really build something there. Don't you think?"

"I feel like something in between is more my style," Nyx said. "I definitely don't want to be in a densely populated world like this, but I don't want to be on a frontier world, either. I like some comforts."

"Who doesn't?" Alex agreed. "Still, I'm where I want to be. The CDF is my first choice."

"Mine too," she said.

They were shoulder to shoulder, watching the sunlight filter through and glitter off the skyscrapers around them. Alex understood that there were trade-offs to everything. While some people might balk at the idea of being ordered to go here or there and told what to do, he liked the camaraderie of being in the CDF. It was exciting to fly a Fast-Attack Titan MBS, even though it carried a high chance that he might get seriously injured or killed in the process. Above all, nothing could compare to being so close to Nyx. He didn't want to do anything that might jeopardize that.

"It's a quarter 'til nine," Nyx said after several moments of comfortable silence.

"Really?" Alex asked, looking at his own PIL for confirmation. "Where did the time go?"

They hurried back through the hospital and found the rest of the Titan team following a nurse, who was pushing Sly out in a hoverchair.

"Thought we lost you two," Ash said with a wink.

"We found a balcony," Alex said.

"Sounds romantic," Ash teased.

He gave her a look that was intended to be stern, but he couldn't stop smiling. Being with Nyx made him feel happy. When he glanced over at her, she was smiling too.

Chapter 22

"They're on their way to the *Currency*," Loman's assistant VP of personnel informed him.

"And Corporal Lasiter?"

"Discharged this morning. He's with the rest of Cronus Team."

"At least that's one good thing," Loman declared.

The media frenzy had only intensified overnight. There were dozens of new stories being circulated, many with so-called witnesses who described corporate warriors in mechanized battle suits carrying out atrocious acts of violence on the innocent. There was outrage across all the level-three planets. People were forming protest rallies and marching in the streets, calling for massive change.

Loman understood their outrage. If half the things he was seeing on the networks were true, he would have joined them in protest. But the stories weren't true about Ahzco, and Loman was in the unique position to know that as an undeniable fact. Unfortunately, he couldn't prove it since any information coming from private military sources were dismissed completely by the people behind the protests.

His assistant VP was a thin man with narrow shoulders and hair that was both receding and thinning, despite the fact that he was still young. His name was D.J. Harlan. The entire executive team was in a conference room on the one hundred and ninety-sixth floor of the Ahzco building, nicknamed the "War Room."

Loman had four assistant vice presidents. It was a rank equivalent to colonel on the admin side of the security division. Personnel, Munitions & Armament, Logistics, and Research each had an assistant VP to oversee each department. They all had offices on the same floor of the building as Loman, but they were subordinate to him. Colonel Chastain was present, along with Harlan and Margot Murray, who was AVP of Logistics.

Loman was pacing on one side of a long table while everyone else sat on the opposite side working their PILs and making calls to answer questions from the PR department, who were trying to find a way out of the media storm that had seemingly sprung up overnight. Loman had no doubt that whoever was behind the attacks, false information, and bomb threat to the building was also pulling the strings of the protests taking place on a dozen worlds.

"Where is security admin Prince?" Loman said. "We should have heard something from her by now."

"I've got her on a secure line, sir," Harlan said. "Would you like to take it in your office?"

"Yes," Loman growled.

Fortunately, his people knew that he wasn't angry with them; they were all feeling the stress of running the mega-corporation's security division while someone was targeting them at every turn. Loman had kept the news of the bomb threat to a minimum, but his AVPs all knew about it, as did Colonel Chastain, who was busy deploying mechanized squads to the worlds experiencing the worst of the protests. It was only a matter of time before the peaceful actions of the mob slid into more destructive behavior. Loman agreed with Chastain that riots, looting, and destruction of company property was on the way.

Loman left the War Room and felt a pang of loss as he passed the reception desk. A young woman from the personnel department had been floated in as a temporary replacement for Raz Goreman. She was friendly and gave him a curt wave, but it was too painful to return the gesture. Less than twenty-four hours earlier, his good friend had occupied the seat the receptionist was perched on. Unlike Goreman, who had been a hulking giant of a man, she was thin, petite, and looked like a child sitting in their parent's favorite seat. Loman felt tears stinging his eyes. He nodded and hurried on past the reception area.

His new office was down the hall from his original corner office, which had massive windows and spectacular views of the city. The door to his old office was open, the room dark. It was after 0900 and his counterpart--they still had no official title for him--Zan Fordham, still wasn't in. It was just another infuriating problem to deal with. The fact that the chairwoman of the company's board of directors had saddled Loman with the incompetent, arrogant, little manager only made the situation worse.

Loman pulled his own office door open and dropped quickly into the chair behind the absurdly tiny desk. He had a computer interface on the desktop, a port for his PIL, and a display phone. The light on the phone's secure line was flashing. He pressed the button, and Ciara Prince's face appeared.

"Are you safe?" Loman asked immediately. Despite what some people thought and what the news media was promoting to the masses, Loman cared about the people who worked for him.

"Yes sir, things are quiet," Ciara Prince said. "I have news."

"Tell me," Loman ordered.

"No one is naming people directly," she explained. "But I've interviewed three finance administrators who claim that a new entity was started through various off-world shell companies owned by some heavy hitters."

"Who?"

"Francis Parlaon, Rubin Coifmere, Quintessa Vandross, and Lynn Faulk."

"No," Loman said. "What is this entity?"

"It's a registered private firm," Ciara explained. "The business filing states that it's a security company. Sigma Services Corp is what it's called. So far it's only been vested, but with billions of credits. No one knows anything about it."

"A security firm?" Loman asked.

"That's what the paperwork says, but it could be anything, really. Parlaon owns four news agencies through his Matrix Media conglomerate. Coifmere and Vandross control massive hedge funds. We're talking quadrillions of credits—more than the gross domestic income of most planets."

"Why would they go in together on a security firm? That makes no sense."

Loman knew of several good private security contractors that worked much like the CDF for smaller businesses. In some instances they did well financially, but most struggled to stay afloat. Without the production capacity of a large corporation, it was difficult to build and maintain mechanized battle suits. Munitions were expensive, as well. Ahzco manufactured everything his operators needed, with several trade secrets that were worth billions, but it still didn't make sense that four of the richest people in the galaxy would start a security firm.

"It's possible that Lynn Faulk is using our proprietary weapons and MBS designs to build a new company," Ciara Prince said. "But I have another theory."

"Don't make me ask for it," Loman said.

He wasn't normally so short with people, but he had never felt so threatened before. The weight of the civil unrest that threatened to destroy Ahzco was worse than dropping into combat.

"I have it on good authority that we're not the only company being targeted by saboteurs. Is it possible that the point of those attacks was simply to weaken us? Zen Tech is reeling from their losses on Carthage Prime. Word is, they're already looking to beef up their security division with private contractors."

"You mean weaken the larger companies and then step in with an offer to take up the slack?" Loman asked, rolling the idea around in his mind.

"It wouldn't be the first time someone created a problem and then showed up with a fix," Ciara Prince said. "But it might be larger than that. I have teams tracking leads. It's possible that Parlaon is fanning the flames of civil unrest with his media agencies. He's been accused of such activities before."

"True, but that wouldn't benefit the other partners," Loman pointed out.

"It would if the calls for a centralized government were the end goal," Ciara Prince explained. "If it is, they would know we would fight back. So perhaps they weaken us so that we can't stop them."

"And Sigma Services swoops in and buys up the security assets as each of the companies topple due to their government control plan," Loman said.

He felt like he'd just been stabbed in the back. The idea made sense, at least on a conspiracy theory level. It wasn't the first time people had blamed the mega-rich for every evil idea that floated into the mainstream. Still, Loman knew Lynn Faulk. She was a power-hungry woman who considered herself superior to everyone else. It wouldn't take much to convince her that she should be in control of the entire human race.

"This new government would most likely contract with Sigma Services to build their own army," Ciara Prince continued. "Then the group makes billions while propelling themselves into positions of ultimate power."

"I wouldn't have thought it was possible," Loman said.

"Until every level-three planet erupted in civil unrest?" Ciara Prince said. "Believe me, I feel like I've fallen off the deep end. I've never given the conspiracy theories about secret societies and powerful cabals of the mega-rich pulling the strings of power much credence, but..."

Loman let an uncomfortable silence linger as he thought about the emergency board meeting that had been held in the middle of the night. Lynn Faulk had been there, casting aspersions, calling for someone to come up with an answer for the protests taking place. Loman had been accused of ineptitude, but that was no surprise, and the rest of the board members knew about the bomb threat. They were on his side, but time was running out. If Lynn Faulk got her way and pushed him out of the company, Zan Fordham stood ready to gut the CDF and leave Ahzco helpless to stop the new centralized government from tearing the mega-corporation to pieces.

"If you're right," Loman finally said, "we'll know it soon enough. Keep digging, but don't get caught. People this powerful don't pull punches."

"You're saying they won't report me, they'll kill me?"

"That's right. What's a little murder when you're taking control of the entire galaxy?" Loman said. "You watch your back."

"What are you going to do?" Ciara Prince asked.

"I'm going to make sure that if there's a fight coming, we're ready for it."

Chapter 23

The transport took Alex and his team to a landing pad, where an Ahzco shuttle was waiting for them. It was a commercial vessel and much more comfortable than a military craft.

"So you're telling me you didn't eat?" Sly said. He was back to his gregarious self, despite having his entire face wrapped in bandages.

"There were like a thousand reporters," Ash said. "No one was thinking about food."

"That's just wrong," Sly said.

Nyx leaned over to Alex. "I could get used to this," she said.

The shuttle had plush, reclining seats. They hardly even felt the ship take off or pass through the atmosphere before a chime went off and a sign lit up that said *PREPARE FOR ZERO GRAVITY.*

Alex had been pleased to find his rucksack on the shuttle waiting for him. All their luggage had been retrieved from their quarters on Arcadia, and the group was headed into orbit for their next deployment.

"It's pretty nice," Alex said. "I doubt CDF personnel get taken care of this well in most circumstances."

"All the more reason to enjoy it now," Nyx said.

Alex was indeed enjoying the flight. He was tired and his head still hurt, but he was letting the stress of the bomb threat and

Sly's injuries fade as the planet shrank below them. They passed into orbit, and Ash got out of her seat to twirl around the cabin.

"Man, I've missed this," she said.

Alex felt himself floating out of his seat, but the safety harness held him back. Twenty minutes later, the ship docked with the spaceport and they all gathered their belongings and floated out. Ash led Sly. Their controllers were together, talking quietly—and from the looks of them, ready to get back into a regular gravity environment.

Alex and Nyx were the last pair off the ship. They floated out of the shuttle's airlock, through the docking tube, and into the long corridor that extended out from the space station. Gravity increased slowly as they went, so that they barely noticed once their feet were on the deck.

"Where to, team leader?" Ash said in a mocking tone that was playful, not disrespectful.

Alex looked at his PIL, then looked back up. "The *Currency* is docked on arm L, berth 4. It leaves in one hour."

"Then we have time!" Sly said excitedly. "I know you can smell the food. Can we please get something? Anything. I can't go back to ship food yet."

"Did you have breakfast in the hospital?" Nyx asked.

"The tray of food an orderly brought him," Ash said. "And the burrito I got him. But he's never full."

"Come on, you know I'm right," Sly said. "We'll have nothing but processed food for who knows how long. Let's get something."

"Fine," Alex said. "But no more than half an hour. We can't be late."

The spaceport was full of people. There were large kiosks for the various commercial transport companies. People sat in waiting areas while ships prepared for boarding. There were dozens of stores, from tourist trinket shops to high-end retailers selling duty-free goods. There were even more restaurants, some selling snack items and others full meals. Sly settled in at a small table in a sandwich shop. He ordered a full meal with french fries and a milkshake. The rest of the group settled for snacks.

Twenty minutes later, they moved on to a shop that sold snacks for space travelers. Alex bought a bag of chips and a sleeve of cookies. Everyone got something and stashed the goodies away in their rucksacks. Then it was on to arm L, berth 4. They had to show their IDs to a soldier at the entrance to arm L. The corridor was long, and Alex noticed that the artificial gravity didn't decrease the further they went. Two more guards—operators in Patroller battle suits with laser pistols and stun batons—stood just outside the airlock. Unlike the shuttle, the *Currency* was connected directly to the space station.

"Sergeant Alex Evans with Cronus team," Alex told the guards.

"You're cleared," the operator said.

They went through the airlock and onto the ship. It was different from the *Republic* but felt similar. They were on the main deck, and an officer with a data pad was waiting for them.

"You Evans?" the man said.

"Yes, sir," Alex replied.

"I'm Lieutenant Rory Jones, first officer. This isn't a carrier. It's a controller ship. It's smaller than what you're probably used to, but in most respects you'll have more space."

"How's that?" Ash asked.

"Private cabins, for one thing," Rory said, waving them down the hall. "The rec area is smaller, and everything is centralized. We all dine from the same mess hall and use the same fitness equipment. Most everyone here is on a first-name basis. This is the command level and has the bridge, controller stations, comms, and briefing rooms. One deck above us, that's the recreation level. Directly below are crew berths. The bottom level will have your hangars, ready rooms, and engineering."

They followed Rory to a briefing room. It was already half full. The lieutenant introduced Alex to Master Sergeant Taylor Montgomery.

"Oscar Company is the resident MBS squad," Lieutenant Jones explained. "Cronus Team is a three-person group of Titan operators."

"Welcome aboard. Call me Monty," the Master Sergeant said.

"The captain will be in to address everyone in just a few moments," Jones explained. "I've got to return to the bridge to oversee departure, but I look forward to getting to know you all better."

"Oscar Company is eighteen strong," Monty said. "We're certified on everything but the Valkyrie and Titan."

"I guess that makes us your flight jockeys," Alex said. "Call me Ace. This is Sly and Ash."

The master sergeant nodded as they took their seats. Nyx had joined with the other controllers, who were clustered in the back of the room. Alex knew that most controllers didn't like to get overly friendly with their operators. His group was an exception, but they needed time with their colleagues. He doubted they would get to spend as much time together as they had over the past week and a half.

"Your man okay?" Monty asked after Ash led Sly to a seat and got him settled.

"He suffered some facial burns recently," Alex said.

"Ouch."

"Yeah, but he'll be fine. The bandages come off tomorrow, and he should be cleared for duty in a few days."

"Any idea where we're headed?" Monty asked.

"I heard the Skandia system," Alex said.

There were things he couldn't share, but he felt comfortable with that small nugget of info. The captain was due to give them a briefing in a few minutes, and Alex guessed that she would make their destination official.

"We just came from a two-year stint in Waygo system. It was quiet," Monty said, "but they don't bring Titans on board unless they expect trouble."

"Protests," Alex said. "Are your people online?"

"The ship's got access to Ahzco's network, but we don't bother with it much. What's happening?"

"There's a movement to start some kind of oversight of private military," Alex said. "We were just in the Carthage system."

"Zen Tech," Monty said. "I heard about that."

"Yeah, well, so did the media—only they got their facts all wrong," Alex said. "That's really all I know."

"The captain will give us all the info we need," Monty said. "I don't care much for politics. Just tell me who the bad guys are and point me in the right direction."

"I hear that," Alex said.

He didn't necessarily agree with Master Sergeant Montgomery, but he understood the sentiment. In his short career, Alex had been privy to much more than he wanted to be. Joining the CDF had been his dream, but not because he had any interest in the administrative or business side. He wanted to help people, to defend those without the means to protect themselves. But he wasn't excited by the prospect of combat, either. Whenever he thought of fighting, Newt's face appeared in his mind—not the joyful, optimistic, friendly face that Alex wanted to see, but the waxy, lifeless face Alex had seen when they got Newt's MBS open. The stakes were high in any combat scenario.

They settled into seats. The briefing room was set up like a lecture hall, with rows of descending seats and a podium down front. There were crew members in the briefing room too, and Alex noticed that people tended to gather in clusters according to job and rank.

When the captain entered someone shouted, "Captain on deck!"

Everyone got quickly to their feet and stood at attention. The captain was a dark-skinned man with teardrop-shaped eyes and a square jaw. His head was shaved and gleamed under the lights of the briefing room. His officer's uniform wasn't tight, but Alex could see the captain's muscular physique. He went straight to the lectern and spoke with a booming voice.

"At ease. Find your seats," he said. "For those of you who are new on board the *Currency*, I'm Captain Christian Poe. We've been ordered to the Skandia system."

Monty nodded in Alex's direction, a slight compliment to show he acknowledged that Alex had shared useful information.

"As you may know," Captain Poe continued, "The Skandia system has a level-one planet with two moons that are in the process of colonization. One orbits Skandia Seven, the other orbits the tenth planet in the system. There are also a spaceport and two scientific space stations in the system. At the moment there is civil unrest on the planet, and our job will be protecting the Ahzco facilities on Skandia Seven."

A hand went up near the front of the auditorium. Captain Poe stopped and nodded for the hand-raiser to speak.

"Isn't there a law enforcement group on Skandia Seven?"

"There is," the captain continued. "Skandia Seven is an FTA planet with a freely elected, representative government. They have their own police force and a volunteer, military-style planetary guard. We will not attempt to control or replace them. We are going into the system to monitor the situation on the ground. If it becomes volatile, we will send our operators in to protect our assets only, unless assistance is asked for by the local government."

Another hand rose, and Captain Poe paused for the question.

"What are they protesting?"

Captain Poe cleared his throat before answering. "The protests are anti-corporate military demonstrations. Private military and planetary ownership are being targeted. And calls for a galaxy-wide central government to rein in corporate defense forces like the CDF appears to be the end goal. Our job is not to join the political fight. We are peacekeepers only. The protests on other worlds have grown violent, and Colonel Chastain has ordered us into the Skandia system for the purpose of protecting our people and the company facilities."

"But won't there be other corporate forces in the system?" someone else asked, this time without bothering to raise their hand.

"Yes, that is highly likely," Captain Poe said. "Varner Enterprises has the largest holdings on Skandia Seven, but there are more than a dozen mega-corporations with facilities on the planet and dozens of smaller companies that could have military personnel in the system. We will not engage with other defense forces. Nor will we do anything that might be recorded and used to further the protests. Am I making myself clear?"

The entire room answered in unison. "Yes, captain."

"Very good. We have two days to reach the Skandia system. When we arrive, I want this entire ship on high alert. Operator teams will be ready to launch at a moment's notice. When we are on station and have assessed the situation, I will share my thoughts with you all. Until then, we have a job to do. Let's make sure it gets done with efficiency and excellence. That is all."

The captain left the podium, and everyone stood up. The noise in the room grew loud with everyone talking. Monty waved

Alex toward the door. "Let me show you the ready room and your quarters."

"Roger that," Alex said, making sure Ash and Sly were with him.

They followed the master sergeant out of the auditorium and down a hall to an enclosed stairwell.

"There's no lift?" Sly said.

"Just stairs," Monty said. "It's good exercise."

"Not if you can't see," Sly said.

"Quit whining—I won't let you fall," Ash said.

"Famous last words," Sly lamented.

They made their way down one level and dropped off their rucksacks in their newly assigned private rooms. They were tiny, narrow rooms with a bed and desk that folded out from the walls. There wasn't enough room to have both the bed and the desk open at the same time, but they weren't forced to share rooms and that made it seem luxurious. There was a double locker in each one and a tiny lavatory in the back.

"Shower facilities are at the end of the hall," Monty pointed out.

"Luxury at last," Sly said.

They went down to the lower deck and were shown the ready room, which was a lot like the one on the carrier ship *Republic*. There were lockers, padded benches, a smaller briefing area, and bathroom facilities. Just down the hall they found the hangar where the mechanized battle suits were kept. The Titans were in a smaller compartment with an emergency access hatch. One of the technicians explained the reason.

"Once you're set in the Titans, we can drop you directly out of the ship," he said, with more than a little pride. "The floor splits open and the clamps just let go."

"Sort of like a trick door," Sly said.

"Better make sure your suit is sealed up before they open it," Monty said.

After the tour, they took Sly up to the med bay to check in. The ship's medical officer insisted on removing the bandages and checking Sly's progress. Alex and Ash went up to the rec level. There was a fitness area, the mess hall, communication bays, and the observation deck.

"Sly won't be happy there aren't food vendors," Ash said.

"I guess you can't have it all," Alex replied as they watched the glistening planet of Arcadia grow smaller and smaller.

"Think we'll have trouble on Skandia Seven?"

"I hope not," Alex said, thinking of his family. "It's sort of like being sent in to fight with your hands tied behind your back."

Chapter 24

Things didn't improve in Arcadia. Fortunately, most of the residents were too busy to protest, but the news was closely and carefully monitored. When Loman left the War Room around midday, he met Zan Fordham coming out of the executive elevator.

"Where the hell have you been?" Loman growled.

"Don't take that tone with me," Zan said in a haughty voice. "I was at an emergency meeting with chairwoman Faulk."

"You don't work for her, Fordham," Loman said. "If your loyalty isn't to Ahzco, we can fix that right now."

"My loyalty is to the company, and not just a single division. You are what's wrong with mega-corporations, Haley," Zan said with a sneer. "All you care about is your own power. You have no thought or consideration for how your operators conduct their affairs."

"Excuse me?" Loman said.

"You heard what I said. You and your ilk have run these private militaries for far too long. But things are changing."

"Is that right?" Loman demanded.

"Yes! And responsible companies are changing with the times. We have to listen to our customers and become the company they want."

"I didn't realize that Ahzco was looking to turn over operations to the fickle whims of society at large."

"There are a lot of things you don't realize," Zan said. He was smaller than Loman and not imposing in the least, but he leaned in close and pointed a finger in Loman's face. "Changes are coming. I hope you're ready for that."

Loman didn't respond, and Zan waddled past him. The smaller man's hands were shaking. He wasn't a threat physically—and maybe he was nothing but a pawn in Chairwoman Lynn Faulk's power games—but he knew things that Loman didn't know. Loman stepped onto the lift and hit the button for the lobby. He was tired, dirty, and in desperate need of a shower, but leaving the office, even for an hour, felt irresponsible.

His own hands were shaking a bit as he pulled out his PIL. A stiff drink and a few hours of sleep was what he needed, but there was no time. The CEO was terrified. The board of directors were furious. Every division was scrambling to ensure that the company weathered the media storm. Loman had spent all morning making deployment assignments and writing out memos to his senior officers. The entire galaxy was watching them. Protecting their employees and assets had never been more difficult. He had to ensure that they did nothing aggressive, and with every big company in the same predicament, it was only a matter of time before they began to step on one another's toes.

Loman brought up the available security personnel on Arcadia and found exactly what he was looking for. There was an undercover infiltrator, Ahzco's special term for corporate spy, waiting for reassignment. Loman sent his handler a quick message. It shouldn't be too difficult for the infiltrator to worm his way into Zan Fordham's life and discover all the manager's secrets. Loman had no doubt that Lynn Faulk was up to something; the only question was if she was dumb enough to reveal her plans to the likes of Zan Fordham.

An hour later, after he had run back to his small, luxury apartment to shower and shave, Loman returned to the Ahzco building in a fresh suit. Food was being catered in, and while Loman was hungry, he didn't really feel like eating. The acid in his stomach was already churned up from the stress of the situation. There was nothing more he could do. His people were forwarding reports to the PR department regarding the CDF's various engagements so that Ahzco's marketing people could combat the misinformation spreading through the global networks like wildfire. Loman couldn't help but admit that they had stumbled into a perfect storm.

At the next emergency board meeting, people were yelling and looking for someone to blame. Loman was the largest target; it was his division that was directly under fire by the media and being used as a catalyst for a new government that would slice and dice mega-corporations in the name of fair and equitable commerce. It was a farce, of course. Ahzco wasn't a monopoly and only held twenty to thirty percent of any market share they were involved in, but that was more than most other corporations. If the axe was about to fall, Ahzco would be one of the first to be shattered under its weight.

But no one in the company was to blame. Loman knew that for a fact, but he couldn't prove it. Even if he could, pointing out Lynn Faulk's shady dealings wouldn't really change anything. Everyone knew she was up to something. Every VP now had a counterpart loyal only to Faulk. Zan was Loman's, but every department head had someone lurking in the shadows, looking for ways to push them out of the company. What didn't make sense to Loman was why she wanted to destroy Ahzco. Lynn Faulk was a major shareholder, and if the department heads were fired, their replacements would almost certainly run the company straight into the ground. She would lose billions of credits. And if she wanted to have more power, running Ahzco like a fascist dictator would only work if the company retained its status. He had thought that perhaps she wanted control of his CDF since they had the most advanced battle suits in the galaxy. While other companies focused on drones, Ahzco had spent their efforts supporting the men and women who served as operators. Having drones in combat wasn't as efficient as a living, breathing person in the field. Loman's MBS's capitalized on the operators, enhancing their control of the war machines until they was like an extension of themselves.

It was a powerful army, and without an outside authority to answer to—as the media was so obsessed with pointing out—no one person should have control of it. Unlike what the media reported, Loman was neither singularly in charge nor without oversight, and his operators had the last say in what they did and how they followed orders. Yet the media portrayed the CDF as if they were cold-blooded killers.

Loman realized now that unfettered control of Ahzco's CDF wasn't Faulk's endgame. She didn't want control of just one army—she wanted to control them all. If her cabal was really behind the calls for a new, central government linking all the inhabitable worlds, they would quickly gain control of the largest fighting force in the galaxy. Those that opposed them would be crushed, their remaining assets absorbed into the new central army. The fact that the public at large couldn't see that was a complete mystery to Loman.

His agents could find the proof, but he didn't know if it would be enough. There were times when the truth didn't matter. Once minds and hearts were set, nothing would stop the rich and powerful from the complete domination they were obsessed with gaining over the galaxy. He didn't know what megalomania drove some people to want to rule over everyone and everything. History was rife with such attempts, going all the way back to the first planet humanity had sprung from. Few ever came close to success. Most were destroyed from within long before they achieved their goal, but that lesson didn't stop new generations from trying. Humanity had taken to the stars, spreading across the galaxy, but there were still those who wanted to bring each and every person under their heel.

Loman wondered which of the incredibly rich magnates would move to the front to become the figurehead of the new government and which would stay hidden the shadows, striking like vile serpents at anyone who came too close. And how many innocent lives would be lost in the struggle that was surely to come. If there was one constant about humanity, it was that people rarely agreed on any one thing, and when they did, it was never for long. Loman had the means to fight back. The entire CDF was willing and able, but he had to bide his time. He couldn't look desperate or cold-blooded. The key to victory would be holding out; if they could survive long enough, the jackals would turn on themselves and rip their new control state to pieces.

Chapter 25

After his tour and checking in with his team, Alex returned to his berth. The display on the wall above the fold-out desk showed a countdown: they had just over forty hours until they reached the Skandia system. There was plenty of time to catch up on his rest.

The bed folded out easily and had a ten centimeter-thick foam mattress. Clean sheets were waiting inside his locker. He made the bed, stripped out of his civilian clothes, and crawled into it. The lights were voice-activated. He turned them off but left the display screen on, which showed a view of space outside the ship. They were far enough from Arcadia and the dozens of solar-powered space stations in her ring of orbit that he could see hundreds of stars. They were mere pin pricks in the dark blanket of outer space, but there was something soothing about lying in the comfortable bed and listening to the low thrum of the ship's engines, the only light being the glow of stars—even if it was an artificial replication of them.

The next thing Alex knew, he was waking up.

"Show me the timer to reach the Skandia system," he said as he sat up on his bed.

The stars faded a little, and bright red numerals appeared. There was only twenty-six hours of flight time remaining. Alex realized he'd slept for fourteen hours straight. His stomach growled, and his muscles trembled as he stretched. After cleaning himself up, he went searching for food.

"You should really check your messages every once in a while," Ash said, hurrying up behind him as he stepped into the lift.

"I was sleeping," Alex said, but he pulled his Flex PIL from his pocket and snapped it onto his wrist.

The PIL activated, the screen coming to life. There were a variety of messages. Most were simple shipboard notifications, which he didn't really care about, but there were a few from Ash and Nyx. He scrolled through them, only half-listening to Ash.

"The ship's not bad," she said. "Just a lot smaller than I expected. The controllers love it."

Alex read the message from Nyx. She had already eaten but wanted to know when he woke up. He typed out a quick message and sent it back to her.

"How's Sly?"

"Aggravated," she said. "The doctor took off his bandages today, but he's insisting that Sly have light therapy. He'll be in the med center all day."

It didn't take long to reach level four, and Alex headed straight to the chow hall. Ash tagged along, but while he ordered himself a full breakfast, she settled for a protein shake. His tray of eggs, bacon, fruit, and pancakes looked like it was decades old. The eggs were scrambled but had a dull white color to them. The pancakes were wrinkled, and the fruit was bland and tasteless. He ate it all anyway and drank the orange-flavored beverage that tasted somewhere between water and actual juice.

"Missing the food on Arcadia yet?" Ash asked.

"It's a trade-off," he said. "I'd rather not be on such a crowded world."

"It's odd that while all their food is imported from off-world," Ash said, "somehow it's still fresh."

"It's a mystery," Alex said.

"You think we'll get time on Skandia Seven?"

"I hope so," Alex said. "My parents are there."

"I thought you grew up on a no-name planet," Ash said.

"I did. NP8261. We called it the Rock because that's basically what it was."

"Level two?"

"Level three," he said. "The air was toxic. Almost no indigenous life."

"Sounds lovely. How'd your family get to Scandia Seven?"

"My father works for the company," Alex said. "He was transferred right after I got recruited."

"Perfect timing, huh? At least they're on a better world now. Skandia Seven is only at a fraction of its population capacity. There are a few large cities, but the rest is farmland and natural ecosystems."

"Someone's been doing her homework," Alex pointed out.

"There's nothing else to do on this boat," Ash lamented. "You were sleeping, Sly's in the med center all the time, I've already worked out, and to be honest, the locals aren't all that friendly."

"The crew?"

"Oscar Company," she said. "They don't really act like they want us here."

"That's odd," Alex said. "Maybe they're just not used to new people if they've been here a long time."

It didn't take Alex long to begin picking up the cues that the *Currency* wasn't like other ships. Looking around the small chow hall, he could see clear divisions between crew, controllers, and operators. It was a small ship, and maybe that's what made the segregation so obvious, but Alex could tell people on board rarely spoke to or participated in activities outside of their own specialties. Everywhere he went, he got strange looks from the other crew members on board. When he and Ash met up with Nyx an hour after Alex's breakfast, what he learned surprised him.

"Everything is shared," Nyx pointed out, "so there's an unwritten code of conduct."

"Yeah, don't even think about speaking to someone outside of your specialty," Ash said. "People were looking at me like I had two heads."

"Operators and controllers aren't really supposed to hang out," Nyx said. "Every specialty has common times in the mess hall, the gym, and the rec spaces."

"Seriously?" Alex asked.

"I'm not subscribing to the segregation, obviously," Nyx said. "But that's what I've gleaned."

They were in a small room between the chow hall and the larger recreation space. The small rooms could be reserved for meetings or games. Nothing on the ship felt very military to Alex, but he was still getting his bearings.

"Even within specialties there's some serious cliques," Ash said. "It feels like high school all over again. The operators in

Oscar Company won't talk to me if they can help it. And unless you're in the hangar, you can forget about the technicians."

"There's a hierarchy," Nyx said. "Ship officers are at the top, although they like to act like no one else is even on board."

"And then the controllers," Ash said with a shrug. "Hey, I'm not judging, I'm just pointing it out."

"It's a control ship," Nyx. "There's more space and tech dedicated to our jobs than just about anyone. After us is the ship's enlisted crew."

"Which leaves us squarely at the bottom," Ash said.

"But we're all members of the CDF," Alex said. "We have one mission, which we can't do without everyone else."

"It's an isolated environment," Nyx said. "From what I can tell, the crew assigned to this ship have been here a long time."

"Don't they get leave?" Alex asked.

"Yes, but they've slid into a way of coexisting that keeps them separate," Nyx said. "And we're the outsiders."

"It probably doesn't help that you like us," Ash said. "My controller hasn't spoken a word to me since coming on board."

"A lot of controllers are introverts," Nyx said. "They like distance between them and everyone else."

"Well then, all we can do is make ourselves useful," Alex said. "There's no benefit to sitting around and complaining."

Making themselves useful was much harder than Alex imagined. Nyx went back to the controllers, doing her best to fit in with both groups. Alex and Ash, on the other hand, had nothing to do. Even when they volunteered to help prep the Titan MBS's, the technicians refused. The operators on board followed a strict schedule: eating at certain times, working out, lounging in the recreation center. It soon became clear that they were expected to be in their cabins a majority of the time.

When Sly was finally released, he came out of the med bay with giant, dark glasses.

"What are those?" Ash asked.

"Shades for my eyes," Sly said. "I'll have to adjust to regular light slowly."

"You look like an old man," Ash proclaimed. "You've even got wrinkles."

"Those are scars," Sly said. "And they're supposed to fade over time."

"It's good to see you back to your old self," Alex said.

They congregated in Alex's tiny room. Ash and Sly both had the exact same berth, but after hanging out in Alex's room on the *Republic*, it was a tradition that no one thought to change.

"It could be worse," Sly said.

Alex had the overhead lights off, and the only light source was the display screen. His bed was folded down and his friends were perched on it, their backs against the bulkhead.

"We're isolated on a tiny ship," Ash said. "I can't imagine worse."

"I'm just saying—at least we're not stuck working eighteen hours a day," Sly went on. "I, for one, am just glad to be alive."

"Oh good grief," Ash complained. "Are you actually telling me that you have a new lease on life after your accident?"

"I was almost killed," Sly said.

"You're too hardheaded to die from a single explosion," Ash said. "Besides, I'd much rather go out in a blaze of glory than die from a thousand cuts."

"No one's dying," Alex said. "Just remember: this assignment is temporary."

Chapter 26

They'd all been keeping tabs on the protests, which continued to grow. Some were even becoming violent. The level-one planets all had security forces which served as law enforcement, but the protesters had the advantage of numbers. It wasn't even close to even, and despite having superior firepower, no one wanted to use weapons on unarmed civilians, no matter how nasty the protesters became.

They reached the Skandia system without incident and joined four other private military ships in orbit. Alex had hoped that they would be deployed upon arrival—not because he was craving trouble, but simply because he was bored. Unfortunately, they were put on permanent standby, with absolutely no contact with the planet. Alex could see reports coming out of Skandia Seven or circulating on the planetary network, but he couldn't message his family.

Four days in, and their tempers were growing short. Alex worked out hard every day, but he felt like he was growing soft. There was simply not enough to do to keep them occupied, and he spent most of his days sitting around, worrying about his parents. The protests on Skandia Seven hadn't grown violent, but he knew it was only a matter of time. A steady stream of news stories continued to crackle across the networks like lightning in a storm. There were stories of atrocious war crimes. Videos of innocent civilians getting caught in the crossfire between two groups of mechanized fighters were hard to watch, and yet he couldn't stop watching them. He was as obsessed as the protesters, even though he knew that he had never been taught or trained to kill indiscriminately. On Carthage Prime, he and the rest of the operators in Tunis had fought over the spaceport, but they had been careful to warn the civilians and move them out of harm's way.

The false narrative about CDF operators made him angry. The commentators and reporters obviously knew nothing about Ahzco's corporate defense force, and yet they made their outrageous claims appear to be absolute truth. Alex wanted to join the conversation and set the record straight, but he was forbidden. Strongly worded memos had come down from the CEO, Ian Gentry, not to respond in any way. But as each day passed and the lies grew more outrageous, keeping himself in line was becoming harder.

Finally, near the end of the fourth day in orbit around Skandia Seven, orders were given for deployment. Alex, like all the other operators on board, was ordered to the ready room near the MBS hangars.

"Any idea what's going on?" Sly asked. He was fully recovered and just as anxious as everyone else for something to happen. They didn't want to fight or hurt anyone, but they all despised sitting idly on the ship while there were people on the planet calling them all murderers and baby killers.

"None," Alex said.

He, Sly, and Ash rode the lift down together and headed straight for the ready room. They were already in their compression fatigues, which they wore all the time just in case they were called to action. Half of Oscar Company was already in the ready room, loitering near their lockers. Alex slipped his ID lanyard from around his neck. His only other belonging was the Flex PIL that was currently wrapped around his left forearm. He left it on and went with the others over to the rows of chairs in the briefing area.

There was only room enough for Oscar Company in the seats, so Alex and his friends stood at the rear, arms crossed, waiting for someone to tell them why they were put on alert. The news reports from the planet seemed no different, from what Alex could tell. Some businesses had been burned and some stores looted, but no all-out fighting had been reported.

Master Sergeant Taylor "Monty" Montgomery was standing near the display screen. He looked calm and unfazed by the order for the operators onboard the *Currency* to stand by, as if he'd done it a thousand times before. The screen suddenly lit up, and the group of operators all fell silent. Ash elbowed Alex, who was scrolling through news stories and hadn't noticed the screen.

"Operators," First Lieutenant Rory Jones said. On the screen, Skandia Seven appeared from orbit and began zooming down. "The decision has been made to deploy to Oslo to protect the MBS manufacturing plant there."

The image continued zooming, as if the camera was falling down toward the city, and stopped on a huge structure . The building was nondescript; it could have been a warehouse or any type of manufacturing facility. There were no smokestacks belching dark pollution into Skandia Seven's clear skies, and the area around the building was clean and neat. There were cargo containers neatly lined up in one area and a well-designed outdoor space with bright green grass surrounded by picnic tables.

"Protestors in Oslo are currently demonstrating outside the government building, which is over twenty city blocks from this manufacturing plant," the lieutenant explained. "Unfortunately, we've picked up chatter on social media about possibly targeting the plant. Oscar Company will take up stations on the edge of the manufacturing property as a show of force that will deter protesters from doing anything violent or destructive. Titan team, your responsibility will be here, where most employees utilize the public underground transport system."

The image shifted slightly away from the plant and focused on a nearby entrance to the citywide transit system. The area was open, and the image showed people moving in and out of the underground. Some looked like businesspeople hurrying to their next appointment, but there were also shoppers and people simply going about their lives. Defending the area looked difficult; there was nothing to use as cover or protection should a firefight ensue. Employees would have to cross the open square from the entrance to the underground, cross a wide street, and then travel down a sidewalk to the entrance of the manufacturing plant's fenced-in property. The route lit up in yellow.

"This is probably the most vulnerable area should the protests move against Ahzco's facility there in Oslo," Lieutenant Jones continued. "If that happens, your Titans will need to escort employees to and from the underground transit. Any questions?"

"Why not just put a few Destroyers on that route?" Monty asked. "Make it a show of force?"

"Because a show of force is the opposite of what is needed," Lieutenant Jones said. "Bear in mind that every minute you are on-station someone will be recording every move you make. It's become standard practice for these protests to become amateur sting operations. The organizers will try to provoke you. We cannot let that happen. They would love nothing more than to gain footage of the CDF hurting people."

"If they start it, then what should we do?" asked one of the operators from Oscar Company.

"You'll be issued crowd-control and non-lethal armaments," the lieutenant said. "But our best outcome is that you do not use them. To answer your question more directly, Master Sergeant, we cannot block the street or hinder the flow of city inhabitants in any fashion. That's straight from Skandia's Prime Minister, and we're obliged to follow their lead. Bear in mind that this facility cost Ahzco billions to construct and contains even more valuable MBS components inside. Losing this plant would be a major setback in the CDF's ability to maintain security in the future."

"How long are we going down there for?" Alex asked.

"So far, the protests have ended each day at sundown. This plant, however, runs around the clock. The employees there are making room for Oscar Company and Cronus Team to stay onsite. Once we are sure the plant is secure, we'll bring in technicians, but we need full deployment during the daylight hours and security rotation at night."

"Roger that," Master Sergeant Montgomery said.

"All right, get suited up," Lieutenant Jones said. "Oscar Company will board drop ship Alpha, and Cronus team will escort you down. Good luck, operators."

The screen went dark, and everyone stood up. Alex held his friends back and let the other operators return to their lockers.

"You guys ready for this?" Alex asked.

"Beats sitting around and twiddling our thumbs," Ash said.

"Non-lethal weapons is the right move, but I'd feel better with laser cannons," Sly said.

"Just remember: the crowds can't hurt us," Alex said as he unfastened the Flex PIL from around his arm. "We're safe in our battle suits."

"But what if they make us mad?" Ash said, only half-joking.

"We'll figure it out," Alex said. "You guys ready to fly?"

"So ready," Ash said.

"You know it," Sly added.

"All right, let's show Oscar Company why we're the best."

They left their PILs in their lockers and crossed over to the Titan area of the ship's MBS hangar. The Titans were too tall to get into without help. The technicians had portable steps set up. Alex climbed them easily, then swung himself into the suit. A technician appeared beside him.

"Do you need anything, Sergeant?"

"No, I'm good," Alex said as he synced his INC to the Titan's control systems.

The technician gave him a thumbs-up and retreated down the steps. Alex pressed the button to engage the Titan's systems and slipped his arms into the weapon-control harness. The human-shaped battle suit closed up around him, and he felt the emergency padding inflating around him until he was held tightly into position.

"Nyx, you copy?"

Loud and clear, her voice sounded in his mind. When he'd first synced with a battle suit using his INC, Nyx's voice had sounded like his own. It was as if he was thinking to himself, hearing his own voice in his head. But over time, Alex had trained himself to hear his controller's responses in her own voice.

"Show Cronus One ready for launch," Alex said.

Roger that, Cronus team is locked and loaded, Nyx said. *All systems green. Power levels are fully charged. Weapons systems on safety mode.*

"Speaking of weapons," Alex said, "what have we got?"

Laser blasters are at mandatory minimums, which means you can stun someone if they're close. You have smoke grenades, tear gas, and auditory bombs to disperse crowds. The soft-alloy repeating cannons have been loaded with lightweight sponge rounds. They're painful but non-lethal.

"Great, maybe we can hold the crowds off with harsh language," Alex said.

Don't even joke, Alex. You can't use your weapons unless you absolutely have to. The protesters want to see you lose your cool. Once you do, it will be all over the networks, and odds are, you'll be out of a job.

"Perfect," Alex said. "We'll just go down and make ourselves moving targets for the locals to shoot at."

He wasn't angry with the situation he was going into as much as frustrated with the situation he was leaving. The last thing he expected when he joined the CDF was to discover prejudice and acrimony between specialties. No one had insulted him outright, but there was plenty of division on the ship. Everyone was fighting to get ahead of someone else. There was very little trust or respect. It came as no surprise that every ship was different, but on the *Republic,* he felt like part of a larger team. That sense of belonging made him feel confident. On the *Currency* there was no camaraderie—only competition and a phony class system that made Alex angry.

Sixty seconds till launch. Once you're outside the Currency*'s artificial gravity, take up positions around the drop ship.*

"Copy," Alex said before mentally switching to his team frequency com-link. "You guys ready to drop?"

"Yes, team leader," Sly said.

"Affirmative," Ash replied.

"Good, let's do this by the numbers. I'll take position over the shuttle. Ash, you're starboard side. Sly, you're port."

Thirty seconds, Nyx said.

Everything had been moved out of the small chamber where the Titan battle suits hung from clamps. A yellow light began to flash as the outer door sealed.

Pressurizing, Nyx explained. *The floor should be opening.*

Alex's head didn't actually move to look down at the Titan battle suit's feet, but he gave the mental command, and the suit's cameras panned down as if he had leaned forward and looked below him. He could see the floor splitting open and retracting. The glow of the planet was bright beneath them.

"Wow, would you look at that," Sly said.

Ten seconds. Nine, eight, seven...

Alex felt a sense of anxiety. He needed to do something, but until the clamps released him, all he could do was wait.

...three, two, one, mark!

The clamps released, and Alex's stomach flipped as the ship seemed to shoot off above him. The Titan's systems came alive. Navigation locked in on every vessel within a hundred kilometers of his position, and Alex could almost feel the huge planet spread out beneath him.

"There's the drop ship," Ash said.

She was the first to soar toward the ship that was already en route to planetary entry. Alex and Sly followed, each moving into position.

"Anyone following us?" Alex asked Nyx. He had full access to the radar information from the *Currency*, but he was focused on staying on course with the drop ship. Her job was to scan the instruments. If there was a problem, she would alert him immediately.

Negative. You're clear. No one else is moving.

Alex knew there were other ships from various mega-corporations in the system. The drop ship would be at its most vulnerable as it made entry into the planet's atmosphere. A well-timed strike could take a vessel out and make it appear that the ship had merely broken apart under the stress of entering the planet's gravity. They were escorting the drop ship just to add a little security. And while every company's defense forces were under attack and scrutiny by the protesters on a dozen planets, it didn't mean that one wouldn't take a shot at an Ahzco vessel if the opportunity presented itself.

It felt good to fly again, although piloting the Titan MBS through space felt less like flying and more like playing a game. In zero-gravity, there was no feeling, no sense of movement. It was like he was sitting still and the galaxy was moving around him.

"Are we the first ones going in?" Sly asked.

"Who knows," Ash responded.

"I'm betting other businesses have security forces on the ground," Alex said. "They just didn't launch from orbit."

The change from orbit to atmosphere was subtle, but Alex felt it. He went from feeling nothing to feeling a gentle tug deep in his stomach. The planet was so huge at that point that it was all Alex could see. The heat reading, which showed up like a digital gauge on the screen of his mind, showed the exterior of the Titan suit heating up. Alex couldn't actually see anything with his eyes inside the suit. Everything was projected into his brain by his INC, and his brain translated it so that in his mind's eye he could actually "see" the feed from the suit's external camera. Any readings appeared in opaque overlay at the edge of his field of vision.

You've got a good entry window, but the atmosphere is thick.

"You can say that again," Alex said.

He was feeling the planet's gravity, and while the Titan was merely falling and not actually flying, it was still shaking and rocking. He was grateful for the tight squeeze of the suit's inflatable padding.

He clenched his teeth and waited out the rough entry. Smoke and flames billowed up around the drop ship, which was falling faster due to its greater mass. Alex and his team were slower than the shuttle and caused less friction. The frigid air of the upper atmosphere fought against the friction caused by their rapid entry through the various gasses and dust.

Suddenly everything settled down, and Alex gave his controls a slight test to ensure that he had the ability to fly the battle suit. She responded perfectly—even the tiniest nudge on the joystick brought immediate results. He felt a sense of freedom that nothing else had ever compared to. Even free-floating in a zero-gravity bubble didn't feel as incredible as piloting his Titan in atmo.

He heard Ash whoop for joy, and Sly was laughing as they reformed around the drop ship.

Passing ten thousand kilometers.

Alex checked his airspeed and altitude readings before giving his weaponized arms a quick test. They moved freely, the power charge and ammunitions reading full.

"Once we pass two thousand meters, I want to pull back from the shuttle and begin a slow, spiraling descent," Alex said. "Let's get a lay of the land."

Just not too low. A battle suit might be a tempting target.

They passed the threshold and began slowing down. The Ahzco factory was in an industrial complex with green space between the buildings. Alex didn't know if Skandia Seven was tech- or manufacturing-heavy, but he could appreciate how well thought-out the design of the city was. He saw tall buildings in the distance. There was a definite city center with a suburban sprawl. Alex was from a planet with nothing outside of the colony. People sometimes took rides outside the colony on wheeled vehicles, but only for the opportunity to see celestial objects or break free from the confining colony, which was over seventy percent underground. The idea of having space to spread out and roam was foreign to him, but he was thrilled to think of his family living here. He could imagine his younger sister walking to school without a rebreather or his parents going on a picnic in a park with grass while fluffy white clouds drifted across the blue sky overhead.

"Can you believe this place?" Alex said.

What do you mean?

"It's so beautiful," Alex said.

That's exactly what every hardened warrior says when they see Skandia Seven, Nyx said with a giggle.

"It's only the second level-one planet I've ever seen," Alex went on, undaunted by her playfulness. "It looks incredible. So much green."

All right, but you need to focus, Alex.

He realized what she was saying. It was easy to get caught up in the moment seeing something new, but he had to keep his mind sharp.

"Thanks," he said, then switched on the team channel of his com-link. "Let's maintain altitude at eight hundred meters."

"Check," Ash said.

"Holding at eight hundred meters," Sly replied.

Alex's teammates were contrasting personalities. Ash was the embodiment of act first and think later. Sly was more reserved, although he wasn't slow to react or afraid of charging headfirst into danger. He was also more comfortable with structure, while Ash was always testing boundaries. Still, he felt lucky to have them at his side. They were loyal and capable. He felt safe knowing they were watching his back.

The drop ship has landed.

"Good, open a line to Monty's team. We need to coordinate our coverage of the plant."

Done.

Alex circled the massive plant. He was high enough to be able to see for miles around and could identify the government building. He could see the protesters too, but they seemed more like one large organism than thousands of individuals. They were moving through the city streets, swarming around buildings. Alex couldn't be sure where they were going, but he couldn't rule out the Ahzco factory.

"Master Sergeant, we have movement," Alex said.

"How far out?"

"Five, maybe six klicks," Alex said. "They could be heading this way."

"I've got it," Monty said. "Let's get into position and see what happens."

Alex continued circling and watching while the ground-based MBS's spread out across the property. The roof of the factory was reinforced, and the industrial elevator inside was large enough to accommodate Monty's Destroyers. He kept most of his units on the ground but put one on each corner of the main building.

"All right, we're all settled in," Monty said. "It's just a waiting game now."

Alex, we just got word that the protestors are moving to the transit entrance near the Ahzco building, Nyx said.

"How long until the workers are done for the day?"

There's a shift change in two hours. We're monitoring their social media, which seems to be how they're communicating.

"Team leader," Ash said, "should we take positions on the ground? If they fill up the square around the transit station, our people won't be able to get through."

"No," Alex said. "Let's let the crowd see us and Oscar Company. That may be enough to hold them back."

"Nothing like staring the down the barrel of an auto-cannon," Ash said.

Just keep in mind that they want you to attack, Nyx said.

"Not all of them," Alex said. "I doubt most of these people want anything to do with us. They're just out protesting what they've seen."

You think they're being used?

"By the organizers, at least," Alex said. "I'm hoping when they see that we aren't going to respond to their insulting rhetoric that maybe they'll get bored and go home."

"That's what I love about you, Ace," Ash said. "You're a glass half-full kind of guy."

"Here they come," Sly pointed out as the first protesters arrived in the square that was directly across the street from the factory.

I guess we'll find out.

Alex knew Nyx was right. He could only hope that he was, too.

Chapter 27

Loman sat alone in the corner of an old diner. It was crammed into a tiny space just below ground level of an old building on the edge of the historic district. The restaurant, a family-owned establishment that had passed from one generation to the next for over a century, was known by a small but loyal following. Their specialty was tamales cooked in a tomato-based hot sauce that infused the spicy meat and soft corn wrapper.

In the past, the diner had offered a full menu, but after decades the other items had been trimmed from the establishment's offerings until only tamales remained. Every patron got a plate of tamales, but that wasn't why Loman was such a loyal customer. His primary reason was for the privacy it offered. The diner had one row of booths with tall dividers in between. When the diner had first opened, the street outside had been busy with land vehicles rushing past and hundreds of pedestrians going in and out of the building. To compensate, the owners had spent time soundproofing the walls to keep the noise out. As a happy coincidence, the soundproofing also worked inside the diner, making it difficult to overhear conversations in the other booths. Loman knew he could have a private conversation in the diner without being spied on.

The owners also prided themselves on privacy, but not because they recognized it as a boon to their patrons. The diner was one of the few speakeasies in the central district. Liquor could be obtained in other ways, but Loman appreciated the privacy of the diner. A plate of tamales and his flask filled with gin was worth more than credits to Loman. He had already eaten his food, and the hot sauce was scorching his digestive track, but the VP of security for Ahzco was a glutton for punishment. Across the booth from him, Ciara Prince slid onto her seat as silently as a shadow.

"You have news?" he asked.

"Some," she said.

A tall, skinny man wearing an old-fashioned paper hat and a dirty apron slid a plate of tamales in front of Ciara along with a bottle of sparkling water. The bottle was cloudy with condensation. Ciara looked at the food and waited for the man to leave, which he did. The waiter, who was also a cook, a busboy, and an underground distiller, shuffled off without a word.

"You eat this?" Ciara Prince asked skeptically.

"What's the news?" Loman asked.

"Sigma Services made their first offer."

"To who?"

"Fellerman's."

"They took a big hit last year when that volcano erupted on Kells Superior."

"They've been seeking a reinvestment," Ciara Prince said. "They agreed to sell their fleet of Hoplite mechanized battle suits, along with all their remaining munitions."

"At pennies on the dollar, I suppose," Loman said.

"There weren't many offers coming in," Ciara said, toying with the food on her plate but not actually eating it. "My sources tell me that part of the deal was a private security contract to protect their assets."

"They sell their MBS fleet and get protection at the same time?"

"That's right."

Loman nodded. It made sense. It was easier to buy someone out and offer to protect them if you knew they wouldn't need it. The moguls behind Sigma Services didn't waste money, even though they could afford to easily. Loman had to admire the gall it took to buy Fellerman's fleet of MBS's only to lease it to the newly formed central government for twice what they paid. And Fellerman's would be one less private army to subdue once they were in power.

Loman had already deduced that Sigma was behind more than just the bomb threat. They had attacked Ahzco's colony ship and the recreation world Apex Purrin. They wanted to destabilize the mega-corporations and reduce their fighting forces. It was a sound strategy for a hostile takeover.

"There's trouble brewing in the Askerria sector," Loman told her. "Rumor has it that Lewan Enterprises is pulling out."

"Why would they do that?" Ciara asked. "It's the richest source of platinum in the galaxy."

"Raids on their shipping lanes, the instability of the planet, the loss of their primary vendor...no one really knows."

"If they lost their vendor and they were incentivized to leave the sector, every other company would fight to take control," Ciara said, thinking through the idea. "It would be a great way to reduce the armies that a government would have to fight in order to gain control."

"It's an incredible coincidence," Loman said. "And I don't believe in coincidence."

"Neither do I," Ciara said. "I'm not going to eat this."

"It doesn't matter," Loman replied as he swiped his ID and punched in a big tip on the payment reader. "What does matter is how we can stop this coup."

"It can't be a coup if there's no existing sovereign to topple," Ciara said.

"Should we even be fighting this?" Loman asked.

"Do you think anyone should be in charge of governing an entire galaxy?"

"No," Loman said. "Most planets can't get along with one another. Government is inherently corrupt. But the question is, do we have a reason to fight? If there's no chance of winning the fight, what good does it do to try?"

"You don't really believe that," she replied.

"What I believe could cost the company trillions, not to mention the lives that would be lost if we take part in an interstellar war."

"What is the alternative?"

"We sell," Loman said. "Shut down the security division. Break the company up and sell it for top-dollar before a government entity forces us to do it without compensation."

"Spoken like a greedy SOB," Ciara said.

"The question that leads us to is," Loman went on as if he hadn't heard a word she said, "are we ethically bound to hold Ahzco together? Would laying off thousands of operators, controllers, technicians, admins, and researchers be morally wrong?"

"I would land on my feet," Ciara said.

"Others wouldn't," Loman said. "If the rumors about the Askerria Sector are true—or even possibly true—Gentry and the BOD will insist that we send ships and operators."

"Despite the fact that we're already stretched to the breaking point and the entire galaxy is outraged at the fighting between private armies?"

"Of course," Loman said. "From a purely financial perspective, it's worth the risk."

"What if you tell them about Sigma Services and the cabal of ultra-wealthy moguls pushing for a central government that would break up the company?"

"Without proof—airtight, undeniable proof—we can't reveal what we know. Not to the board. Gentry is too unstable; we can't trust that he would keep the information to himself. Besides, Faulk has me half out the door as it is. I can't give her more ammunition to fire at me."

"So we have to appear as if we don't know," Ciara Prince said.

"The question is, how do we do that?"

"By hiding our strength in plain sight," Ciara said. "We send as many units to the Askerria Sector as possible, but we hold them back. We don't engage. The focus will be on the fighting, not on our forces lingering on the edge of the system."

"To what end?"

"So that when we do have to fight," Ciara said, "we are ready...with our full strength."

"And in the meantime, we have to find out what this cabal is up to. There has to be a way."

"Figure that out, and we save the company," Ciara said. "Save the company, and we save the galaxy."

"Even if no one ever knows what we did," Loman agreed.

"Even so," Ciara said. "It's what we do."

"Indeed," Loman said. "It is indeed."

Chapter 28

The protesters filled the open square around the public transit entrance and even spilled out onto the street. Airborne transports had long since replaced ground vehicles for personal conveyance, but shipping still moved on the ground. Fortunately, the street between the large Ahzco factory and the square wasn't a busy avenue.

"The local law enforcement people are here," Ash said.

Alex watched, hoping they would order the crowd to disperse, but all the local law enforcement officials did was reroute traffic away from the scene.

"Why don't they send these people home?" Sly asked. "Do they really have a right to demonstrate anywhere they want?"

"Might makes right," Ash said. "There are just too many of them."

Alex knew she was right. There were more people packed into the square than he had ever seen in one place.

We're coming up on shift change, Nyx said. *If we don't find a way through the crowd, the factory will have to be shut down.*

"All we can do is try," Alex said.

He began to descend toward the crowd. It felt frightening and unnatural. His instincts were to move away from such a large crowd, yet he trusted in the Titan battle suit to protect him. They were pointing and shouting at him. He could hear some of the taunts, but he didn't pay attention to them. It was possible that some of the people in the crowd could have weapons, but the armor on the Titan would repel small arms fire. What Alex didn't want was to incite panic. If people got hurt—even if only because the crowd panicked and hurt their own—Ahzco would be blamed. When he was less than thirty meters from the ground, he hovered.

"Activate the external loudspeakers," Alex said.

The Titan battle suit was built for battle. It had external speakers that would make him heard over the sounds of explosions, gunfire, or the screams of the wounded. That wasn't the kind of thinking Alex needed, and he forced himself to remain positive.

Speakers are on. Whatever you say, they'll hear.

Alex took a breath and spoke clearly. "Make room below me."

The crowd reacted with anger. They were outraged to be given an order, especially from the likes of him. The Titan battle suit looked robotic, but in the shape of a man. Only the arms were different. Multiple gun barrels protruded from the shoulders of the battle suit and pointed down at his sides. Alex knew that many of the protesters were staring at the guns and wondering if they would erupt with fire and hot metal to kill and maim. Alex rotated his arms up, so that he had the weapons pointing toward the sky instead of the crowd.

"I have to land and escort Ahzco employees to their workplace across the street," Alex said, his voice booming through the square. "Please make room."

He was just above the entrance to the transit underground, which was a descending staircase surrounded by railings with an arched sign over the front. The crowd continued to protest. It was impossible to make out what any one person was saying. With a thought, Alex activated his low-level laser, but instead of firing beams of focused light through the laser cannon, he transferred the electrical current to the armor of his battle suit. He could see blue arcs of electricity snapping and popping over the front of the suit like tiny bolts of lightning.

"Please be aware that touching my armor will result in shock that will stun or possibly injure you. All I ask is for room to land."

The people on the fringe of the crowd screamed insults and curses, but those closer to Alex looked scared.

"I will not hurt anyone. I am not here to challenge your right to protest. I only want to help the innocent employees of the Ahzco facility reach their workplace unharmed."

Alex saw the crowd move. It was slow. Many people were shoving to make way as he slowly descended, but there were so many people in the square that it took time to move them.

"Well, that's a fancy trick," Ash said.

"It's working, Ace," Sly said. "They're moving."

Alex switched off the public address system and activated his com-link.

"Take positions by the front entrance," he ordered. "We'll move the people coming into work first, then take the ones leaving down to the transit station."

"Roger that, team leader," Sly said.

"Nyx, tell me they have room to land," Alex said.

They do, for now. The crowd is spreading out, but they'll give you all a wide berth after your light show.

It wasn't just a harmless display. The electrical current creeping across his armor would shock and stun anyone who touched him—but it wasn't a normal feature of the Titan battle suit. Alex didn't expect anyone outside of the designers or other Titan operators to know he had manipulated the battle suit. It felt like an innocent action that might help him accomplish his mission.

He landed in a growing open space directly in front of the transit entrance and shut off the laser power rippling across his suit. Almost immediately, objects came flying toward him.

Incoming! Nyx warned him.

Alex had expected no less. Some of the objects were harmless—rotten fruit, eggs, water balloons—but others were more potent, like stones and bricks. All Alex could do was stand and let his armor take the hits. Most of the objects missed him entirely. They flew over his head or wide of his armored body. Alex still had his weapons pointed upward, which made him an even bigger target, but the crowd was in constant motion. The throwers were bumped and jostled, and many were just lobbing their supply of trash in his general direction. Unfortunately, some of the projectiles hit innocent protesters. There were shouts and angry cries of outrage.

Alex looked down at the bottom of the wide stairs that led to the public transit station. A group of nearly sixty people stood looking up, obviously trying to decide if it was safe.

"I've got workers here," Alex said. "I'm going to bring them up and start the escort."

Copy. I'll alert Oscar Company.

Since he wasn't focused on landing his MBS, Alex could toggle through his communication options. He activated the public address system once again.

"Ahzco supports your right to assemble and demonstrate," Alex said, his amplified voice booming across the square. "We have no desire to use force of any kind, but we ask in turn that you allow our workers to continue supporting their families by moving to and from their work site without interruption or abuse. Ahzco employees, please join me at the top of the stairs."

The Titan battle suit was an intimidating MBS. In most cases, people didn't get too close, but the courage of the mob emboldened some individuals. One appeared out of the crowd wearing a long coat. He pulled out a rifle of some sort and pointed it at Alex.

"Take this, baby killer!"

The weapon was a projectile device that fired a group of pellets, all of which ricocheted off Alex's armor and peppered the crowd. The ricochet had cost the pellets their deadly force, but they pelted the crowd in a painful fashion. Some even broke the skin.

As the mob began to scream in anger, Alex lowered his right arm, aiming his weapon at the man whose face had gone from fury to fear. He started backpedaling, but the crowd behind him pushed him away. Alex could feel the danger. The entire crowd—thousands of protesters—were on the verge of panic. If he fired, as he had every right to do, it would do more than incapacitate a violent protester. It would send the crowds running in every direction. People would get shoved, tripped, and trampled on.

Some would be injured, others killed. Alex couldn't let that happen.

"Remain calm," he said, his voice amplified and booming across the crowd. "There is no need for panic or violence."

The man with the gun raised his weapon again, racking another load. He looked terrified, and yet he brought his weapon to bear again.

"Your weapon cannot penetrate my armor," Alex said. "It will only ricochet onto the innocent."

"Burn in hell!" the gunman screamed.

He followed his call for condemnation with a second round from the weapon he held. It was pointed up, loosely aimed at the Titan's head. Alex reacted on pure instinct. He spun around and ducked just as the man fired. He was fast, but not fast enough. Half the spray of pellets missed him entirely, shooting up and past Alex to impact a building on the opposite side of the square. Unfortunately, several of the pellets still hit Alex's armored head unit. They ricocheted off the Titan without damaging it but then flew into the crowd. One hit a woman's head and gouged a bloody furrow across her scalp. She screamed as blood flowed down the side of her face.

Perhaps it was pent-up tension or the danger from the gunman, but Alex was certain the sight of the bloody woman was a catalyst to the fear and outrage the crowd felt. Screams and shouts filled the air as people began to push and shove each other. The protesters were suddenly in a rush to escape and get away from the site of their demonstration. Signs were dropped, all civility forgotten, as the crowd rushed away in every direction.

Alex panned the crowd looking for danger, but there was none he could see. The real danger was to the crowd of protesters. There were too many people crowded into the square, and once their resolve broke, they hurt one another in their rush to get away.

"Holy smokes," Sly said. "They're running over each other."

"What should we do?" Ash said.

"Nothing," Alex replied. "We'll only make things worse."

Alex, keep those workers in the stairwell.

He knew she was right, but as he turned toward the stairs, he saw the frightened workers climbing up, trying to see what was happening. Alex dialed down the volume of his public address speakers before engaging the workers.

"Stay here," Alex said. "It's not safe."

The workers nodded. There seemed to be more arriving every minute. The entire staircase was lined with them. In the square, people were still rushing to escape. Alex saw several injured protesters. They needed medical attention, but in his Titan battle suit there was nothing he could do for them.

"Are we calling for medical assistance?" Alex asked Nyx.

It's been called in by the locals. You have to get the workers moved to the factory before law enforcement shuts the area down.

"Right, good thinking," Alex replied.

There were still dozens of people in the square and the street beyond, but none were moving toward him. He felt safe enough leading the employees across to the gates of the Ahzco-owned facility.

"All right," Alex ordered. "Let's go. Nice and easy. Move straight to the gates."

The workers didn't need to be told twice. Alex stood back, watching for any signs of danger, but the protesters had dispersed and the only movement was from those trying to help the injured.

"Workers headed your way," Alex said over the tactical channel.

"Copy," Master Sergeant Montgomery said.

"We see them," Ash said.

"Sly, follow these workers inside and get those who are leaving."

"Yes, team leader," Sly replied.

Alex watched the group moving off in a line. One caught his eye. The man was already well past him by the time Alex caught a glimpse, but his gait was unmistakable; it was his father, Bruce Evans.

Chapter 29

It took half an hour before the last stragglers from the plant made it across the road and into the transit entrance. Some even chose to walk home rather than take the underground train. Law enforcement and first responders had come into the square to see about the injured. Alex had watched them carrying people away on gurneys equipped with repulsers. With a push of a button, the gurneys rose up to waist height off the ground and were easily pushed toward the ambulatory areas.

Was that a success? Nyx asked.

From a purely tactical standpoint, the mission to get the workers to and from the Ahzco factory had been a success. None of their people were hurt. None of the MBS's were damaged, although Alex probably had some chipping on his armor from the gunman. But only time would tell how the media would describe what happened. Alex doubted that it would be a favorable or accurate account.

"Who can say?" Alex said. "Odds are, no matter what we did, people would blame us."

The entire incident—especially the woman with a bloody face—kept replaying in his mind. He didn't even feel like flying and instead plodded across the square. The locals were eyeing him with suspicion and fear. The law enforcement officers were in armor and had riot gear, but their gear was nothing compared to the mechanized battle suit.

When he reached the gate, Ash and Sly were waiting for him.

"We should keep one person up in the air. We can take turns," Alex said.

"I'll do it," Ash said.

She launched herself straight up like a rocket. Alex couldn't help but watch. The Titan battle suit was a thing of beauty. It reminded him of a comic book superhero.

"The danger is past for now," Alex said. "We can work in shifts just like the factory workers."

"One on, one off, one on standby?" Sly said.

"Yeah, that sounds right. You mind if I take the first break?"

"Not at all, team leader. I'll move up to the roof of the factory."

He could have gone in and ridden up in the industrial lift, but instead he jumped into the air, activated his repulsers, and glided up to the rooftop. Alex walked to the entrance of the large manufacturing plant where Master Sergeant Taylor Montgomery was meeting with a group of people from the factory.

"We've got space for all of you," a woman in a business suit was saying. "Charging capacities too. I've already got our people setting it up."

"We got lucky today," Monty said. "If a crowd that size tries to get onto the property, we'll be forced to fight."

"I understand," she said.

"Sergeant Evans is in charge of the Titan team," Monty said.

"I'll have one Titan in the air on overwatch," Alex explained, "and a second on standby. We'll escort the workers, but it might be better to keep all essential personnel on the property."

"We're making arrangements for that," the woman said. "We've got a safety bunker, but it isn't big enough for everyone."

"This time of year," a burly man in dark coveralls spoke up, "people could camp out on the lawn.'"

"It's warm enough. I'll make sure that's an option for people who want to stay," the woman said. She was clearly in charge of the facility. "We can rotate through the bunker's bathroom facilities."

"Any idea what the protesters will do next?" asked the third member of the group of workers. He had on a clean, white, button-up shirt with a Flex PIL on his forearm. Alex guessed he was some type of engineer.

"There's no telling," Alex said. "But it was their person who brought a weapon and fired on us. If things escalate, it could get ugly."

"We should be able to keep unauthorized personnel away from the property and protect the workers on site," Monty said.

"It's those who want to go home that are in danger," the woman said with a sigh. "I understand. We'll start making preparations and scaling down production."

"Can I see the recharging stations?" Alex asked. "And the area you've designated for us?"

"Of course. Frank will show you around, Sergeant," the woman said, indicating the man in coveralls.

"This way," the man said. He was gruff, with a no-nonsense attitude. Alex followed him toward the factory building.

"Your people build mechanized battle suits?" Alex said.

"Actually, no. That's a common misconception. Ahzco Robotics builds the suits. We just service and repair the robots."

They went through a large overhead door and into what appeared to be a fabricating workshop. The walk space was wide enough for a delivery truck, and Alex had no problems getting through. There were several people working at their benches, which were lined with tools.

"We have replacement parts," Frank explained, "but sometimes we need parts custom-fabricated. We keep twelve fabricators on staff."

He led Alex through a set of thick but transparent doors that slid apart as they approached. The interior of the factory was not what Alex expected. Growing up on NP8261, he had been to his father's workplace many times. The repair shop—or garage, as the workers referred to it—was dark, dirty, and cramped. This factory was the complete opposite. It was light and airy with well-designed manufacturing lines that were actually rows of automated building machines. Robotic arms rose up from the ground beside the conveyor belts or hung from the ceiling. There were no people near the machines, but Alex saw a long room enclosed in glass, with computer stations where men in white shirts sat monitoring the robotic building process.

"Engineers make sure things are running correctly," Frank said, pointing to the glass-enclosed room. "At the far end is storage and shipping. We have laborers who move the battle suits off the line and prep them for shipping out to the field."

"And what do you do?"

"I'm in charge of the mechanics who fix the robots," Frank said. "Most of the time it's damn boring. We do regular maintenance, but the place runs smooth. You can say whatever you want about Ahzco, but don't knock their robotics division. They make quality machines."

"The battle suits aren't bad, either," Alex said.

The gruff mechanic actually chuckled. "It's good to see you can keep a sense of humor, Sergeant. Things around here haven't been very fun the last week or so. There's a lot of tension in Oslo."

Alex followed the mechanic around the edge of the building. The assembly lines filled the center, but there was still a lot of empty space, leaving plenty of room even for an MBS that was almost four meters tall. They circled around the machinery and passed a room with a lightning bolt warning sign.

"That's the powerplant for the factory," Frank explained as they moved past the doorway. "We were able to rig up recharging stations in the next room."

They went inside what appeared to be a storage area. It was a long, rectangular room with charging stations along one wall. Cots were being set up by a group of men in coveralls on the side opposite the charging stations.

"It may not be four stars, but we're glad to have you," Frank said, waving at the space. "I'm assuming your technicians are on their way down."

"They will be," Alex said. "In the meantime, can you have someone help me out of this battle suit?"

"Sure," Frank said.

He waved over a couple of the workers who were setting up the cots. They plugged in the Titan and got it charging.

"Nyx, I'm getting out of my battle suit," Alex said. "But I'll stay synced up in case you need me."

Copy that, she replied.

He pressed the button to disengage the Titan battle suit but left it on standby mode so that he could access all the suit's functions. Alex guessed he could probably even operate the suit without being in it, but only if he was close by. Otherwise he might lose connectivity, which would be disastrous for whatever mission he was trying to accomplish. One of the mechanics leaned a ladder against the Titan and held it steady while Alex crawled out.

"Good to finally meet someone who uses these things," the mechanic said.

"Thanks for your hard work," Alex said. "We'd be in real trouble if not for you."

"Well, I don't build them," the mechanic said. "I just help maintain the robots who do."

"Still, it's appreciated. I was hoping that you might be able to help me. I'm looking for a mechanic named Bruce Evans."

"Sure, I know Bruce. Good man. He's over in the repair shop tinkering around. You know him?"

"I do," Alex said. "Can you show me?"

The mechanic nodded. He led Alex toward the door and shouted at his superior. "I'm taking the sergeant over to the repair shop. He knows Bruce."

"Fine, but stay with him," Frank said. "This is a working factory. I don't need people running around and getting hurt."

They walked out the door of the room that had been set up for the operators and their MBS's. The factory was louder than it had seemed to Alex inside his suit. It was easy to forget how much work the Titan did to protect him, even from loud noises.

"My name's Theo," the mechanic said. "How do you know Bruce?"

"We were on NP8261 together," Alex said.

Theo led him to another room that was almost identical to the one being set up for the operators. The lights in the room were bright, the floor clean. There were work benches and large chests full of tools. Several people were inside. Most were watching one man work on something. Alex recognized his father right away. Bruce had his back to his son and was working on a piece of machinery while the others watched. It was obvious at a glance that the other mechanics were all younger than his father. It didn't surprise Alex that Bruce was teaching them something.

"There," Bruce said. "Now, once you get the wiring harness situated, you'll need to make sure that nothing is out of place. Otherwise you run the risk of a wire getting too hot and burning through or shorting out. If you don't cut corners —"

Alex interrupted him. "... you'll save time in the long run."

Bruce turned around, saw his son, and a huge smile creased his face. He wasn't a big, burly man like Frank. Bruce was thin and wiry, but strong. He was also shorter than his son. Bruce rushed forward and threw his arms around Alex.

"What are you doing here?" Bruce said pulling back.

"Following orders," Alex said.

Bruce stood back and looked at Alex for a moment. There was pride on his face. Then he turned to the other mechanics in the room. "This," he said, "is my son. Alex Evans."

Chapter 30

"You were one of the Titans?" Bruce asked his son.

"I was the one at the entrance to the transit station," Alex admitted. "I didn't see you until you had passed by me."

"Alex," Bruce said, his joy transforming to concern. "That was dangerous. You were shot."

"The Titan suit has thick armor," Alex said. "You should know that, dad."

They had moved outside and were sitting at one of the picnic tables that lined the large park-like green space. Alex had never seen his father looking so well. His face had more color than Alex had ever seen.

"Well, yeah, I guess I should, but I never considered my son being in one of the suits. I thought you were still training."

"We were, but we got deployed to Carthage Prime."

"I've heard some bad things about that system," Bruce said. "What happened there?"

"We had prospectors on the ground, and we were sent in to protect them," Alex explained. "Then a group of Zen Tech battleships arrived and drove our support carrier out of the system. They launched kamikaze drones and tried to take control of the colony. We attacked as they tried to land their drop ships. It wasn't a perfect ambush. People died...one was my friend."

Alex had to pause for a second to keep himself from breaking down. There were moments when Newt's face was so clear in his mind. He still felt guilty that his friend had died. Alex should have known better than to just rush into battle without ordering Newt back into a reserve position. If he had, his friend might still be alive...but Alex would probably be dead. That would have been okay with him at just about any other time, but in that moment, sitting across from his father, he was so glad to be alive.

"But none of the deaths were civilians," Alex pressed. "I've heard the news reports too. The landing pads were destroyed, and some of the supplies stored in their warehouses were damaged, but we didn't kill the colonists. Plus, the company is rebuilding and replacing what was damaged or lost."

Bruce nodded. He had worked for Ahzco almost his entire adult life. He was proud of the company that had paid him a living wage for so long, but there was always doubt. On NP8261, his family had been safe, together, well fed, and for the most part, without complaint for over fifteen years. Yet their hometown had been a company town, keeping the employees there at a level of poverty that made leaving almost impossible. But it was his son that he trusted, and if Alex said the news reports weren't true, then that is what he would believe.

"Can you come home?" Bruce asked.

"No," Alex said. "Not unless things calm down and we can get some leave. I really shouldn't even be out of my battle suit, but being a sergeant has its privileges."

"Sergeant?" Bruce said, noticing the triple stripes on Alex's uniform for the first time. "When did that happen? You haven't even been in the CDF for a year yet!"

"We were all promoted to corporal after our first mission," Alex said. "I was team leader, and some of my ideas were used in the battles to hold off the Zen Tech forces. I got a field promotion during the fighting, and then afterward it was formalized."

"My gosh," Bruce Evans said. "Who knew you would be so good at soldiering? Your mother worries, but she's also proud. We have a little house with our own garden. She walks Jasmine to and from school every day and has already got vegetables ripening on the vine—not that we need to grow our own food. And I'm officially the second mechanic here. I've got more seniority than just about everyone else in the factory."

"They're treating you well?"

"It's amazing. The younger guys really listen when I'm teaching," Bruce said. "Who would have thought? Me, a teacher? But there really isn't much to do here. So Frank rotates everyone through different shifts and makes sure that we keep up our skills. My experience in the field is a bonus here. I couldn't be happier."

"That's fantastic," Alex said. "Does Jas like her school?"

"She's thriving, Alex. She really is. I felt so guilty for getting stuck on the Rock for all those years, but it's paying off handsomely now. Just don't get yourself killed. Your mother would never get over it."

"Neither would I," Alex joked. "But I love what I'm doing. It's a dream come true."

They spent the entire evening talking, but eventually Alex and his father both had to return to work. Alex's Titan was completely charged when he returned. The mechanics helped him back inside, and Alex checked in with Nyx.

The drop ship is on its way back down.

"Has there been any aggression from the other ships in the system?"

No, but a few have sent teams down after they saw us do it. No individual fliers, just shuttles.

"So we don't need to escort them?" Alex asked.

I don't think so. But it might not hurt to be in the air.

"I agree. On my way," Alex said.

The only drawback to the charging area was that Alex was forced to walk through the building to get to the exit. The Titan battle suit could move at speed when necessary, but there was a chance it might damage the floor, so he forced himself to walk.

"Sly, get moving. We need to watch for threats to the drop ship," Alex said.

"Already flying, team leader," Sly replied.

The drop ship is over twenty-five thousand meters. ETA twelve minutes.

"Thanks, Nyx," Alex said.

As soon as he was out of the factory, he took to the air with a small crowd of laborers, fabricators, and mechanics watching.

"What's going on, Cronus?" Master Sergeant Montgomery asked over the tactical channel.

"The drop ship is returning, Master Sergeant," Alex said. "We just want to be up in the air on the off chance somethin—"

Alex was cut short by a warning alarm. It blared in his ears, and a red warning flashed in his vision.

Missile in the air! Nyx declared.

Alex was still climbing, and he turned, trying to find the weapon. He wasn't sure if it was tracking him or one of his teammates.

"Evasive maneuvers!" Alex ordered.

"It isn't coming after us," Ash said.

Alex finally caught sight of the weapon's contrail. It was streaking upward higher than his team of Titans. The realization sunk in with sickening finality.

"The drop ship," Alex said.

They're firing countermeasures.

"Who the hell is shooting at us?" Sly said. His voice was loud, and Alex heard a note of fear in it.

"It came from the city," Ash said. "I saw it come up from a cluster of buildings."

"Keep climbing," Alex said. "They could target us next."

The drop ship cut her engines. She's in freefall.

"What about that missile?"

It's tracking the countermeasures.

Alex held his breath, waiting for the report from the missile. There was nothing they could do to stop it, and he felt helpless.

"Keep tracking for more missiles," Alex told Nyx.

I'm on it.

"Who would shoot at us?" Sly said. "It has to be the protesters."

"That was a ground-to-air missile," Ash said. "How do supposedly anti-military protesters get their hands on one?"

It was a good question. Odds were good that they didn't go looking for it. Someone was most likely using the group to cover their criminal behavior. But that was someone else's concern. All Alex needed to worry about right now was staying alive.

"Stay alert," he warned his team.

"Roger," Ash said.

"You know it," Sly said. "I wish we had weapons that were actually lethal. If the bad guys can shoot at us, I want to be able to shoot back."

The missile passed the drop ship. It's still tracking the countermeasures.

"That was fast thinking on the pilot's part."

Wait, no, the missile's turning. They've cut power on the engines, and the missile is turning back. They're passing seven thousand meters.

"If that ship gets hit, the wreckage will rain down on the city," Ash said. "It could kill who-knows-how-many innocent people."

"Not to mention the crew and passengers," Sly said.

Alex was only twenty-five hundred meters up. There was still no way to intercept the missile, but he knew they had to do something.

"Keep climbing. We might be able to help," Alex said.

It's going to be close. The pilot is firing more countermeasures and changing course.

Alex knew what it was like to have a missile chasing him down. There was a sickening helplessness knowing that the missile wouldn't stop or change course.

An explosion above them made his heart sink. The missile had found its mark. Smoke billowed from the drop ship, which was small but visible to Alex as he flew. The ship was mostly intact but dropping like a stone.

The drop ship is gone, Nyx said sadly.

"No it isn't," Alex said. "Cronus team, on me!"

What are you doing?

"The missile took out the cockpit and controls, but most of the ship is still intact."

It must have been a low-yield warhead. The passengers could still be alive.

"We're on our way," Alex said, switching to his team channel. "Let's see if we can get under it."

"You want us to get between a falling spaceship and the ground?" Sly asked incredulously.

"Yes," Alex said. "We'll use the electromagnets in our suits to connect to the hull, then use our repulsers to slow the descent. We might even be able to guide it somewhere friendly."

"You're insane," Sly said.

"I love it," Ash said.

"It's the only hope those passengers have," Alex replied.

"And if we don't have enough thrust to keep it from crashing?" Sly asked.

"Then maybe we can keep it from killing anyone else," Alex said. "We have to try."

Hurry, Alex. Once it drops below two thousand feet, your suits won't have enough thrust to stop it.

"Get the suit ready to connect," Alex said. "I'm almost there."

Ash was the first to reach the drop ship. It was in a spin, falling bottom-first and remaining mostly upright.

"We should connect at the same time to keep from unbalancing the ship," Ash said.

Passing four thousand meters.

"Sly?" Alex said.

"Right behind you, team leader," Sly said.

They moved into position just below the falling ship.

"Activate our electromagnetic capabilities," Alex ordered.

He felt the new EM waves radiating from his Titan and the others. There was a moment when nothing happened. They were all falling, but all they could do was wait for the ship to get close enough that their suits would be drawn to it.

Three thousand feet, Nyx warned.

"Come on, come on," Alex whispered.

Suddenly he felt a sudden jarring collision and heard the metal-on-metal thump as his Titan battle suit connected with the drop ship.

"Engage thrusters and repulsers!" Alex ordered.

He brought his controls to full throttle, which didn't seem to slow them down at all.

Passing two thousand meters...It's working Alex, the ship is slowing down.

"Is it slowing down enough?"

I think so, but Alex, how are you going to get out from under it?

Toby Neighbors

Alex hadn't thought his plan all the way through. Perhaps it was possible that they could flip the ship over. The passengers should all be strapped in.

"Is it possible that once we get control of the ship, we could flip it over?" Alex asked.

I'll do the calculations, but I doubt it.

Alex was near the front of the ship, on the bottom but close to the ruined cockpit. Ash and Sly were behind him. He knew what he would have to do.

"Let's just get it slowed down," Alex said. "Once we have it under control, we'll fly it to the Ahzco factory."

And then what? Alex, you have to get out of there. There's nothing more you can do.

Alex ignored Nyx. He didn't like the idea of crash-landing with a spaceship on his back, but there wasn't a better option. When he was close to the ground he would just have to try to jump out of the way. It sounded ridiculous, even to him, but he didn't have a choice.

You're at one thousand meters. Airspeed is continuing to decline.

"Let's move it back to the plant," Alex said over the tactical channel. "Oscar team, we're headed your way with the drop ship."

"Copy, Cronus One. Standing by."

"You might want to get some emergency measures ready," Alex replied.

"Already done, Ace. Just get that thing on the ground, and we'll take it from there."

227

Getting the drop ship on the ground wasn't the problem; keeping it from killing his team or the survivors inside was another issue. They weren't flying the smoking hulk—what they were managing was a guided fall.

Five hundred meters.

Alex could see the factory and the surrounding property.

"Ash, Sly—on my mark, we break free," he ordered.

"Roger that, team leader," Sly said.

"Just say the word," Ash added.

Two hundred and fifty meters. Alex, what are you going to do?

"Let's set it down on the grassy area," Alex said.

"Setting it down is being generous," Sly remarked.

"Any landing you can walk away from, right?" Ash said in a jovial tone.

"That's right," Alex said, although he knew the odds of walking away were almost zero.

One hundred meters.

There was no time left. Alex knew he would either survive or he wouldn't. At least he was home. His parents would know his fate.

Fifty meters.

The grass was so green. It looked inviting. Alex decided there were much worse ways to die.

Twenty-five feet.

"Go, go, go!" Alex ordered.

Ash broke to starboard, Sly to port. Alex could see the ground rushing up at him as he dropped, but there was no escaping the ship on his back.

Chapter 31

Ale—

Silence. He couldn't see or move. The Titan's internal padding held him fast, and he could scarcely breathe.

"Nyx," Alex said, the words sounding strange and muffled.

There was no reply. For a few seconds he wasn't sure what was happening. He knew the ship had fallen on him, but he didn't know if he was alive or dead. There was no pain, and he could feel his body when he struggled to move, yet there was no movement. He opened his eyes and saw no light, not even the video feed being translated by his brain. He tried to call up the Titan's systems, but there was no response. The MBS was dead, which meant he was either dead or about to be.

If the Ahzco mechanized battle suits had one flaw, it was the ventilation system. His Titan had air tanks, but without power the valves shut down, leaving him with only the air in the cavity of the battle suit, which didn't amount to much. If a Titan went down, as his had, the operator could only survive a few minutes.

Fear clawed at Alex's brain. He didn't want to die—it was too soon. There were still so many things he wanted to do: see his family's new home, kiss Nyx, travel the galaxy, try new things, have a family of his own...yet there was nothing he could do to change his current situation. Struggling was useless and would only burn through what little oxygen he had left more quickly.

If he was going to survive—assuming he wasn't already dead—he would have to be rescued. He was in a good place.

People knew and cared about him. His fear was so strong that he could feel himself trembling all over. Yet a spark of hope remained: Ash, Sly, his father, Master Sergeant Monty—they were all there. They would fight for him. They would do their best to rescue him. He used every mind-controlling technique that Master Sergeant Grossman had taught him on Helena Prime. Still, Alex felt himself slipping toward mind-numbing panic.

All he could hope for if he was dying was that there had been survivors on the drop ship. The pilots were gone, that much was certain. What Alex couldn't know was how much damage the cargo area of the drop ship had sustained from the missile. He had bet his life that there were survivors on board the ship—innocent technicians who spent their time and energy making sure the Titan battle suits were charged, loaded, and fully capable whenever he was needed. They deserved to live. The drop ship pilots had died trying to save them, and Alex's Titan team had done all they could.

His mind replayed their actions. He couldn't help but wonder if they should have taken a different approach. Maybe they could have stopped the drop ship's descent by latching onto the sides, but he hadn't thought of that in the moment.

He was still replaying their rescue attempt in his mind when he felt a vibration. It was slight, and he was afraid that he had imagined it—but then he felt another. Hope bloomed in his chest like dawn after a long, terrible night. He was still alive. The new sensation proved that, if such a thing was provable at all. And something was happening to the ship. He hoped it was more than just the passengers being rescued. He wanted to be saved, to believe that his friends were doing everything in their power to reach him.

Another vibration was followed by the unmistakable sound of metal creaking. It was muffled, but Alex heard it. With his Titan MBS powered down, hearing anything outside of it was hard. The suit had audio pickups built in so that a person speaking to him could be heard, the sound picked up by the suit and amplified for his ears. But there was so much metal and insulation around Alex that sounds had to be very loud to be heard. He could scream for help and no one would hear him.

There was clanking and definite contact with his suit, but Alex was having trouble identifying it. His mind felt foggy, and concentrating on any one thing was suddenly hard. He wanted to close his eyes. Having them opened didn't make a difference. It was too dark to see anything anyway, and closing his eyes felt good.

Movement! There was a sudden, jerking motion, like being dragged. But that made no sense to Alex. He couldn't comprehend what was happening. There was also banging—a dull thumping. Alex tried to make sense of it all, but it was impossible. All he wanted now was to close his eyes, drift away, and forget about everything.

Another sound of metal rending. It was louder than before —a creaking groan followed by a banging rattle. Something was changing. It was odd, and Alex couldn't identify it at first…a new sensation, perhaps. His mind was slowly beginning to clear, and he realized he could smell dirt. That was odd to him. His mind couldn't comprehend where the aroma of dirt and grass was coming from. On NP8261, he had smelled dirt every day of his life. The colony was mostly underground. Dirt, dust, and the dank stench of mildew were common enough. But this was different. It was richer somehow—clean despite being dirt.

Another wrenching sound, and Alex could hear voices seemingly from far away. He couldn't make out the words or who was speaking. It all jumbled together in his foggy brain, but he could tell someone was talking. Was he dying or being saved? It didn't make sense.

Then, with a pop, the Titan suit was wrenched open. Sunlight flooded Alex's eyes and felt like hot needles. Someone grabbed him and pulled his body out of the mechanized battle suit.

"Get him some water," a familiar voice said.

Alex lifted his hand to block the sunlight. It was late in the day, but the light still seemed harsh to Alex. He saw a shadowy face above him—a familiar one.

"Dad?" Alex said.

"We are not telling your mother about this," Bruce Evans insisted.

There was laughing, and someone handed Alex a paper cup filled with cold water. He took a sip, then a deep breath, and his mind cleared.

"You want to tell me what you were thinking?" Bruce said.

Alex looked at the drop ship. It was scorched and smoking on the lawn. One corner was lifted on jacks, and his Titan battle suit was still half-crushed under the weight of it.

"The passengers?" Alex said.

"They're alive," Bruce said. "Shook up, scared, but alive, thanks to you."

An all-terrain Destroyer MBS was gaping open nearby. Master Sergeant Taylor Montgomery was speaking to the facility administrator, then walked over to where Alex lay propped on one elbow.

"Well, that was about the damnedest thing I've ever seen," Monty said. "Any idea who fired that missile?"

Alex reached out a hand, and Monty pulled him to his feet. "No," Alex said. "I could guess, but that's all it would be. How are Ash and Sly?"

"Fine, they're still flying. We all thought you were dead. If not for your old man, you'd still be buried under that ship."

"I hoped the dirt would give you enough cushion to survive," Bruce Evans said.

"I'm glad he was right," Monty said. "But your suit is toast."

"Thank you," Alex said to his father, who shrugged.

"If I hadn't tried, your mother would never forgive me," he said with a grin.

"It will be dark soon," Alex said. "What's the plan?"

"We're doubling up the watch," Monty said. "There's been no demonstrations or protests at night, but that could change. Someone is getting serious about getting rid of us."

"Yeah," Alex agreed. "I need to talk to my controller."

"You can use my rig if you want," Monty said. "Once the technicians get over being shot out of the air and crash-landing, we can probably get you into another MBS, but for now I don't mind trading off."

"Great," Alex said. "That works for me."

Alex walked over to the Destroyer. The tank treads had been switched to wheels more suitable for an urban setting. He climbed up and sat on the top, his feet down inside the battle suit. He didn't need to activate the entire thing to sync to its computer system and bring up the communications system. Fortunately, Monty's controller had taken a break with him out of his suit, so there was no strange voice in Alex's head.

"Nyx, do you read me?" Alex said.

Alex? You're alive? Nyx replied over the com-link.

"Yeah, they pulled me out and cracked open the Titan battle suit. It was touch-and-go with the O2 levels, but I survived without losing too many brain cells."

Are you injured?

"Negative. The suit is totaled, but it protected me just the way it's supposed to."

Thank God, Nyx said. *I was so worried when I lost contact with you.*

"I'm sorry," Alex said. "That wasn't such a good plan."

You're okay, that's all that matters.

"What about that missile? Any intel on who fired it or where it came from?"

Hang on, Nyx said. He could hear her hands working the controls of her station. *The ship's weapon recognition software listed it as a Miryll Systems 82 heat-seeking ground-to-air missile.*

They're fired from shoulder-mounted weapons and can reach thirty thousand meters. It's old weapons tech, but effective.

"Miryll Systems? I've never heard of that."

They were acquired by a larger company, who in turn was bought out by another. They stopped making the 82HS decades ago. Someone has found or stolen an old armory's outdated weapons.

"That doesn't really give us a solid read on who was behind the attack," Alex said. "If the protesters have that kind of weaponry, we could be in trouble here."

Agreed, Nyx said. *We've sent word to HQ, but it could be days before we get word back. In the meantime, we keep doing what we're ordered to do.*

"All right. Well, my Titan is down. I'm not sure how long it will be until I get another."

I'll be standing by, Alex. When you need me, I'll be here.

"Thanks," he replied. "That's good to know."

He disconnected from the Destroyer's systems as the sun began to set in earnest. He needed to talk to the technicians and find another battle suit—fast.

Chapter 32

"We have the suits, but no computer systems to run them," Sergeant Owens was the head of the operator technicians group and had flown down to the planet to help maintain the MBS's being used by Cronus Team. Another group of technicians was in charge of the MBS's being used by Oscar Company.

"So they won't work," Alex said in frustration.

"We do the main build, all the hardware," said Frank, the head mechanic. But the power system is built at another facility, the computer systems are designed at yet another facility, and all the wiring is done someplace else. In fact, there are multiple plants creating the different battle suits. We specialize in the Titan and Valkyrie suits exclusively."

"So they won't work," Alex repeated himself.

"Not with what we have here," the tech said.

"Hang on," Bruce Evans spoke up. "We have all the parts we need to rebuild the suit."

"I'm sorry," Owens said. "Were you not paying attention?"

Bruce grinned. "Let's all play nice, shall we, young man? I'm referring to his original suit. It has all the wiring and computer hardware. We would have salvaged the suit for parts at any rate. Why not use them with one of the new suits fresh off the line and get him back in the game?"

"Can we do that?" Alex asked.

"No," Owens said.

"Yes," Frank said with a grin.

"It's impossible. We don't have the schematics," Owens insisted.

"We don't need it," Frank said. "The ruined suit is our model. We just pull things off one, record where and how it all fits together, and put it into the new suit."

"Weapons too?" Alex asked.

"Sure," Bruce said. "Why not?"

"That's not how we do things," Owens insisted.

"Well, we're not technicians," Frank said with a grin. "We're mechanics. It's how *we've* been doing things for thousands of years."

"We could probably even make some suggestions about making them better," Bruce said, purposely goading the tech.

"The Titan is the most advanced mechanized battle suit in the galaxy," Owens said. "I don't think it needs improving."

"He's joking with you," Alex said. "If you work together, I'm sure you can do it."

"My guys are digging your suit out from under the drop ship right now," Frank said.

"I have to get approval," Owens said.

"Then let's go get it," Alex said.

Bruce pointed them to the admin building. It was a small, two-story building with windows that overlooked the green space beside the huge plant. The head administrator was Cathy Brown. The rest of her team had already gone home for the evening when Alex entered her building. The bottom floor was a waiting area with two models of what the plant produced. A tall FA Titan and the bulkier AR Valkyrie stood like sentinels on either side of the room. There was a glass-enclosed presentation room on the first floor, a break room, and a lavatory. Stairs led up to the second floor where the administrative staff had offices. Alex led the way into Cathy Brown's office.

"How can I help you?" she asked, without looking up from her computer display.

"We need to contact the *Currency* in orbit," Alex said.

"Yes, we can establish a link to the ship in the conference room downstairs," Brown said. "And we'll just leave it up so that your people can use it whenever the need arises."

Ten minutes later, Alex and Sergeant Owens were alone in the glass-enclosed room. There were several displays built into the conference table, but they stood in front of a large wall display where the captain of the *Currency* appeared.

"Sergeant Evans, that was a heroic effort," Captain Poe said. "Thank you for saving the technicians. I'm glad to see you are unharmed."

"My Titan suit saved my life," Alex said. "Unfortunately, it was damaged beyond repair in the process."

"So, we're a man down. Tell me you have a solution," the no-nonsense captain said.

"Actually, the mechanics here at the factory believe they can salvage what they need from Sergeant Evans' Titan to refit one of their new battle suits off the line," Owens said.

"Interesting," Captain Poe said, his eyebrows furrowing together and creating deep creases across his forehead. "What do you think, Sergeant Owens?"

"It's not a project I would attempt, but I can't see the harm in trying," Owens said. "Sergeant Evans can't use his original Titan battle suit. If there's a chance we could get a new one running for him, I think it's worth the effort."

"Very well. I'll approve the project on my end. Keep me updated."

"Yes, Captain," Alex and Sergeant Owens said at the same time.

"So," Owens said once the screen went blank, "I guess we're doing this."

"Yeah, I hope I didn't step on your toes."

"You really trust these guys?"

"The older one is my father," Alex said. "So yeah, I trust him with my life and that of my team."

"Well, I, along with every technician who came down, owe our lives to you and your Titans. Let's go get started."

The mechanics already had the crushed Titan MBS out of the ground and into the factory. The mechanics were taking pictures and laying all the electrical components out on a separate table, marking each with a tag. Several fabricators were busy cutting off anything they saw as usable from the crashed drop ship. Alex was amazed by their creativity and work ethic.

"They don't let anything go to waste," Alex said.

"I guess not," Owens said "Fortunately for all of us, none of the munitions on your old Titan are volatile. Otherwise, they might blow themselves up."

"How's it going?" Alex asked his father.

"Good. We're having fun," Bruce said.

He had the sleeves of his coveralls rolled up, revealing his sinewy forearms and a tattoo of his wife's name, Penelope, on the inside of his left forearm.

"We'll have to fabricate some of the connectors," Frank pointed out. "Your suit was crushed, and we had to cut more than few components out. But we haven't seen anything yet that we can't fix."

The technicians were gathered close to the table but stayed out of the way. They answered questions about what specific parts did, but they didn't try to help with the salvage. The mechanics from Skandia worked with deft hands and an eagerness that Alex hadn't expected. They were skilled laborers who loved a challenge and who didn't get to do much work in the regular run of business at the plant. It was clear that they were all tinkerers in their spare time. Alex remembered seeing his father take things apart and put them back together again. He made their lives on NP8261 better than most because of his knack for fixing things.

"What happens when your shift is over?" Alex said.

"Oh, we aren't leaving," Bruce said. "You couldn't get these guys out of here. I've contacted your mother and sister. They're both anxious to see you, but until we're sure the plant is safe, I've told them not to come."

"That's smart," Alex said. "I want to see them too, but I'd never get over it if they got hurt."

"Well," Bruce said. "Keep in mind, your mother and I feel the same way about you. So be careful. You don't have to be a hero."

Alex nodded. He never set out to do heroic things, but like his father, he simply couldn't stand to see a task unfinished. And his new skills made it possible for him to do more than most. Still, he was starting to see things from his parents' perspectives; he didn't want any of his team members to get hurt, and that meant he should be careful too.

After a while, watching the mechanics work bored Alex. It wasn't that the project wasn't interesting, but he didn't like being on the outside, watching others do things. He was a hands-on type of person, only he didn't have the skill to build things like his father. The concepts didn't interest him enough to really apply himself to mechanical work. Alex could appreciate what the mechanics were doing, and he knew he couldn't replicate it. He trusted their abilities and instead of hovering over them, he decided to go find out what was happening elsewhere.

In the room set aside for the operators to rest and recharge their MBS's, Alex found Ash napping. He felt bad that she had stood watch all day, and because his suit was damaged, he wouldn't be able to take a shift. He made sure that food was being brought in for his team and Oscar Company. The administrator, Cathy Brown, had already seen to it. So Alex found his way up onto the rooftop. Master Sergeant Monty was there in his Destroyer, with the top open to the cool night air.

"Anything happening?" Alex asked.

"Negative," Monty replied. "It's quiet in this part of the city. What time is the shift change?"

"Eleven PM local," Alex said. "But most of the workers aren't leaving."

"Yeah, well, I bet the engineers are," he said with a grin. "I've seen a few looking like they've seen more than enough excitement for one day."

"Can't say I blame them," Alex said as he looked out over the city lights.

"You gotta love this level-one planet air," Monty said. "If there is one thing I miss on a CDF ship, it's fresh air."

"Where are you from?" Alex asked.

"NP9701, originally. My family was second-generation on a Zen Tech colony."

"No breathable air, I suppose," Alex said.

"No, you could breathe it, but it was thin. You always felt out of breath. And the planet is too close to the system star. Desert conditions on the poles, but lots of natural resources."

"Have you always worked for Ahzco?"

"No," Monty admitted. "Zen Tech recruited me, got me off that hothouse planet, and I jumped at the chance—but Ahzco pays better. We've got better toys, too. Zen Tech is trying to catch up, but they don't have the talent on the R&D side."

"Well, maybe you can retire here one day," Alex said. "There's still plenty of space on this planet."

"Wouldn't that be something?" Monty said with real enthusiasm. "A no-name planet rat moving up in the world. Anything is possible."

"I grew up on NP8261," Alex said. "My father worked for the company. When I got recruited, they transferred him here."

"Your whole family got to a level-one planet because the CDF wanted you?" Monty said with surprise. "Damn, that's what

I'm talking about. See, that's the difference between Zen Tech and Ahzco. Around here, people respect what we do. We're not just numbers and a bottom line."

"Tell that to those protesters today," Alex said.

"You know I would," Monty replied. "But they wouldn't listen. Their minds are already made up. The facts don't mean anything to people like that."

"What does?" Alex asked. "How do things ever change?"

"Money and influence," Monty said. "A hundred actual CDF operators could tell the truth, but it only takes one celebrity to sway public opinion. A singer or actor says we're killing babies, and that's all most people will ever believe."

They stood silently for several minutes staring out over the city.

"You have thoughts on what we do if the protesters return?" Alex asked.

"You mean the violent ones?" Master Sergeant Montgomery asked.

"I'm saying I think someone, probably in the group of protesters, fired that rocket at our drop ship today," Alex explained. "And my fear is they won't stop."

"In that case, we stop them," Monty said.

Chapter 33

Nyx was still at her station. Her work wasn't nearly as strenuous as Alex's, and she was determined to be at her station when he needed her. In the meantime, she and almost everyone else on board who wasn't busy with another task were monitoring the planetary network. More stories were pouring in about the protests. Charities were springing up like weeds in a vacant lot. Most disturbing of all were the news stories about the demonstrations in Oslo. Nyx clicked the link to unmute the video report on her workstation computer.

"I was horrified," said a bedraggled woman with dried blood in her hair and on the front of her shirt. "They showed no concern for basic human decency. I was just there to protest Ahzco's deadly use of force. They make those horrific war machines right here in Oslo. We don't want any part of that. I wasn't doing anything, when suddenly that monster pelted me with something so hard that it cut my scalp."

"The operator in a battle suit did that to you?" the news reporter asked. The look of shock on his face was almost comical.

"Yes," the bedraggled woman said. "He ordered us to leave, then began pelting us with tiny projectiles. I don't know what they were, but I know what they can do."

"How did you respond?" the reporter asked.

"I ran. We all did. What else could we do? We were there as a peaceful demonstration to communicate our belief that private militaries are out of control. I had no idea they'd turn violent against us."

"Outrageous," Nyx said angrily.

"What?" asked another of the controllers.

"This woman is blatantly lying about what happened down there," Nyx said.

"Yeah, it's on all the news services. Unfortunately, there's no video surveillance in that square. The protesters can say whatever they want."

"That was my operator in the crowd," Nyx said. "Someone was shooting at him with a projectile weapon. The pellets ricocheted off his armor and hit some of the people in the crowd, but it was unavoidable."

"You're preaching to the choir," the other controller said. She was a short woman with a round face and chin-length, pink hair. "But what can we do?"

Nyx stood up, realizing there *was* something they could do. She marched out of the controller section of the ship and went straight to the bridge. There were several senior officers at their stations, including Captain Poe. She waited until he looked up and noticed her.

"You need something, Sergeant?" he asked.

"I have an idea that I wanted to run by you," Nyx said, "when you have the time."

"Is this a private matter?"

"No, Captain," she said.

"Very good. Join me."

She walked to the pit in the center of the ship's command center. The captain was studying the plot, which showed the *Currency's* position and everything around them, including the planet, on a round display table. There were nearly a dozen ships in orbit. Each one was listed with a designation. One side of the large, round display table had the designations for each ship listed. A quick glance showed that eight ships were from various mega-corporations. The other four were from major news agencies.

"See anything unusual?" Captain Poe asked.

Nyx frowned. "Four news ships? I didn't know Skandia had the population to support that many large news agencies."

"They don't," Poe said. "These are from the major planets further in the galactic arm."

"What are they doing here?"

"That is the question I've been asking myself for the last four hours," Captain Poe said. "The only thing I can fathom is that they know something I don't."

"Like what?" Nyx asked.

"I read your file, Sergeant West. You have high marks in creative reasoning. Your work at the academy was flawless. There's even a note from Colonel Chastain regarding your part in the strategies used on Carthage Prime."

Nyx didn't know what to say. She liked to think that she was a valuable member of the CDF, but she didn't always think of herself that way. She was almost embarrassed to know that Captain Poe had read up on her.

"Thank you, sir," she said.

"Don't thank me, help me. What do they know?"

Nyx didn't have to think about things for long to see what he was getting at. "You think they have something planned?"

"The protesters, perhaps," Captain Poe said. "They've sent word."

"Something more than the rocket they launched at our drop ship?"

"Yes," he replied. "These news ships have only been in orbit a few hours. If that rocket was all they had, they would have saved it for their audience."

"They're going to do something that might hurt our operators," Nyx said. "We have to warn them."

"I've already sent word. The actions of your Titan operator were impressive, to say the least. I'm glad he survived."

"Sergeant Evans is fearless, sir. It's a pleasure to work with him. In fact, I had an idea to combat the news stories. I'm sure you've heard that the protesters are blaming us for the injuries in the plaza."

He nodded, never taking his eyes off the plot.

"Sir, it is possible to record the video feeds from their MBS's. We could use the footage to refute their claims."

"I'm not sure that would change the hearts and minds of the people on the ground," Captain Poe said. "But we'll let greater minds decide that. Do what you need to do to record the footage—everything we can get from Oscar Company and Cronus Team. I'll make sure it gets to Colonel Chastain."

"Yes sir, thank you," Nyx said.

"Thank you, West. I appreciate it when my people take the initiative."

She saluted and left the bridge, feeling light on her feet. She had been gone from her console too long, but she had an alarm set to vibrate her PIL if she had an incoming message. So far, all was quiet, so she decided to grab a quick bite to eat. Odds were good that she'd be spending hours at her console. She needed to make the most of any time away from her station.

The mess hall was on the upper level of the ship, but there was a food dispenser just outside the bridge. She swiped her ID and got a sandwich wrapped in paper, a yogurt cup with fruits and nuts, and a bottle of mineral water. With her food collected, she returned to her station. There was still no word from Alex. She hated that his Titan MBS had been damaged. She felt cut out of the mission because she couldn't communicate with him. She was used to regular reports and knowing exactly what was happening at all times. She leaned back in her chair, looking around the divider between her station and the one where Ash's controller worked.

"Anything?"

"All's quiet," the woman said. "My operator just went offline for six hours. I'll be back."

Nyx knew six hours of sleep was the most a person could hope for during a combat op. Their mission was to keep the employees safe and protect the Ahzco property on Skandia Seven. Their enemy wasn't another combat force but rather the mobs of people protesting their very existence. There was no way to predict when or how they might strike. The more she considered why four major news agencies would send interstellar ships to the Skandia system, which already had its own news reporting service, the more she agreed with Captain Poe. Something was in the works, and it had to be significant. No matter what, she wanted to be connected with Alex when it happened.

It wasn't just about the excitement of the mission, although Nyx loved working with Alex during combat. It made her feel not only important, but also vital to his success. She felt that she was part of the mission, part of what was happening, even if she was hundreds of kilometers away on the control ship.

If an attack was coming, she needed to be connected with Alex. Being cut off from him when the drop ship fell on him was almost more than she could take. She had feared for his life, though she felt certain he was still alive. If she ever got to the surface of Skandia Seven, she would track down Bruce Evans and hug him. Nyx loved her parents and knew they cared deeply for her, but she wondered if her own father would have had the same presence of mind and the technical skills to save her.

She ate her meal in silence, hardly tasting the bland food. She continued to monitor the networks, very aware that no stories of the rocket that had been launched at the drop ship were being reported. She had heard people say that news agencies had agendas or only reported one side of most events. She knew everyone had their biases, but it seemed impossible to think that no one cared about the truth. Unfortunately, it seemed every news service had a script they were sticking with no matter what. She didn't know where that left her or the CDF, but she trusted there were good people tackling those issues. Her focus and attention remained on Alex and his Cronus team. That's all she needed to think about until they were all safely back on board the *Currency*.

She only wished he would contact her soon. Until then, there was nothing she could do.

Chapter 34

"It's ready," Bruce said.

It was half past midnight. The protesters hadn't returned during the late-night shift change. There were fewer workers for the graveyard shift, half as many mechanics, only two fabricators, and just a few engineers. The lines shut down for several hours so that the tracks could be lubricated and safety checks completed. But none of the mechanics had left during the shift change; they had worked nonstop on the new Titan MBS.

The electrical system was in place, the weapons were loaded, and the power supply connected. All that remained was to turn it on and see what happened. Alex climbed the ladder, leaning against the side of the battle suit. He dropped inside and took a deep breath. There were nearly twenty people standing around, watching to see what would happen. The technicians had overseen the work and seemed confident it would work, but until the power was activated, there was no way to tell.

"Here goes nothing," Alex said.

He pressed the button to engage the power supply. Normally, the battle suits were online and all systems running before Alex arrived at the hangar, but the new Titan MBS had to be booted up for the first time. The suit made a whirring noise but didn't close up. Alex was afraid something was wrong. The EM waves from the suit were strong, but he waited to sync with the system. Several of the technicians were holding handheld scanners, checking the systems from a distance. In most MBS hangars, there were cables that could be hooked into the suit to give them instant access to every onboard system, and advanced computers calibrated the suits to exact specifications—but in the factory, everything was being done one step at a time, with only Alex's observations and feedback.

"Power's up," said Owens, the chief technician for the FA Titans.

"How long should it take the systems to boot up?" Alex asked.

"Several minutes," Owens said.

"Just relax," Frank, the head mechanic, announced. "Nothing's smoking yet. We're okay."

Before Alex could respond, the suit closed up around him. He felt the suit's impact cushions inflating around him. In that moment, he was reminded of the MP Defender he had climbed into after pulling out the wounded operator on NP8261. His life had changed that day, and he was hopeful that things would go well. He let his mind sync with the suit's computer system. It snapped together, the way two magnets connect, and suddenly he was acutely aware of every system in the battle suit. Power was at optimum level. Communication was online. Weapons were in safety mode. Flight systems were cycling up. And a firm connection with ship control was being made.

Alex toggled on the suit's external speaker system. "Everything looks good for now."

His voice projected from the suit in a crystal-clear audio. He took a step, turned around, and rotated the gun arms. Everything worked flawlessly.

"All systems are working," Owens said, the surprise unmistakable in his voice.

"We're professionals here," Frank said. "What'd you expect?"

"Let's go outside," Alex said. "We need to test the flight systems."

"All right, let's get the safety equipment ready," Frank said. "We can't let Bruce's son get cooked on our watch."

Alex marched out through the factory. He was in the fabrication shop before the suit finally connected with the control ship *Currency.*

Alex? Are you there?

"I'm here," Alex said. "How are things looking on your end?"

All systems are green across the board. I'm so glad you're back online. Have there been any developments down there?

"Negative," Alex said. "It's quiet. No problems at shift change. We've got units all around the property. There's no movement in the sector around us."

Good, but stay alert—the captain believes something is afoot. There are four major news agency ships in the system.

"Really?" Alex asked. "What would bring them to the Skandia system?"

That's what we're trying to decide. The consensus is that something is going to happen.

"Something pre-planned?"

Probably. A public relations event that we aren't privy to.

"And what if that *event* is an attack? Are we going to just take it on the chin?"

Do you have another idea?

"Actually, yes," Alex said. "I should sync with the news ships and see what I can find out. If they're planning something, it would surely be on their computer systems."

Perhaps, but don't you have to be close to do that?

"I do," Alex said. "I'll have to make orbit."

We have to get the Captain's permission, and he'll insist on knowing why. VP Haley expressly ordered you not to let anyone else know about your abilities.

"So we just do nothing?"

Can't you sync with the protesters' computer systems?

"Only if I know who they are and where their computers are set up. The demonstrators aren't carrying tech with them. Where do I begin?"

They both fell silent, thinking about the problem. Once Alex was outside and the mechanics were ready with safety equipment on the off-chance that something went wrong with the battle armor, Alex launched himself into the air. He flew straight up for a hundred meters, then turned and banked with ease. The suit was perfect. He rotated his guns, had Nyx change the weapon loads from orbit, let her take control of navigation, and after a few minutes he returned to the ground.

"It's perfect," Alex said.

"Unbelievable," Owens said.

"Never a doubt in my mind," Frank declared.

"Be safe, son," Bruce said.

"I will. Get some rest. The protesters will likely be back in the morning," Alex said, before launching back up into the air. He toggled his com-link from the suit's external speakers to his team frequency. "Sly, report."

"That you, team leader? In a shiny new battle suit?"

"Affirmative. What do you see?"

"Nothing," Sly said. "It's been quiet all night."

Sly was flying between two and three hundred meters above the factory, keeping an eye out for any signs of aggression, but fortunately there were none.

"We have reason to believe that there will be an attack," Alex said. "My guess is that the protesters have something planned. I want you to catch a few hours of sleep and have your Titan recharged."

"Roger that, team leader," Sly said. "I didn't get a chance to tell you earlier—I'm glad you're okay."

"Me too," Alex said. "Get some rest while you can."

I have an idea.

Alex switched his com-link to the private setting that only Nyx could hear. She was the voice in his head and could speak to him at any time, no matter what else he was doing with his communication system. His voice, on the other hand, had to be transmitted to her via the com-link.

"What's that?"

There's a news affiliate not too far from your location, Nyx explained. *If you can isolate the EM waves from their servers and sync to them, you might be able to find out what they know.*

"It's worth a try," Alex said. "Send me the coordinates."

His brain translated the data into a direction. He didn't know how exactly he knew where to go—he just did. The news affiliate was only eight kilometers from the Ahzco factory. The Titan battle armor had no exterior lighting, and he was high enough above the city's ambient light to be practically invisible in the night sky. Connecting to the news affiliate's servers wouldn't be difficult, but finding out what was being planned would be like searching for a needle in a haystack. Still, he had to try. Just because a task was difficult didn't mean he could discard it. They needed to know what was coming, and Alex was their best chance of finding out.

Chapter 35

"We have something," Ciara Prince said.

Loman was in his office. Another benefit to the tiny space was the lack of ways people could spy on him. There wasn't much in the little room: just a small desk, his chair, and the computer equipment. There were no decorations, no seating for guests, and not even a window to look out of. He had come to depend on the security of his tiny space.

Ciara Prince had become Loman's chief investigator and his only trusted confidante within the company. She was loyal because she loved her work. Money didn't interest her. She had zero desire to marry or have children. Uncovering secrets was her passion, and as long as Loman Haley continued to give her juicy assignments, she was loyal to him and the company they both served. She was young, dark-skinned, and attractive when she wanted to be, plain when she didn't. She was the perfect investigator, with patience and an innate sense of trustworthiness that made people want to open up to her. She was in a small privacy booth, transmitting on a secure line. Loman could see her face but nothing else about her surroundings.

"Tell me everything," Loman said.

"We found a video blog with Lewan Enterprises' head of security in the background."

"Norma Basher?"

"Correct. She's with a man we haven't been able to identify. The two are having what I'm sure they believe to be a private conversation."

"With someone close enough to hear them recording a blog?" Loman asked.

"No, the blog was recorded at a city park on Angelinos Three, not far from the Lewan Enterprises headquarters."

"Okay," Loman said, sounding skeptical.

"We were able to zoom in on the pair in the background, enhance the video, and used a lip reader to translate what they were discussing."

"Which was?"

"An offer. Completely off the books, of course," Ciara Prince said. "You're going to owe me big time for this one."

"I'll gladly pay up," Loman said. "I always do. What were they discussing?"

"A plan for Lewan Enterprises' withdraw from the Askerria Sector."

Loman didn't respond at first. If what she was telling him was true, it was a major coup. In his experience, if something sounded too good to be true, it probably was.

"You checked out this blog?" Loman asked. "This is starting to sound like a setup."

"Our spies in their company reported that Basher was having frequent meetings out of the office," Ciara explained. "In fact, it was written up that she was being recruited by another mega-corp by our own analysts. That may be true, to a degree—only it isn't another company recruiting her."

"It's the cabal," Loman said.

Ciara Prince nodded. "We still haven't identified the man she met with, but we have concluded two important things. One: he isn't affiliated with any major companies. And two: he's funded by Sigma Services."

Loman sat back in chair. He couldn't believe what he was hearing. Had Ciara Prince really found the agent behind the scenes of all their troubles? Of course, if the man really was with Sigma Services, he was simply a pawn in the machinations of the rich and powerful—but to have a target was such a relief that Loman felt his stress and worry lifting from his shoulders.

"You're certain? It could be a red herring. They have to know we're searching for them," Loman said.

"I'm certain he gets his funds from the same group who started Sigma Services," Ciara Prince said. "We spoke to several vendors outside the Lewan HQ building and they reported seeing Brasher go into the park. My team did an extensive search for recordings posted to social media in that park on the days we know she went there. We were hoping to catch sight of her, perhaps find out what she was up to. We have several confirmed clips of her moving through the park from various pictures and video posts. In all those, she is merely caught in the background, but our facial recognition picked her out easily."

"Your methods are impeccable," Loman said.

"Thank you, sir. We did look into the video blog. It seemed too good to be true, but the blog is real. The woman recording it has a loyal following—nearly six million people watch her videos each week. It's been up for nine years and has hundreds of recordings. They're almost all the same: just her, in front of the camera, giving her opinions about things. She likes to do the videos from different locations, mostly outdoors."

"So the video is legit, and Brasher made a mistake," Loman said.

"It certainly looks that way. The blogger doesn't advertise where or when she'll be filming. On the video, Brasher is meeting with the Sigma Services agent from beginning to end."

"You're saying they were already discussing things when this blogger made the video?"

"Yes, sir. If they were trying to mislead us, odds are good they would have entered once the video began. We're looking into the blogger's finances now, but there don't appear to be any ties to any mega-corporations. Her finances are clean, too. If she took a payoff to be in the park that day, we haven't found evidence of it."

"I want her approached and questioned," Loman said. "Nothing aggressive—unless you discover that she was part of a plan to send us down the wrong track."

"Yes, sir. I've got my people in place," Ciara said.

"You anticipated the order?"

"Yes, sir. It's the only way to be sure. I'm sending in Ted with some Thiopental. He can slip it into her drink and get the truth without her ever knowing she was questioned."

"Excellent," Loman said. "Now tell me exactly what Brasher and this man discussed."

"It was an offer. Lewan Enterprises would get financial compensation for pulling out of the Askerria sector now, and once the new government is in place, a guaranteed permit for exclusive mining in the Askerria sector."

"So they aren't really giving it up?" Loman said. "That makes sense."

"There's more, of course. Brasher will be tapped to be the first commander-in-chief of the new government's military forces."

"Not surprising," Loman said. "The new government is already working deals under the table."

"Power tends to corrupt," Ciara said.

"And absolute power corrupts absolutely," Loman added. "At least we know we were right. The cabal wants us to waste our resources fighting over the Askerria Sector."

"Should we share this information with the other companies?"

"They won't believe it coming directly from us. They'll think it's a ploy to keep them from trying to take control of the mineral rights in Askerria."

"So maybe we leave it out somewhere they can find on their own?"

"If they're smart enough to see it," Loman said.

"And if they're not?"

"Then they can kill each other. I don't care about saving other companies. But when the new government comes after Ahzco, we'll be ready."

Chapter 36

Alex hovered over a midsized building. The roof was cluttered with parabolic satellite dishes, antennas, and long-range transceivers. There were more EM waves coming from the building than any place he'd passed over in his flights across Oslo.

The electromagnetic waves coming from the news agency sounded like the pounding thrum of club music. There were people inside the building sending and receiving messages, despite the late hour. Alex closed his eyes, which was an impulse that didn't affect his ability to see, since the Titan's external cameras fed the information directly into his brain, bypassing his eyes completely. Closing his eyes helped him concentrate.

Syncing with regular computer systems that weren't designed for use with his Implanted Neural Controller was a little like forcing a new key into a lock. It worked, but it took a little more effort. He let the EM waves transform from sound to information as they poured into his brain. There was so much data, and with more coming in every second, it was a little like flipping through the pages of an old-fashioned book, looking for a particular word or phrase. He needed to settle into the computing system and force it to find what he was looking for.

"I'm in," Alex said.

You haven't been sighted. The streets are quiet.

Nyx was using the ship's surveillance cameras to keep watch. Despite the city lights, it was too dark to get a normal picture. Nyx had to use infrared camera and watch for heat sources that might move in the general direction of where Alex hovered. If someone fired a rocket at him, the way they had at the drop ship, odds were good it would kill him, and Alex was glad that Nyx could watch his back, even from thousands of kilometers away.

He discovered a search algorithm and forced the rest of the noise from the building's massive computer servers out of his mind. It was like trying to hear just one type of instrument in a vast orchestra, but he knew he could do it because he had done it before. Syncing with interstellar ships was much easier because the massive computer systems were very clearly defined to control the various aspects of the ship, such as navigation or life support. The news agency, on the other hand, was constantly receiving and sorting data from all over the planet and from various satellites that connected Skandia Seven to the galactic information network.

"I'm ready to do a search."

Look for messages regarding the protests.

Alex did as she requested and got thousands of hits. The protests against private military were generating hundreds of news stories every day.

"We have to narrow it down," Alex said.

It won't be a general message to the masses. Filter out news stories—we're only looking for messages. It will most likely be a mass mailing, probably from an anonymous source, not a person's name. Look for something with a jumble of letters and numbers sent to a group.

Alex had used computers all his life, but he had never studied them or tried his hand at programming or hacking. Nyx was much better versed in computers and how they worked. Her advice narrowed the messages down to three.

"This looks promising," Alex said.

The first message was a request for mention in stories and reports. The message was supposedly from a charity to help the families of those harmed by private military violence, but Alex recognized it as a scam. The second message was from a source that called itself *The People's Voice* and was full of instructions such as words to use, calls to action, and a layout of the ideas people should promote with their news stories. Alex had often heard people complain about news agencies or social movements that sounded more like they were reading from a script than reporting actual news. The second message seemed to be exactly that.

The final message was less clear; it was a short message that had been sent from an anonymous source.

EXPECT ACTION AT VARIOUS LOCATIONS ON SKANDIA SEVEN IN THE SKANDIA SYSTEM, FTA801.

The send date was a week prior, and after listing various mega-corporations with holdings on Skandia Seven, another date was given.

"It's today," Alex said. "I don't know what it is, but something is going down today."

You're sure?

"It's an anonymous mass mailing that says, 'Expect action at various locations on Skandia Seven.' It lists over a dozen companies, including Ahzco. And the date at the end is today."

There's nothing else?

"No," Alex admitted.

Run a search for the person who sent it.

Alex did as she instructed. The sender was a long jumble of letters and numbers. There were no other messages from that particular sender and no information that he could find about the identity of the person who had crafted and sent the message.

Alex didn't stick around. He had gotten all he was going to find at the news agency. Whoever was planning things wasn't dumb enough to put their plans into writing, but the advantage of surprise was lost. Alex didn't know what they were planning, but he knew when and where. If they were going to attack an Ahzco facility, it would be the MBS plant. He disconnected from the news agency and started back toward the factory, ignoring the searing pain that had sprung up behind his eyes.

"Nothing," Alex said to Nyx. "Just the one message."

So we still don't know what they plan to do?

"We can infer from the message that the protesters—or someone using the protesters for cover—plan on striking several of the businesses on that list. Perhaps all of them. Does Ahzco have any other facilities on Skandia Seven?"

Just one moment...There are three distribution centers, basically just big warehouses full of Ahzco products waiting to be shipped to retailers all over the planet. I think the PIL division has a few retail stores in the bigger cities, but that's it. The Titan/ Valkyrie plant is the only manufacturing facility.

"It wouldn't hurt to notify the warehouses that something is suspected and that they should heighten security," Alex said.

I'll contact them myself. But what are you going to do?

"Make sure we're ready," Alex said. "That's all we can do. Hopefully there won't be anything we can't stop in its tracks now that we know about it."

Just be careful. I need to alert Captain Poe.

"Go ahead. We've still got over an hour before the sun rises down here. I don't think the protesters want to do anything in the dark. They want the entire galaxy to see us burn."

Chapter 37

"A source?" Captain Poe asked. It was the first time he had given Nyx his full attention. "What source? From where?"

"Someone on the ground," Nyx lied. "They relayed the message to one of the employees."

"And what did this message say exactly?"

"To expect action today. It listed several companies, including ours."

He looked skeptical.

"I can't say for certain, but it sounds like someone at the local news agency decided to warn us," Nyx said.

Captain Poe clearly wasn't convinced. "It didn't say what this action was? It might not be anything at all, Sergeant."

"I realize that, and hopefully whoever warned us has warned the other companies. I just thought it might be prudent to warn them ourselves."

"Do we have a copy of this message?"

"No, sir."

"Then we do nothing," Poe said. "Our forces are on alert. If the other companies are smart, their people will be ready. Our responsibility is to Ahzco alone. Without proof, the other companies won't believe us, anyway."

"Yes, Captain," Nyx said.

She hadn't really expected him to alert the other forces in the system, but she had to give him the option.

"Is your operator back in full battle armor?" Captain Poe asked.

"Yes, he is, sir."

"Very good. Return to your station and remind all our operators that we are on high-alert. If the protesters have something planned for us today, I want our people ready for it."

Nyx saluted. Captain Poe merely turned back to his plot. He was a good officer but seemed more interested in protecting his ship than the Ahzco factory on Skandia Seven. She hadn't really expected him to care about the other businesses. From a purely capitalist point of view, if the other mega-corporations suffered losses, Ahzco stood to benefit. But Nyx didn't want to see anyone hurt. It was a bit of a catch-22, considering she was a sergeant in the CDF, but she saw her job as a means of protecting people, not hurting others.

When she got back to her station, she put on her headset and checked in with Alex. "I'm back," she said.

"Good to know," Alex replied. "I've just been discussing our situation with Master Sergeant Montgomery. He had a good idea."

"What was that?" Nyx asked.

"We're going to set up as many of the Titan battle suits as we can before the sun comes up."

"They aren't ready to fly yet," Nyx said. "What do you mean set them up?"

"They have dozens of battle suits just waiting to be boxed up and shipped off-planet," Alex said. "They aren't operational or armed, but the protesters don't know that. We'll put them up around the property to make it seem as if we have more forces than we actually have."

"It can't hurt," Nyx said. "A greater show of force might cause the crowds to back down."

"At the very least, we give them more targets to shoot at. The next shift change is just after sun-up. We'll make sure the employees are all as safe as possible inside the factory. After that, we'll just have to wait and see what happens."

"I wish I could do more. I feel helpless."

"You're not. No one likes waiting around for the battle to begin."

She knew he was right. There were things she could do, things that only she could do to help him in a fight. An operator could only do so much in a battle suit, which was exactly why each one was paired with their own controller; plus, two minds are better than one. She knew him better than anyone else, and together, they used the state-of-the-art Titan battle suit to wage war against anyone threatening to harm Ahzco employees. With the mechanics and fabricators who stayed on site through the late shift, the factory could have as many as a hundred innocent employees in harm's way. Whatever she could do to keep them safe—even just sitting and waiting—was worth it.

It just wasn't easy.

The *Currency* was in a geosynchronous orbit above the city of Oslo. Its surveillance cameras were pointed down at the city and able to zoom in right on the factory. As the sun rose, she could see the factory workers had set up nearly twenty extra Titan battle suits. They were spaced along the chain-link fence that surrounded the property.

She checked the time. The first daily shift started at 0700 local time, and her computer showed that it was twenty minutes until seven. The first of the employees would start arriving at any moment. She made sure that she could see the square where the city transit station was located. Alex and Ash were in the air, watching for any signs of the protesters. So far, all was quiet. The employees arrived in in small groups of three or four. Many of the mechanics who had stayed behind at the factory to help with Alex's battle suit took the opportunity to leave.

While Nyx was focused on the factory and the transit station, someone else was watching the city. An announcement came over the ship's speakers: "Protesters are beginning to organize near the city municipal complex."

"Alex, we have visual confirmation that the protesters are gathering," Nyx informed him.

"Copy, we're ready."

She didn't see how they could be ready for something they couldn't predict, but she admired his courage.

The day slowly unfolded. After a brief rally, the demonstrators at the Oslo municipal complex dispersed. Nyx worried that she and Alex were wrong. Mid-day passed. The stress of wondering what was coming and lack of sleep combined to make her feel ill. Her stomach hurt, her head was aching, and her eyes burned. It was hard to continue staring at her computer screens, which only showed the seemingly normal daily life of people on a level-one planet going about their business.

She leaned her head against the divider between her console and the next. Before she knew it, Nyx had nodded off.

Chapter 38

Alex was bored, tired, and growing more frustrated with every moment that slowly ticked by. He was certain that he was right about the message he had found at the news agency—but just because someone sent such a message didn't necessitate that something would actually happen. Perhaps their plans had fallen through. The dispersing of the protesters certainly seemed to back that idea up. Or maybe it was all a hoax, just an effort for an out-of-the-way planet to get a little more attention. Still, no matter how hard Alex tried to dismiss the warning, he couldn't shake the feeling that something was headed their way—something dangerous. Something no one would see coming.

It didn't help that his father was there. Alex had spoken to everyone, from the employees to the chief administrator. The plant was shut down, and most of the employees had been sent home. But as the day passed without incident, Alex began to worry that Ms. Brown would reopen the facility. What if she lost patience, and an attack came right when the workers for the evening shift arrived at the factory?

"Heads up, I've got a child with a backpack approaching."

The warning was given by one of Oscar Company's operators out on the southwest corner of the property. Alex, Sly, and Ash were all patrolling from the air. The approaching child looked to be a preteen with a novelty backpack.

"Looks harmless," Ash said.

"We can't take any chances," Alex said. "Stay alert."

"I think we got bad intel," Sly said.

"There's no one here," Ash added. "No protesters, no media, nothing. It's a waste of time."

The child continued walking down the sidewalk along the Ahzco property fence. He looked up at the battle suits with more than a little fear, but didn't stop.

"What are we, the kiddy police?" one of the operators from Oscar Company said.

"He looks dangerous," someone else added.

"Looks can be deceiving," Monty warned. "Let's not—"

"He dropped his backpack!"

The warning came from another operator. Alex was watching the scene from a hundred meters overhead. The child had shrugged out of his backpack directly across from the public transit entrance and was sprinting toward the stairwell.

"Cut him off," Alex said as he dove down toward the plaza.

Ash was faster and landed right in front of the entrance. The kid skidded to a stop, looking terrified. Alex landed fifteen meters to his right, and Sly was came down on his left. The com-link had erupted in chatter, with Master Sergeant Montgomery barking orders for everyone to move away from the backpack.

"We aren't going to hurt you," Ash said. Her Titan's external speakers were loud in the silence and echoed off the stone walls of the surrounding building.

"What's in the bag, kid?" Sly asked.

Instead of answering or even trying to run away again, the boy dropped to his knees and covered his head with his arms. Alex turned back toward the property, noticing just how close to the factory that section of fencing was. If there was a bomb of any size in the bag, it would blow the fence apart and knock a hole in the side of the factory.

No one saw the real attack coming. It shot up out of the public transit entrance and hit Ash in the middle of her back. Alex didn't see the weapon, and the explosion knocked him off his feet. He hit the brick-covered square and rolled. The unexpected nature of the attack had caught him completely off-guard. When he looked up, Ash was facedown just a couple meters from the cowering child, and the back of her suit was charred black, smoking, and twisted.

"Ash!" Alex shouted.

What happened?

Nyx sounded groggy, but there was no time to ask if she was okay. Alex was on his feet and running to his friend. A thermobaric grenade shot up and out of the darkened stairwell that led down to the public transit train. Sly was moving toward Ash, as well. They both hesitated and ducked. The grenade arced over the square and dropped toward the factory. Before it hit, Alex shot a canister of teargas down the steps into the transit station.

He and Sly were beside Ash's fallen MBS when the grenade hit. Fire blossomed along the rooftop of the building, and the ground shook from the explosion. The factory, like many of the buildings in Oslo, was made from granite blocks. They rippled like water under the stress of the blast, and a large section of the wall and roof collapsed inward.

Alex's first thought was of his father, who had stayed despite Alex's warnings. He and several other mechanics felt like they could be of use and decided to stay. Alex knew his father just wanted to be near his son if violence broke out, but Alex wanted the exact opposite. Before he could do anything at all, small arms fire rained down on them from the rooftop.

"What is happening?" Sly shouted.

"We're under attack!" Alex shouted back. "Stay with her."

He jumped into the air, activating the repulsers on his suit which propelled him straight up. One weapon arm was loaded with tear gas canister, the other was a fully auto projectile cannon loaded with sponge bullets. It infuriated him that he couldn't fight back with equal force, but he used what he had. The auto cannon roared to life, spewing the collapsible, non-lethal bullets onto a crowd of people on one rooftop. They dove for cover, but most weren't fast enough. He saw several topple to the roof, their weapons flinging from their hands.

More bullets were pinging off his armor. Alex turned in midair and fired at the second group, just as the explosives in the backpack went off. A pressure wave slammed into Alex, who had to fight to keep from crashing his Titan battle suit.

Alex!

There was no time to answer. He had to feed power to the suit to keep it airborne and above the buildings.

"Another bomb," Alex snarled.

Reports are hitting the network. There are attacks all over the planet.

Alex didn't have time to even consider attacks elsewhere. The sidewalk where the backpack had been was gone. In its place was a crater that took out the entire street and part of the plaza. The factory was falling down, smoke rose like an angry black cloud, and a huge fireball was rolling up into the sky.

When Alex turned back to the gunmen on the rooftop, they were scrambling to their feet, but only to flee. He wanted to mow them down again, but it was no use. The bullets he had at his disposal were meant to repel a crowd, not capture or kill anyone. Alex looked down to check on Sly, but he was gone. Looking back up, the sky was clear. Sly was nowhere in sight.

"Sly? Where are you? Do you read?"

"I'm on my ass," he said. "The shockwave from the explosion knocked me down the stairs."

"Are you okay?"

"I'm alive but taking fire. Permission to engage?"

"Granted," Alex said.

With one last glance at Ash, who still lay prone on the cobblestones of the plaza, Alex shot upward.

"Ash is down," Alex said on the private channel to Nyx. "She's not responding."

I'll check on her. Where are you going?

"This might not be over," Alex said.

He was circling the property. A group of people with rifles on the far side of the factory were taking pop-shots at the MBS's of Oscar Company. Alex had to circle the billowing cloud of smoke and dust thrown up by the wreckage of the factory. Only one corner of the massive building still remained upright. It took all of Alex's willpower not to rush down and search for his father. In the Titan battle suit, he was helpless. The Titan had no arms—only weapons—and no way to start moving the rubble to search for survivors.

"Master Sergeant Montgomery, what's your status?" Alex asked over the tactical channel.

"I'm down...Ace...I can't...move."

Monty's voice was strained. He was obviously in pain, and even though Alex hadn't spotted him yet, it was clear that he had been caught in the blast. All Alex could do was hope his battle suit's armor had saved him. At least he still had power and could communicate.

"Where are you, Master Sergeant?"

"Under...the wreckage...the blast threw me...back."

"You're in the factory?"

"Affirm...ative," he groaned.

"We'll get to you as soon as the threat is neutralized." Alex came at the fighters from the air, pelting them with sponge bullets. Most threw down their weapons and ran for cover, but a few recognized the non-lethal ammo couldn't hurt them permanently.

Alex left the stragglers for Oscar Company, who could target them more effectively than he could. As he circled back around, there was white smoke billowing from the entrance to the transit station.

"Sly?"

"On my way out," he replied. "Had to use tear gas to clear the platform. The fighters have fled down the tracks."

"That's good enough. We've got to help the wounded now."

Alex, Ash's suit is completely offline. There's no way to know if she survived.

"We have to get her out of that suit, Sly," Alex ordered.

"I'm on it. I'll have to bail out of my Titan though."

"Do it," Alex said. "I'm going to help the people trapped in the factory."

Chapter 39

Alex made two more passes, searching for threats of any kind. There were none, but he saw smoke rising from other parts of the city.

"Tell me what you're hearing," Alex said.

There are reports from around the planet of attacks on large corporate holdings, Nyx explained. *Terrorist-style bombings, mobs of gunmen, and a Rhine Company manufacturing plant was driven into by a massive delivery truck. There are casualties being reported, but no one knows for sure what is happening. There's looting in most of the cities. Warehouses and retail stores are being broken into and set on fire, and their goods are being destroyed.*

"All right, I've got to leave my MBS, but I'm staying linked. I'll be able to hear you. If there's danger, let me know. You're our eye in the sky. We have to try and save the people in the factory."

Roger that, Cronus One. Be careful!

Alex didn't have the time to reply. He had just landed and popped open his battle suit. Climbing out, he was two meters off the ground. He jumped down, falling to his knees and rolling over his shoulder. He came up on his feet and started running toward the factory.

"Dad! Dad!" Alex shouted.

There was no answer. The only sound was the crackle of fire and the whir of the Destroyer's electric engines as they approached. Alex looked over his shoulder. There were three members of Oscar Company behind him. One popped the battle suit open and stood up.

"Sergeant, where do you want us?"

"Get out of those Destroyers. We have to dig them out."

Alex didn't wait for the operators from Oscar Company to comply. He ran to the wreckage and started looking for movement. He saw an arm sticking out of the rubble and ran toward it. Unfortunately, the arm wasn't connected to a body. Alex felt his stomach heave, but there was no time to be sick. Somewhere in the wreckage and debris of the factory, his father needed him.

"Sergeant?" said a corporal with "Hanes" printed on his compression fatigues. He was leading two other operators who had left their Destroyers to help.

"Over there," Alex said, pointing to a large heap that was covered in metal beams, twisted sheet metal, chunks of foam insulation, and molded plastic. "Master Sergeant Monty is there. We have to dig him out and get him out of his MBS."

"Roger that," Hanes said. "Let's go."

He was followed by a male and a female operator, and the three of them began pulling and tossing the debris away. Alex wanted to search for his father, but he knew he should help Monty. The master sergeant was still alive, and Alex had no idea about his father.

Emergency help is on the way, Alex.

The sound of sirens could be heard echoing throughout the city.

Sly is working to get Ash out of her suit. No updates yet.

Alex began to move debris with the corporals from Oscar Company. Time passed. Before Alex knew it, the sun was setting. Sly had gotten Ash out of her Titan battle suit, but she was unconscious and couldn't be woken up. First responders had taken her to the hospital, and Sly had joined Alex working to free the men and women trapped in the rubble of the factory.

Four members of Oscar Company had been caught in the blast or trapped when the building fell. Three had been on the roof when it collapsed, but two of those Destroyers had managed to drive free of the wreckage. The other had landed upside down, but the operator was unharmed.

Master Sergeant Montgomery's Destroyer was crushed, not unlike Alex's old Titan. One of the veteran operator's legs was gashed in the attack, and he had lost a lot of blood, but Alex felt confident he would survive. They found another wounded operator, and one was dead when they finally got the Destroyer open.

It was late into the night, and they had been moving debris for hours before the first mechanic was found. Nyx had filled Alex in on the attacks worldwide; they were being called rage-fueled riots, but Alex knew better. They were well-timed, coordinated attacks by groups who had been supplied with weapons and instructions on how to use them. The small arms fire was useless against mechanized battle suits, but in other locations there were multiple deaths from the attacks.

Alex was exhausted and filthy when they pulled the first mechanic from the rubble. He was unconscious, but alive. Two more were found soon after.

"Bruce Evans," one of the men said, his face coated with a thick layer of dust and grime. He was leaning on Corporal Hanes and being helped toward a first aid station. Alex heard him talking as they moved past him. "He told us to get under the conveyor belts where the battle suits are made. It's the only reason we survived."

Alex felt a spark of hope; his father had known what to do. Surely if any of the mechanics survived, he had. Alex continued digging with renewed strength. Six mechanics were pulled out alive. Three others had been found dead near the same section of the factory. It was almost midnight when someone called to Alex.

"Sergeant Evans! Hey! Over here."

It was a corporal named Sansabar, a woman with large eyes and a dark complexion. She and the rest of Oscar Company had worked hard to find the survivors. Alex moved to her side, stumbling and crawling over the mounds of debris. A large metal beam was pinning down a chunk of metal. It looked like a Titan chest piece. From a gap between the metal and the crumpled edge of the conveyor, a hand appeared.

"Alex," a husky voice said. "You're okay?"

"Dad!" Alex shouted. "Are you hurt?"

"No, nothing serious," Bruce Evans said. "But you've got to get us out, Alex. Frank is hurt. He's bleeding, and I can't stop it."

"We're working on it, Dad, just hang on," Alex said.

When he turned, Corporal Sansabar already had cargo straps in hand, ready to pull the heavy steel beam away. They attached the straps to a line connected to one of the Destroyers, which was pulling the large parts of the wreckage out of the ruined factory. It took a few minutes to get everything secure.

"We're about to start moving the big stuff," Alex said to his father. "Don't move."

"Okay, okay," Bruce said. "Just hurry. We're losing him."

Alex waved, and the Destroyer started pulling. The metal groaned, then shifted. The debris pile around the conveyor where his father was sheltering shifted. Alex could only hope nothing was falling in on his father or smashing him with the awful weight of the heavy beam.

Once the Destroyer had pulled the steel beam away, Alex rushed back and hefted the piece of metal that had dropped down beside the conveyor belt and trapped his father underneath. It was heavy, but Alex was fueled by the need to get his father safely out of the wreckage. He lifted it slightly, turned, and let it drop to the ground. Bruce Evans was under the conveyor belt, hunched over the prone figure of Frank, the head mechanic, who looked pale and had Bruce's belt wrapped tightly around his upper thigh.

"He's lost a lot of blood," Bruce croaked.

"We'll take him," Sansabar said, as Alex helped his father crawl out from under the conveyor belt.

Bruce Evans looked like an elderly man. His back was hunched, and his hair was white from the dust. Alex held him, trying not to rush him out of the cramped position he'd been stuck in for hours. It was obvious that Bruce was in pain, but his only concern was for his friend.

"Franks leg got cut," Bruce said, panting a little. "It's deep. I tried to make a tourniquet, but he needs a doctor."

A pair of EMTs with an emergency hover-gurney got Frank onto their floating device and started checking his vitals. Alex heard one say that his heartbeat was weak. Alex had Bruce sit on a mangled machine to catch his breath and let the muscles in his back and legs loosen up a bit before they tried to crawl out of the piles of debris from the fallen factory.

"Is he going to be okay?" Bruce asked.

"They're taking him to the hospital, dad. I'm sure he'll be okay. We're taking you there too." Alex helped his father to his feet, pulled one of the older man's arms across his shoulders, and started helping him navigate their way out of the wreckage.

"How many made it?" Bruce asked.

"Eight counting you and Frank," Alex said. "The others said you told them what to do."

"I heard the explosion," Bruce said. "Protocol in the mines was to get under something once the ground started shaking."

"Those men owe you their lives."

"They wouldn't have stayed if not for me," Bruce said. "They would have been home with their wives and children. There were a lot more than eight of us in here. All those technicians you saved from the drop ship—they were in another part of the factory."

"We'll find them," Alex said.

Unfortunately, he knew that most were dead. They had been in the section where the MBS chargers were, and it just happened to be closest to the massive explosion. A few might survive, but they were badly injured. Many had been ripped apart in the blast or crushed to death under the rubble.

"Your mom won't like this," Bruce said, before lapsing into a fit of coughing.

"She'll get over it," Alex said. "Especially once she learns that you're a hero."

"That's not true," Bruce said. "You're the one out there risking your life."

"I'm just doing my job," Alex said. "And this time I really messed up."

"This isn't your fault."

"I knew it was coming, and yet I failed to stop it," Alex said.

Sly just finished another patrol. There's no sign of the attackers.

Nyx's voice in his head was usually welcome, but at that moment he didn't want to hear her. He didn't want to think that the people responsible for so much carnage and death would go unpunished. Alex thought of the young boy, perhaps only ten or eleven years old, who had carried the bomb and left it on the sidewalk beside the factory. In the battle that followed, the boy had disappeared. It made him ill to think that someone who was supposed to love and protect him would willingly put his young life at risk for their twisted political ideology.

When Alex and Bruce reached the first aid tent, an EMT sat Bruce down and began checking his vitals.

"Your blood pressure is high, and your pulse ox is low, Mr. Evans. I think it's best if we send you to the hospital for a thorough exam."

"No, no, I'm fine," Bruce said.

"Got to the hospital, Dad," Alex urged him. "You can check on your friends, and Mom will be able to find you there."

"She won't be happy."

"She will," Alex insisted. "You're alive, and that's all that matters."

Alex watched while his father was loaded into an ambulance along with another man with a bandage on his head. The ambulance rose up on repulser engines and hummed quietly away toward the city.

Was that your father?

Nyx was watching him from above. He looked up.

Is he going to be okay?

Alex gave her a thumbs up, then went back to helping the emergency workers dig through the rubble.

Chapter 40

Loman had been at the office since 0600 and decided to go home eleven hours later. He was waiting on the lift, thinking of all the things that still needed to be done. His job had only become more demanding as of late, and he was beginning to wonder why he was fighting so hard to keep things the way they were. He could just resign and live the rest of his life on the savings and investments he had. It would be a comfortable life, too, on any world—or maybe even a luxury space station. He was enjoying the fantasy of spending his days lounging by a pool with a view of a nebula while attentive servers kept the gin martinis coming throughout the day. It was a pleasant daydream, which was interrupted when the lift door opened and Loman saw his counterpart, Zan Fordham, already inside. The elevator had been coming down from the top floor, which meant Zan had been with the CEO, Ian Gentry.

Loman might have waited, but the elevator could take a long time to travel down nearly two hundred floors and back up. He stepped inside and saw that the button for the lobby was already lit up.

"Calling it a day," Loman asked as the lift doors closed and the elevator car started descending.

"I have a dinner meeting," Zan said.

"Really? With who?"

"That's really none of your concern."

"Actually, it is. We're counterparts—I'm the executive vice president of security, and you're a misplaced manager trying to take my job."

The civility between Loman and Zan had ended the moment the VP saw Zan agreeing with the media about Ahzco's military's heavy-handed treatment of civilians. It had occurred the night Zan had taken out Alex Evans and his Titan team. When the group of operators and controllers had refused to talk ill of the company, Zan had done it for them. Since then, Loman had stopped trying to manipulate the little, rotund manager. Instead, he made sure that Zan knew exactly how he felt about him.

"At least you won't be surprised when the board throws you out on your ear," Zan said with a sneer.

"And then what will happen?" Loman said, whirling around suddenly and moving dangerously close to Zan. The smaller man tried to back away, but he was stuck in the corner of the lift car.

"What?" Zan sputtered.

"What will happen when I'm gone, Zan? Are you going to take over? You don't know the first thing about security. You don't know or care about how we do things. You've been here for over a month, and all you do is waste time and money. Look at what you're wearing!"

He was wearing what amounted to a bed sheet with sleeves and leggings. It hung limp around his protruding middle and looked ridiculous.

"This is a Brumar suit, custom-tailored," Zan said.

"You're a fool," Loman said. "Just a pawn in a game I doubt you're even aware of. Let me tell you what happens here the moment I am pushed out of the company: the entire security division will be shuttered."

"That's preposterous," Zan said, but his voice was trembling.

"And if this asinine central government comes to power, the entire company will be broken up. Not that you'll have a dog in that fight, because once the security division is folded, Lynn Faulk will no longer have a need for you."

"You don't know her," Zan said. "She respects me."

"She's using you. If you can't see that, then you deserve what's coming. I hope you're putting as much of the money you're throwing around into an off-world account as you can. You're going to need it."

"You're just bitter," Zan said. "Resentful."

"You're damn right I am," Loman said. "Our company— no, the entire galaxy—is under threat, and you could be helping, but instead you're too busy trying to be popular with the "in" crowd. Those people don't care about you. They're using you, just like Lynn Faulk is using you. They'll never think of you as one of them, Zan. And when the money is gone, they wouldn't spit on you if you were on fire."

"You've lost it," the smaller man replied, swiping at the sweat springing out on his upper lip. "You're crazy."

"Maybe so," Loman said, turning back around and wishing he could return to the dream of idling his days away at a luxury space station.

The truth was, Loman didn't really care about luxury or material possessions. He was a man of action who found fulfillment in doing his job. That didn't mean he didn't enjoy a drink at the end of the day or being able to travel as freely as he did as the VP of a mega-corporation, but he honestly thought he was doing what was best for Ahzco. He believed in the free market and in protecting the people who made Ahzco such an incredible company: the employees.

The lift came to a stop on the ground level, and both men got out. Zan hurried past Loman, who reached the large, revolving door that led out of the building's lobby just behind the smaller man. There were two transports waiting in the courtyard. One was a small, economy transport, the other was a large, executive, luxury vehicle. Loman watched Zan crawl into the larger transport and shook his head at the waste. Loman didn't mind the finer things in life, but Zan hadn't earned the money he was spending. Everything he did was paid for by a company spending account, which Lynn Faulk had insisted on. Zan was there to disrupt things, distract Loman from his work, and report back everything he did to Lynn Faulk. Fortunately for Loman, Zan wasn't good at spying and was more interested in spending money doing any actual work.

Loman climbed into the economy transport and gave the pilot his home address. Then he pulled his PIL from his coat pocket and swiped it on to read the news reports of the day. The transport lifted up and began moving across the city. He hadn't gone far when Loman's preferred news app finished downloading the latest headlines. The first thing he read made him feel like he couldn't breathe.

RIOTS BREAK OUT ON SKANDIA SEVEN. MEGA-CORPS TARGETED BY ANGRY MOBS SEEKING AN END TO PRIVATE MILITARIES.

"Take me back!" Loman ordered the pilot.

"What's that?"

"Back to Ahzco HQ building. I have to go back right now."

Chapter 41

It was late at night when the last unaccounted-for body was found. Alex, Sly, and eleven members of Oscar Company worked tirelessly with first responders digging through the rubble until every person who had been in the factory was found. The chief administrator, Cathy Brown, was on site working with the EMTs and keeping track of every person. She knew them all by name and made sure no one gave up before every person was accounted for.

Once they were finished, the first responders from Oslo moved on. The operators gathered together. Four were still in their battle armor standing watch, but the rest collapsed onto the grass of the green space, exhausted after hours of rescue work.

"We going to the hospital?" Sly asked

Alex didn't want to move. Every muscle in his body ached, and he was so tired he felt sick. Administrator Brown moved among the operators, handing them bottles of water.

"Yeah," Alex replied to Sly. "We should."

"Thank you for everything," Cathy Brown said as she handed Alex a bottle of water.

"We failed," Alex said.

"No," she replied. "You did your job. You stayed the course, and you saved lives. More importantly, you made a connection with the people here. And that is something that can't be bought or manipulated by the media."

Alex wanted to respond by asking what good it did, but he was too tired. He sucked greedily at the bottle of water and let the cool liquid rush down his throat, which was coated with dust and dirt.

"We need to check in with the *Currency*," Alex said.

"The admin building is practically untouched," Brown said. "The terrorists targeted the factory and nothing else."

Alex wanted to point out that they also targeted Ash and every operator on the property. Even the empty Titan battle suits, which had been set up like toy soldiers in an effort to deter the attack, had been shot with small arms fire. Most had fallen over after the bomb had gone off that destroyed the factory.

"Stay here," Alex said. "I'll make the report. Get orders, and then we'll go to the medical facility and check on our people."

"Roger that, team leader," Sly said. He poured some water on his face and rubbed it dry with the sleeve of his compression fatigues.

Alex got slowly to his feet and then followed Cathy Brown across the lawn toward the blocky, two-story building. They pushed through the entrance and went straight to the conference room. Ms. Brown checked the connection, and they waited a few minutes for Captain Poe to appear. He looked tired.

"Sergeant Evans," Poe said. "You look like hell. What's the latest?"

"We got the last of the workers out of the rubble. There were twelve survivors among the workers. We lost both technician teams. A few are still alive but seriously injured. They were evacuated to the local hospital. Master Sergeant Taylor Montgomery was injured, along with four other members of Oscar Company. Two were killed in action. The rest are here with me."

"Well, not the most successful mission, but at least you survived. Any word on our wounded?"

"No, Captain, we'll go to the hospital soon," Alex said.

"Your operators showed exceptional bravery," Cathy Brown spoke up.

"Thank you, Administrator Brown. I wish we could have done more. Unfortunately, with our drop ship down, I'm going to have to ask for your help a bit longer."

"The administration building is still intact," Cathy said. "They can bivouac here until they're needed elsewhere. I'm sure the mechanics saved by the operators will be glad to help out with their battle suits."

"Power is going to be an issue," Alex said.

"All right, see to the wounded and get me an update," Captain Poe said. "I'll do my best to find transport for Oscar Company and Cronus Team back to the *Currency*. Until then, remain on the property and see to your MBS's."

"Yes sir, Captain," Alex said.

The image disappeared, and Alex turned to Cathy. She started talking about getting them food and transportation, but Alex's attention was diverted to movement behind her. They were in the conference room that had a full glass wall dividing it from the waiting area and the building's break room. Alex grabbed Cathy Brown by the shoulders and pushed her down. He dove on top of her as bullets ripped through the glass, which shattered into thousands of tiny shards and rained down on them. Alex immediately rolled, pulling Cathy Brown with him, as close to the conference table as the row of chairs would allow.

Alex's ears were ringing, and beside him Cathy was screaming, but the shooting suddenly stopped. Alex looked up and saw a lone gunman. It was a man with a thick beard. Alex saw the dark whiskers glistening with oil. He didn't look like a criminal—in fact he looked almost as terrified as Alex felt. The weapon he was carrying was some type of ancient-looking submachine gun. The fully automatic, miniature rifle had a short barrel and a folding stock. The breech was stuck open from one of the shell casings that had jammed. The shooter was looking at the weapon as if it had betrayed him.

Without a conscious thought about what he should do, Alex rolled away from Cathy Brown and rose to his feet. He ignored the stabs of pain from the glass shards and dashed toward the gunman. The man looked up, horrified, but managed to raise the gun like a club. He swung it at Alex's head, but the operator was faster, ducking low to tackle the gunman around the waist. The two men went down, and the real struggle began. Alex had no weapons, and the gunman was desperate. Fortunately, Alex had landed on top of the man and raised up to get the leverage needed to land a solid blow—but before he could, there was a flash of light reflecting off polished metal. From somewhere, the gunman had drawn a knife. He thrust it up toward Alex's throat, but the hand-to-hand combat training Alex had had on the *Republic* on the journey to the Carthage system kicked in. Alex seized the gunman's wrist and twisted. The knife blade turned, and Alex leaned as much of his weight toward the knife as possible. The gunman's arms bent under Alex's weight.

"No," the man wailed. "Don't!"

Alex kept pressing. He could feel the gunman's body shaking beneath him. The look on the stranger's face was pure terror. He wasn't strong enough to hold Alex off, and the CDF operator wasn't going to stop until the threat was neutralized.

"Please," the gunman begged.

He might have dropped the knife and tried to surrender, but Alex's grip on his wrist held the weapon in place. The tip of the blade sank lower and lower, finally pressing into the gunman's chest. He screamed, but Alex didn't stop. The thought of holding back didn't even cross his mind. He was thinking of Ash and Monty, and how his father had nearly been killed by people like the gunman. To them, the attack was simply an activity, a way to show their dedication to a cause. But it had cost lives. The bodies he had helped pull from the rubble were running through Alex's head as he drove the knife down to its guard into the man's chest. With a jerk, the gunman ceased resisting.

When Alex rolled over the man's body a second later, he was certain the gunman was dead. Cathy Brown was sitting up, looking at Alex. There was glass in her hair and several small cuts on her face. The silky blouse she wore was already coated with dust and sweat. There were tear streaks down the grime on her face.

"Is he..."

"Yeah," Alex said, getting slowly to his feet. "You better let me check the rest of the building."

There was no one else in the admin offices, and Alex rejoined Cathy in the lobby. She was trembling, and it was clear that she was at the limit of what she could endure.

"Why don't you stay here?" Alex said. "I'll move the body. We'll clean up the glass and make sure this building is secure. You can go home."

She looked at him, her bottom lip pinched between her teeth. It was the first time Alex had seen her calm demeanor crack.

"Do you think?" she said. "Just long enough to clean up. I could come right back."

"There's no need," Alex said, extending a hand to help her to her feet. "Keep all your people home."

"All right," she said, a clear note of relief in her voice.

They pushed out the doors and started back toward the green space. The property owned by the Ahzco corporation was dark, but Alex could still see the rubble of the factory. Sirens were wailing in the distance. They had been heard off and on all night. Several people Alex had helped from the rubble had been rushed away in ambulances with sirens and lights. The sounds barely registered in Alex's mind.

"What happened in there?" Sly said, approaching in the dark. "Did we hear gunshots?"

"Yeah," Alex said. "But the threat is neutralized."

"It is?" Sly asked.

Cathy Brown nodded but didn't speak.

"What's the word, Sergeant?" Corporal Hanes asked.

"We'll take shelter in the admin building," Alex said. "There's a lot of broken glass inside though. And a body."

"What about visiting the hospital?" Sly asked.

"We can—once we find transportation," Alex said.

"The Destroyers are running just fine," Corporal Sansabar said.

"Yeah, but after tonight we aren't rolling through the city in battle suits," Alex said.

"Why not?" another member of Oscar Company asked. "It's no less than these bastards deserve."

"Not everyone in the city was responsible for the attack," Alex said. "We have to keep our cool."

"Are those sirens coming this way?" Hanes asked.

Alex turned. They could see the flashing lights, and the sirens had gotten louder. He wasn't sure what was happening. Perhaps someone had heard the gunshots and called the authorities. Alex didn't feel bad for killing the gunman; it was completely justified, and not simply because of the attack on the Ahzco factory. His life and that of Cathy Brown had been threatened. Killing the gunman was a clear act of self-defense, yet despite knowing that, he still felt a tremor of fear. His heart rate sped up as several police vehicles flew over the surrounding buildings and hovered in the air at the edges of the Ahzco property.

Alex, what is happening?

He couldn't answer her. His INC allowed him to hear her, but outside the Titan he had no way to answer her question. Plus, he really had no idea what was going on.

"Hands in the air!" a voice boomed from the law enforcement vehicles. "You are being detained for acts of terrorism."

Alex saw the weapons turrets on the Destroyer battle suits, still manned by four members of Oscar Company, swivel to point at the law enforcement vehicles.

"No!" Alex shouted. "Stand down. We all stand down. Do not fire. Everyone out of your battle suits."

He wasn't the ranking officer on the scene. Oscar Company had two members who were sergeant-grade, and both had more seniority than Alex, but they were content to let him take charge. There was a tense moment when Alex wasn't sure that the operators wouldn't open fire on the authorities. The entire group was stressed, exhausted, and looking for someone to blame. The police coming to the scene and treating the CDF operators as if they were criminals didn't help. Things could get ugly very quickly.

"Should we get back to our armor?" Sly asked in a tense whisper.

"No," Alex said loudly. "They aren't our enemy. No one move."

One of the occupied Destroyers powered down, the protective armor opening like a clamshell. Alex breathed a sigh of relief as the others quickly followed a suit. Two law enforcement vehicles landed. Six armored men with rifles got out. They had "OPD" printed in reflective material on their armor. They fanned out around the group of operators.

The second vehicle was an armored transport. He settled on the ground between the rubble from the factory and the admin building. The rear hatch opened, and two more armed men got out.

"Who's in charge here?" shouted one of the law enforcement officials.

"I am," Cathy Brown said. She sounded more like herself as she stepped forward. "I'm the chief administrator of this facility."

"And you have private military on site?" the policeman asked.

"Yes," Cathy replied. "Some are here, some at the hospital. As I'm sure you know, we were attacked today. Our factory was destroyed by a bomb."

"We are detaining all private military personnel," the policeman said, "including armed, private security."

"On what grounds?" Sly asked angrily.

"Acts of terrorism," the policeman said. "Let me be clear. We have been given the authority to use deadly force. If you resist us, we will open fire."

Alex heard grumbling, but no one resisted outright. "We aren't the enemy here," Alex said. "We were trying to protect Ahzco property and employees."

"Looks like you're really good at your jobs," the policeman said. "Get on your knees, lace your fingers together, and keep them on top of your head."

Chapter 42

"Loman, what are you doing?" Ian Gentry, CEO of Ahzco asked as Loman charged through his office toward the door that led to his private landing pad.

"I'm going to the Skandia System," Loman said.

"Do you really think that's a good idea?" Gentry said.

"Our facility was attacked," Loman said. "It's going to happen again somewhere else. You mark my words, Gentry. There will be attacks on every level-one planet. I'm not going to just sit in my office and hope things get better."

"And rushing off to the Skandia system will?" the CEO asked.

"It's the least I can do. You should come with me. Let's show solidarity with our people in the field."

Gentry looked down, and his voice changed. "I...I can't."

"Why not? You're the CEO. You can do whatever you want."

"I have a meeting today with Lynn Faulk," he said.

"So cancel."

"You don't cancel with the chairwoman of your board of directors, Loman. Not if you want to keep your job."

"My God, man, is that really what you're worried about right now?"

"It's what I'm always worried about, and you should be, too."

Loman wasn't sure what he should say. He didn't care about losing his job, but there was a fight coming. Lynn Faulk and her ultra-rich cohorts were determined to take control of the galaxy. Loman didn't know if it was possible to stop them, but he was determined to try. And from the way Gentry was acting, it was a good bet that Lynn Faulk had already gotten to him.

"Well, I'm not," Loman said. "I'm worried about the people putting their lives on the line for this company. I will not let them down."

He turned and hurried through the short hallway and up the flight of stairs. He opened the door to the roof and went quickly to the transport.

"Get me to the nearest shuttle depot," Loman ordered. "I've got to get up to the spaceport."

"Yes sir, Mr. Haley," the pilot said.

Loman sat back in the butter-soft, calf-skin leather seat of the CEO's private transport. Gentry could have shut him down. One order, and the pilot would have refused to take Loman anywhere. But either because Gentry still had a sliver of humanity left, or maybe because he was just a complete coward who was unable to stand up to anyone, he hadn't grounded the transport. Loman was thankful for that.

He pulled out his PIL and sent an emergency message to Colonel Chastain, ordering her to take every available CDF asset to the Askerria sector. Then he sent a message to Ciara Prince, telling her to get word to every mega-corp with military forces: *Warn them about Sigma Services and the secret alliance of moguls.*

Tell them if they want to fight, they can join us in the Askerria sector. Then get somewhere safe. I'll be in touch.

He hoped that was true, and he hoped he would have the chance to see Ciara Prince again. But things were changing, and he knew they would never be the same again. The future would be new and different. All he could hope for was that things would get better, and he was determined to do everything in his power to make it so.

Epilogue

Lynn Faulk walked into the underground conference room. Her people had already run a sweep, and she knew the signal-blocking technology built into the walls, ceiling, and even the floor made the space as private as possible on a world teeming with people and technology.

CEO Ian Gentry was already waiting for her. She didn't smile, but she felt a thrill of satisfaction when powerful men ran to carry out her demands. She had ordered the meeting, and instead of joining the CEO in his large office on the top floor of the Ahzco building, she had insisted they convene in the secret lounge that only the top executives even knew existed. It was deep underground, a secure haven where company policies could be decided in private. Gentry was seated, but he got up hastily and looked like a child being called on the carpet by their parents.

"Ms. Faulk, it's good to see you," Gentry looked around the room.

There was no one in the room but himself, Faulk, and one of her assistants, which were really just bodyguards. The assistant looked like a killer, even in a business suit and dark, computer-aided glasses. Faulk saw Gentry trying not to stare at the bulge under her assistant's coat, where his powerful laser pistol was kept close at hand.

"Gentry, let's talk," Faulk said, sliding smoothly into a chair beside the CEO.

He was clearly nervous, and she guessed he was expecting to be fired. Officially, Lynn Faulk didn't have the authority to fire Gentry or anyone else in the company. She was chairwoman of the board of directors. But if she wanted him gone, no one would fight her over it. Chief Executive Officer Gentry was in charge of running Ahzco and ensuring that it remained profitable, but it was the BOD who set the tone, direction, and vision for the company. Faulk had nothing to do with the hundreds of products Ahzco produced, but she had bought into the company at a steady rate over time. She had the largest percentage of the company's shares —nearly eighteen percent. It was more than any other single person. Entire worlds cost less than her investment in Ahzco. But she wasn't interested in products or things to own; she was a woman of singular focus. That dedication and mental fortitude had driven her to become one of the richest people in the galaxy—not that money was her aim, either. She had more money than she would need for a dozen lifetimes. What Lynn Faulk worked tirelessly for wasn't financial gain or success. It was *power* that she wanted—and not just the kind of power her money entitled her to, nor the kind of power that made Ian Gentry fear for his job. She wanted him to tremble at her feet in fear for his *life*.

"Of course," Gentry said. "What...what's on your mind?"

He was having trouble swallowing. Fear did that to some people, Lynn knew. His mouth was dry, his body full of nervous energy, his bowels watery. Ian Gentry—a rich, powerful man—was essentially quivering before her. She suppressed the smile pulling at the corners of her mouth. It was never a good idea to let her inferiors know she was pleased.

"Rumor has reached me that a bomb threat was issued against the company recently," Lynn said.

Gentry visibly relaxed a little. He was expecting the worst, and he probably thought that Haley's handing of the bomb threat was a win for the executive team.

"Yes, that's true," he said. "We were threatened, but the security personnel was on top of it. They handled the situation without word leaking to the press or even most of the building."

"How did they manage that?" Lynn asked.

She had heard rumors from her own people, but none could explain how or why Loman Haley's people had discovered the plot to blow up the Ahzco building before the bomber had a chance to reveal himself. She had, of course, been partly behind the threat—not that she would ever destroy the Ahzco universal HQ building. That would be bad for business, and while Lynn Faulk could afford to lose trillions of credits, she didn't relish the idea.

"One of the operators sensed the bombs via their Implanted Neural Controller," Gentry said. "It was quite impressive, really. And the bombs weren't actually explosives at all," he went on with a chuckle. "Apparently, the bomber had been scammed. Anyway, when the fake bombs were powered on, the operator sensed the EM waves."

Lynn felt a tremor deep within her carefully constructed facade. Was it really possible, she wondered, for an operator to distinguish EM waves in a city full of electronics? It didn't seem possible to her, but she knew something strange had occurred. Her plan had been to embarrass Loman Haley and push him out of the company. His network of spies and complete control of one of the largest, most sophisticated private militaries made him dangerous to her plans. She didn't need to embarrass him to remove him from Ahzco, but she did need to cause a fissure between the executive VP and the military forces he controlled. That was a key component to her overall aims.

"Who was this operator?" Lynn asked.

"A young man named Ace Evans," Gentry said. "Ace may not be his real name. Loman would know better than me. He's one of Loman's star operators. They were on Arcadia after almost single-handedly winning the victory on Carthage Prime. It was a kind of reward for their excellence in the field, I believe. You know, meet the CEO, tour Arcadia—that sort of thing. They would still be here if not for the protests."

Lynn knew about the protests. She wasn't the mastermind behind them, but she knew who was. Everything was coming together, but the operator was an asset she hadn't counted on. The fact that he could pick up EM waves from the sub-basement was astounding. He was clearly a highly sensitive person, and if his skills with the INC were actually what led to Loman Haley disrupting her plan, then she needed to find a way to bring the operator onto her team.

"Interesting," Lynn Faulk said. "I would like to meet this operator. Ace Evans, did you say? What an interesting name."

"Well, that shouldn't be a problem," Gentry said with a frown. "I'm sure Loman could—"

"No, no," Lynn Faulk said. "Don't bother Loman, he has enough on his plate to deal with. I want you to set up a meeting with this operator. Let's keep it off the books. We wouldn't want the others getting jealous."

"Oh, okay," Gentry said.

"These are dangerous times," Faulk continued. "Our companies could be destroyed if we aren't careful. Millions of people could lose their jobs."

Gentry nodded. She could see his throat moving as he tried to think of what to say. It was obvious that his fear was back, and his mouth had gone dry. Another flutter of satisfaction passed through her.

"In times like these, we need to utilize every asset we have," Faulk said. "And if this operator is as talented as you say, well then, we owe it to our stockholders to make sure he's put to the very best use."

"I see," Gentry managed to say.

Lynn Faulk knew that he didn't see. He was clueless. He was a good manager perhaps, proficient in keeping the cogs turning, but he couldn't see what was so clear to her. Humanity was busy spreading through the galaxy, and a few powerful people would rise to the top of an incredible empire. She planned to be one of those people at the very pinnacle, and Ace Evans would either help her or end up cast aside like every other person she no longer had a use for.

She looked at Gentry. His time was running out, but for the moment he still had some value. The poor pathetic soul would soon be forgotten, just another disgraced CEO. Her star was on the rise, and she was determined not to let anything get in her way.

www.ingramcontent.com/pod-product-compliance
Lightning Source LLC
Chambersburg PA
CBHW052020240626
47153CB00006B/1893